The Bride Goes Rogue

He didn't believe in fate, but no need to get into that now. Instead, he bent and captured her mouth in another kiss, the contact sending a jolt down to his toes. She was eager and sweet, kissing him back with abandon, without guile, and he drank it in like fine wine. The curves of her body fit perfectly with his, even given his height. How lucky he'd been to meet her here—an event with thousands of women.

When they broke apart, she was clutching his coat, her eyes unfocused. He felt a little dizzy himself, actually. Pressing a final kiss to her forehead, he said, "You should go before we lose our heads again. Shall I take you to find your friend?"

Stepping back, she righted her clothing. "That isn't necessary. I know exactly where she's waiting. Do you plan to stay longer?"

He shook his head. "No, I've had enough. I found what I want."

"Me?"

"You."

Also by Joanna Shupe

Fifth Avenue Rebels
THE HEIRESS HUNT
THE LADY GETS LUCKY

Uptown Girls
THE ROGUE OF FIFTH AVENUE
THE PRINCE OF BROADWAY
THE DEVIL OF DOWNTOWN

The Four Hundred series
A DARING ARRANGEMENT
A SCANDALOUS DEAL
A NOTORIOUS VOW

The Knickerbocker Club series
MAGNATE
BARON
MOGUL
TYCOON

ATTENTION: ORGANIZATIONS AND CORPORATIONS
HarperCollins books may be purchased for educational, business, or sales promotional use. For information, please e-mail the Special Markets Department at SPsales@harpercollins.com.

THE BRIDE GOES ROGUE

❧ The Fifth Avenue Rebels ❧

JOANNA SHUPE

AVONBOOKS

An Imprint of HarperCollinsPublishers

Excerpt from *The Duke Gets Even* copyright © 2023 by Joanna Shupe.

THE BRIDE GOES ROGUE. Copyright © 2022 by Joanna Shupe. All rights reserved. Printed in the United States of America. No part of this book may be used or reproduced in any manner whatsoever without written permission except in the case of brief quotations embodied in critical articles and reviews. For information, address HarperCollins Publishers, 195 Broadway, New York, NY 10007.

First Avon Books mass market printing: May 2022

Print Edition ISBN: 978-0-06-304506-4
Digital Edition ISBN: 978-0-06-304406-7

Cover design by Guido Caroti
Cover illustration by Anna Kmet

Avon, Avon & logo, and Avon Books & logo are registered trademarks of HarperCollins Publishers in the United States of America and other countries.

HarperCollins is a registered trademark of HarperCollins Publishers in the United States of America and other countries.

FIRST EDITION

22 23 24 25 26 BVGM 10 9 8 7 6 5 4 3 2 1

To me. To you. To us.
Because these last few years
have been rough.

The Bride Goes Rogue

Chapter One

❧

August, 1895

It was a fine day to ambush a fiancé.

Well, perhaps *ambush* was too strong a word, Katherine Delafield thought as she carefully descended from the hack to the street. She hadn't contacted him beforehand or made an appointment with his secretary, but certainly he would make time for *her*. While Preston Clarke was a busy man, with his many properties, he and Katherine were betrothed.

Clutching her journal, she made her way toward the tall building bearing her fiancé's name. They hadn't seen each other since a brief introduction a year ago during the season. It wasn't until after said introduction when her father informed her about the betrothal agreement between her and Preston. Years ago, when Henry Clarke and Lloyd Delafield were still business partners, they decided their only children would wed once they were of age.

This hadn't come as much of a surprise, as Katherine always expected her father would choose her husband. That was how most marriages worked in their world. What had surprised her, however, was how much she was looking forward to being Preston's wife.

She could still remember spying his tall and striking form across a ballroom, a giant warrior in a sea of bland and banal. With his windswept hair falling over his brow, he'd laughed at something one of his friends said, and she watched his smile transform his face from stern into breathtakingly handsome.

From then on she'd looked for mention of him everywhere. Followed the progress of his company. She even learned the names of his mistresses. At first, she hadn't minded waiting on him to announce the betrothal. But Katherine was more than ready now, and Daddy was tired of fielding her questions about when and where this marriage would take place. He finally urged her to visit Preston and iron out all the details.

This was not a hardship. Details were among her favorite things.

Now inside the ornate lobby, she gave a polite nod to the elevator operator. "Good afternoon, sir. I'm here to see Mr. Clarke."

"Ah, then you're going to the top floor, miss." He closed the iron door and started the lift. "Gets visitors all day long, Mr. Clarke does. None as pretty as you, though."

"That's very kind of you, thank you." She supposed she would be seeing a lot of the building employees in the years to come. "What is your name, sir?"

"Reginald, miss."

"Nice to meet you, Reginald. I am Miss Delafield. Soon to be Mrs. Clarke."

His brows shot straight up. "Well, now! Congratulations. I wasn't told he was getting married."

"Oh, there's been an understanding between our families for years. I'm here today to work out the details."

"Then I wish you luck. He could use a little sunshine in his life, if you ask my opinion. Never seen a man scowl so much."

Poor Preston. She sensed that he worked very hard. She would change all that once they were married and settled.

They stopped and she waved goodbye, then headed toward the office with Preston's name on it. When she opened the door, a secretary looked up from behind her desk. There was a man sitting in one of the chairs in the anteroom, likely waiting for an appointment with Preston, and he stood politely at Katherine's arrival.

"How may I help you, dear?" the secretary asked. "Are you lost?"

No doubt Katherine looked out of place here. She tried for a bright smile. "No, I'm here to see Mr. Clarke."

The older woman blinked. "Do you have an appointment?"

"No, but he'll want to see me."

"Mr. Clarke has a full schedule today, miss. Perhaps we could put you down for next week?"

Oh, no. Next week would not do. She had decided they would do this today, so today it would be.

"Please tell him his fiancée is here."

The secretary's mouth dropped open. "I beg your pardon, but did you say . . . ?"

"Yes, fiancée. Miss Katherine Delafield."

"Fiancée?"

That was happening a lot today. "Yes. He will want to see me."

"Oh, I have no doubt," the secretary said, the edge of her mouth kicking up. "Would you care to wait? He's just finishing up with a meeting. However, I should be able to slide you in before his next appointment."

Katherine glanced at the man already waiting. "But wasn't he here first?"

"Mr. Vance won't mind letting you go in ahead of him. Will you, Mr. Vance?"

"Have I a choice?" Mr. Vance asked, frowning.

"No, not if you want to be seen at some point today."

Mr. Vance huffed and went back to his reading. Katherine assumed the secretary knew best, so she nodded. "That would be lovely. Thank you, Mrs. . . . ?"

"Cohen, dear. It's Mrs. Cohen."

"Nice to meet you, Mrs. Cohen. By the way, I love your dress. That color is very becoming on you."

Mrs. Cohen softened and gave her a wide smile. "Aren't you the sweetest thing? Please, have a seat."

Settling in the empty chair, Katherine placed her journal on her lap and tapped the cover with her fingers. Once this meeting was done, she had a hundred tasks awaiting her in regard to the wedding. Hopefully, she and Preston could come to an agreement on most of the bigger decisions today.

A loud conversation began drifting through the closed door. Katherine wasn't typically an eavesdropper, but she could hardly prevent herself from overhearing it.

"You don't understand, Mr. Clarke. I . . . I cannot lose my home. Where will we go?"

"That is not my problem," another man, clearly Preston, snapped. "You gambled away all your money, took out a loan and used the deed as collateral. When you couldn't pay the bank back, I bought the deed, fair and square. If you have an issue with any of that, take it up with Gotham First National Savings and Loan."

"The bank told me to talk to you!"

"I am not running a charity, Mr. Harris. This is a business."

A heavy feeling settled in Katherine's stomach. Mrs. Cohen continued working, while the man in the chair next to her focused on a stack of papers, both seemingly unbothered by the conversation. Was this sort of thing a usual occurrence around here?

"My family has nowhere else to go," Mr. Harris was saying. "Does that even matter to you?"

Katherine held her breath. Dear God. This was terrible. Did Preston not feel even a tiny bit of compassion for this man and his family?

She couldn't hear her fiancé's response, but the door quickly opened to reveal an older man in an ill-fitting brown suit. He shouted, "I hope all that money keeps you warm at night," over his shoulder just before slamming the door shut and storming out.

Mrs. Cohen rose and nodded at Katherine. "I'll see if he's ready for you, Miss Delafield."

Katherine tried to calm her racing heart and forget what she'd overheard. Preston had a reputation as a ruthless businessman, but perhaps she could soften those rough edges over time.

"Miss Delafield," Mrs. Cohen said a minute later from the open office doorway. "Mr. Clarke will see you now."

Katherine stood and smoothed her skirts, then bit her lips for color. Her friend Nellie claimed this made one's smile appear brighter. Pushing her shoulders back, Katherine walked into Preston's office.

A man rose from behind the desk. He was every bit as handsome as she remembered. More so, actually.

"Miss Delafield."

Lord, he was even bigger up close. He made her, a woman taller than most, feel tiny. Her chest fluttered as she shook his hand. "Hello, Mr. Clarke."

"Thank you, Mrs. Cohen," he said to the secretary, who nodded and closed the door. Then to Katherine: "Won't you have a seat?"

She gracefully lowered herself into a chair, while at the same time taking a peek at the room, curious about her future husband's domain. The office was sparse, with a walnut desk and chairs, bare walls and a giant safe in the corner. He needed some decorations in here, some artwork at the very least. She put it on her mental list to hang some paintings in his office after the wedding. Something serene and soft, like a Manet, perhaps.

Meeting his gaze, she said, "I apologize for coming unannounced like this."

"I admit, my curiosity is piqued." He leaned back in his chair. "What may I do for you?"

She took the list from her journal and handed it to him. "Here are the items on which we must decide. I've been pestering my father with these questions and he suggested I just come to see you. So, here I am." She gave a small laugh, the kind that came out whenever she was nervous.

He accepted the paper without looking at it. "What questions would those be?"

Edging forward, she found her pencil and began reading off her notes in the journal. "First, I'd like to discuss the time of year. Most people prefer the spring, but I quite like the idea of the fall. September, perhaps. We'll decorate with orange blossoms, of course."

He glanced at the paper, his lips parting slightly as he read her list. "Wait, what?"

"You're right," she hurried to say. "Spring might be better. Let's set that aside and return to it later. Now, let's discuss food. I would prefer to hire Louis Sherry over Delmonico's."

He grimaced and placed the piece of paper on his desk carefully. A muscle moved in his jaw as he held up a hand. "Please, we should talk about this."

"Would you rather decide on the music? It's unconventional, but I like the idea of a single harpist for the ceremony."

"You must stop."

Uneasiness compounded in her stomach. Men typically didn't participate in wedding preparations, but she hoped to arrange everything to his liking. She wanted to be the perfect wife. "I know, it seems trivial. Silly little things women like me worry about." She lifted a shoulder. "But I didn't want to get off on the wrong foot by ignoring your input. That is, unless you prefer for me to make all the decisions—"

"I'm not referring to the plans, per se. I'm referring to the wedding. We're not getting married. Not in the spring, not in the fall. Despite what you have been told, this is not happening."

A shiver of fear and embarrassment slid through her. "I don't understand."

"I am not marrying you."

"But . . ." She blinked at him and bit the inside of her cheek. "We are betrothed. Our fathers agreed on our marriage years ago."

"You didn't really believe them, did you? They had no right to make that betrothal on our behalf. This isn't medieval Scotland. We aren't two rival clans that must be joined in marriage to keep the peace. It's nearly the twentieth century."

"I suppose, but I always expected my father would choose my husband. It's how things are done."

"Not for me," he said firmly. "Even if he were alive I wouldn't allow my father to choose my wife."

Air trickled into her too-tight lungs, like they'd been wrapped in twine, and a strange ringing started in her ears. "Is it because of the way I look? Too tall? Not tall enough? Is my hair too plain? My eyes are too close together, aren't they?"

"Good God, no. It's not about how you look. You're lovely. It's about me. I'm not ready to marry anyone. I may *never* be ready to marry. Do you understand?"

There had to be a reason. Most men his age were married. It was what people in their circles did.

"This doesn't make any sense."

"Miss Delafield. Katherine," he said, his tone gentle but firm. "I apologize, but I cannot marry you. I really am sorry if you believed otherwise, but believe me, it's for your own good."

For her own good? And he was *sorry*? This was like a terrible dream, worse than the one where she was running and couldn't find her way home.

Mouth dry, she swallowed. "Perhaps you need more time to come to terms with the idea. I can wait."

His lips flattened into a thin line, the skin above his collar turning a deep red. "I do not need *time*, Miss Delafield. Not a year, not a decade. I cannot marry you, ever. Is that clear enough for you? Or shall I write it down in list form?" He gestured to her forgotten paper on his desk.

Realization hit her like a douse of cold rainwater. She finally understood. He didn't want to marry her.

She had been waiting for . . . nothing. Absolutely nothing. For one year she'd believed herself betrothed, putting off her future until he was ready. How silly. How stupid.

How naive.

Hot prickles gathered behind her eyes, every

breath scraping like needles inside her chest. She couldn't pull enough air into her lungs, and the urge to flee overrode everything else. "I see. I'm terribly sorry for bothering you." She snapped her journal closed and shot to her feet. "I won't trouble you again. Good day, sir."

"Wait," he called behind her, but she didn't listen. She kept right on walking. She'd already given Preston Clarke too much of her time.

She wasn't about to waste one second more.

Chapter Two

❦

"I told you not to make her cry," Mrs. Cohen said as she entered his office.

Preston dragged a hand over his face and dropped into his chair, the wood creaking beneath his weight. "Believe it or not, I did not intend to upset her."

"Is she truly your fiancée?"

No, Katherine absolutely was not his fiancée. His late father had arranged the betrothal eons ago, but everything had changed since then.

"She told you? Why on earth didn't you warn me?"

Mrs. Cohen lifted a shoulder. "You deserve a shock every now and again. It's good for the heart."

"While I'm not up on all the latest medical research, I believe the opposite is true. Furthermore, I should fire you for that."

"But you won't, because I know all your secrets. And your father's secrets, may he rest in peace."

True. Mrs. Cohen had worked for the Clarkes longer than Preston had been alive, and she was indispensable. "To answer your question, no. She is not my fiancée."

"Why not? I liked her father, back when he worked with yours. She's quite pretty. You could do worse."

Yes, she was pretty. Beyond pretty, actually. Tall and stately, Katherine had light brown hair streaked with faint strands of gold. Eyes that sparkled with innocence and decency. Kindness. He felt *dirty* just staring at her.

Preston was far from innocent and decent. Instead, he'd done terrible things, corrupt things, in the name of earning a dollar. His grandfather rose up from the slums of the docks through violence and blackmail, then Preston's father had lost nearly everything before he died. When Preston took over, the Clarkes were mired in debt, and a return to their unscrupulous roots had been required to save the business, their home and their legacy.

No one gained a fortune in this city through honorable and just means.

Soon he'd rebuilt what his father lost and, no matter what else took place, Preston would never allow that to happen again. The worry over their future had nearly killed his mother the first time, and if he had to sell his soul to the Devil himself, Preston would do it to spare her another moment of anxiety.

"You are aware of my feelings regarding that family," he said to Mrs. Cohen. "The idea that I'd marry her is laughable. Lloyd should know better."

"Now, you can't blame Mr. Delafield for what happened to your father. But even if you do, his daughter had nothing to do with it."

Preston knew that, but it didn't change the circumstances. Lloyd Delafield could've helped the Clarkes when it mattered. Instead, he'd refused and dissolved their common business interests, leaving Henry Clarke to drown alone. Preston wanted nothing to do with Lloyd or his daughter. "I'll blame whoever I damn well please—and if you want to keep your job, you'll take my side."

She wasn't intimidated in the least. "You know, you're far too young to scowl this much."

Young? Some days he felt a hundred years old. His business dealings took him all over, a web of connections to the most dangerous and powerful men in the city. He'd made enemies along the way, too. Everyone was fighting for the same bedrock, an equal slice of the pie, and most were willing to do anything to succeed—including him.

God knew timidity and congeniality wouldn't help him erect the tallest building in the world, the plans for which currently sat on his desk.

The Clarke name was about to go down in history.

Had Lloyd heard of the project? Preston shook his head. That transparent bastard. It explained why Lloyd had encouraged Katherine to come here today and finalize the wedding plans. No doubt he was trying to profit from a Clarke's hard work once again.

Well, Preston would not allow it. He'd do everything possible to avoid all Delafields at any cost.

That reminded him . . .

"Send flowers to Mrs. Russell with a card that I'd like to see her on Saturday."

Mrs. Cohen cleared her throat. "Is this because that nice Miss Delafield brought up marriage and now you're running scared?"

Yes. "That is none of your concern. Is Mr. Vance still waiting?"

His secretary peered over her spectacles at him, a disapproving look that never failed to make him feel small. "You should also send flowers to Miss Delafield and apologize for upsetting her."

She was right. Why hadn't he thought of it? "Fine, take care of it. Are we done talking about flowers and parties? May we return to the things that really matter?"

"What could possibly be more important than dealing with the women in your life?"

"There are not *women* in my life," he fired back. "However, there will be one *less* woman in my life if she doesn't quickly send in my next appointment."

She sniffed and walked to the door. "I don't know why I put up with you."

"Because I pay you double what anyone else would."

"Yet it's still not close to what I'm worth."

True. He made certain to overpay Mrs. Cohen to make up for the years when his father hadn't been able to afford her salary. Loyalty prompted her to stay through the worst of it, and Preston intended to reward her for that, daily. He didn't trust many people, but he did trust her. "But where else would you have this much fun?"

"I couldn't say. A funeral?"

Though meant in jest, it reminded him of an all-too-real funeral a few weeks ago. One of Preston's closest friends had descended into a spiral of alcohol abuse and self-loathing, moving from one flophouse to the next, until Forrest had finally stumbled in front of an oncoming train.

The guilt and grief must've shown on his face, because Mrs. Cohen quickly said, "I'm sorry. That was thoughtless of me, considering."

"It's fine." He busied himself by straightening the papers on his desk. "Let's get this meeting with Vance over with, shall we?"

"It's not fine. I shouldn't have said it. You're still in mourning for your friend."

He resisted the urge to pull at his collar. "Must we discuss this?"

"No, but I think you'd be a little less surly if you did."

He rose and went to the corner safe. Spinning the dials, he quickly opened the heavy metal door and surveyed the stacks of cash inside. Three thousand should be enough to bribe Vance, who was currently on Brooklyn's planning commission. Reaching in, Preston took what he needed and locked the safe. "I prefer to be surly, because then people leave me alone and I can get more work accomplished."

Mrs. Cohen threw up her hands and heaved an exasperated sigh. "I'll send him in."

She was almost to the door when it flew open and bounced on the hinges. What on earth . . . ?

Katherine Delafield rushed in. Wisps of brown hair framed her face and her eyes were wild and angry. This was a woman on a mission, an avenging queen. Ready to slay kingdoms—or him. He couldn't move, couldn't *breathe*, as she stalked toward him, right past Mrs. Cohen.

"It took me until I reached the street to realize the truth." Katherine let out a harsh laugh that held no mirth. "There is nothing wrong with me. *You*, Preston Clarke, are the one who has something wrong with him. You are a . . . a heartless clod."

Before he could respond, she tossed her journal onto his desk, where it landed with a thump. "You may keep that. One day, you'll regret letting me go but it'll be too late. I wouldn't marry you now if you begged me on bended knee in front of the whole dashed city. You ruined your one chance at having the perfect life. Enjoy your"—she waved her hand to indicate his office—"work. I hope it makes you very happy."

His jaw fell open while his mind tripped over her words. A heavy weight settled between his shoulder blades. "Katherine, wait," he called, not quite certain what he was about to say.

It didn't matter. She was already marching toward the door. As she passed Mrs. Cohen, Katherine told his secretary, "You really should find a new employer."

"Believe me, I know it," Mrs. Cohen muttered, shaking her head.

When they were alone again, Mrs. Cohen rocked on her heels. "Indeed, what a day this has been. Can't remember the last time we've had this much excitement. Shall I send her another bouquet of flowers with another apology?"

He picked up the journal and started to toss

it into the wastebasket. At the last minute he changed his mind and slipped it into his desk instead. "I don't want to hear another word about it. Send in Mr. Vance."

WHEN SHE RETURNED home, Katherine found her father in the gallery, where the paintings were being taken down off the walls and put into crates. Anger and humiliation brewed in her stomach, enough to burn the back of her throat. She blurted, "Why didn't you tell me he had no intention of marrying me?"

Surprise coasted over her father's features before he said, "Michael, Robert. Give us a minute, will you?"

The footmen departed and Daddy shoved his hands in his trouser pockets. "What did Clarke say, exactly?"

"That he won't marry me or honor that betrothal. He was quite insistent about it. Rude, even. I made a total fool of myself."

Her father's mouth flattened into an unhappy line. "You are not a fool. He's the fool, if he is unwilling to honor this agreement."

"What were you thinking, betrothing me without checking with him first?"

"Henry said he discussed it with his son—at least, that was what he told me shortly before he died."

"I don't know whether Mr. Clarke discussed it or not, but Preston could not have been clearer."

Daddy's jaw tightened and his voice became like steel. "I will sue him for breach of contract, then."

A lawsuit? What did that mean? Would she be forced to sit and listen while a group of lawyers discussed her and Preston in court? Or worse, would she be called to testify?

Wincing, Katherine closed her eyes briefly, imagining that public disaster. Her embarrassment would only multiply. "No, absolutely not. Leave it alone. I want to forget it ever happened."

"Why? This was what his father wanted. Preston should honor that commitment."

She recalled the meeting just before she saw Preston, the callous way he'd treated that man losing his home. "I don't think honor and Preston have anything more than a passing acquaintance. We should leave it be."

"I don't like it. When I was younger, no man would dream of acting in such a disrespectful and callous way—especially not to a woman."

"Daddy, you have to let this go. He's made his position clear and I no longer want to marry him. In fact, I'll run away and join the circus if you try to force me into it."

It was a familiar threat from her childhood, one that made him smile. "I don't like anyone hurting you, Kitty Kat. But if that's how you feel, I won't sue him." He patted her shoulder. "We'll find you another husband, I promise."

"No, please." She sighed and pressed her hands together. "I've thought of myself as Mrs. Preston Clarke for an entire year. I need some time to adjust to the idea that I'm not. Does that make sense? I want to find my own husband."

"There isn't a whole lot of time, Katherine. Already your debut was delayed a year because we were still in mourning over your mother. You know how these things work."

Yes, she did. If she waited too long, she'd be branded a spinster. Unsuitable for marriage.

"I'm not asking for years. Just a little while. Are you in such a hurry to get rid of me?"

"No, absolutely not." He leaned over to kiss her temple. "My job as a father is to see you settled, but I want you to be happy first and foremost. It's what your mother would've wanted, too."

"I know." That reminded her of the room they were in, the paintings being removed from the walls. These were her mother's prized possessions, the result of combing the world for her favorite pieces.

Mama had loved art of all kinds and Katherine could almost feel her mother's presence in this room. She could still hear Mama saying, "There's so much beauty in the world, if we only stop to appreciate it." When she first grew ill, Mama would sit in this room for hours, staring at her favorite paintings.

Katherine was sixteen when her mother became sick. The doctors said the disease was too far along, too aggressive, and they'd been right. After a steady decline, her mother died almost two years later. The ache in Katherine's heart hadn't lessened in all that time. Perhaps it never would. So, what on earth was her father doing? "You aren't selling Mama's paintings, are you?"

"No." He dragged a hand over his jaw. "I can't bear to part with them. However, I can't bear to look at them, either."

"I don't understand."

A shadow passed over his face, one that spoke of grief and loneliness. Katherine recognized it because she felt the same. "They're a reminder of her," he said, "and I would merely like a day or two when I walk by here and don't experience an awful knot in my stomach."

She understood, she did. There were days when the grief grabbed Katherine by the throat and wouldn't let go. But these paintings were a link to her mother, a way of remembering and honoring Alva Delafield. "You cannot do that to her paintings. She wouldn't have wanted them stored, Daddy."

"But she's no longer here. It's up to those of us left behind to pick up the pieces. I cannot—"

She waited for him to finish. When he didn't, she said, "I understand. I miss her every minute of every day. But these are *hers*. She worked so hard to find these. Most galleries would kill to get their hands on them."

There were the romantics and neoclassics. Renaissance era, as well as the ancients. Ukiyo-e prints from Japan. Dutch masters. Even a few works by little-known artists, merely because Mama liked them.

"Katherine, please. I'm not trying to hurt you or your mother's memory, but this will help both of us move forward."

Move forward?

That was an odd turn of phrase. She didn't want to move on from losing her mother, nor did Katherine want to lose this connection to her.

When Mama was well, Katherine had often

trailed her into this room, just to hear the stories about the art and artists. Like the Bonheur that had been Mama's favorite, acquired from a handsome collector in Lisbon. Or the Ruskin Mama received as a wedding present from her parents. The illustrations by Charles Gibson, who became one of Mama's friends later on. Katherine could trace the path of her mother's life through the sketches and paintings in this room.

And Daddy wanted to pack them away?

Surely they could honor these brilliant works of art and avoid shoving them into an attic. "Will you give me a few days to think about it? I don't want to see her things stored. Maybe there's somewhere I can display them, like a permanent exhibit of some kind."

He sighed, indecision on his face. Then he smiled fondly at her. "You always want to do the right thing. That's her doing. You're considerate and kind, just as she was. I suppose a few more days won't hurt."

"Thank you." She threaded their arms together and put her head on his shoulder. They'd grown close after Mama's death, their shared grief like a tether between them. "I love you."

"I love you, too. Want to talk more about what happened with Clarke?"

"Goodness, no. I can't remember everything I said, I was so furious, but I definitely gave him a dressing down."

"Good. Sounds like he deserved it. There are rumors about him, but I never expected Henry's son to turn into such a scoundrel."

"*Scoundrel* is too tame a word. One thing's for certain, Preston Clarke would've made me miserable."

"It's a shame. I had such high hopes after you first met him. I swear, you had stars in your eyes. It reminded me of when I met your mother, the feeling that I'd found the perfect woman."

Except this was wildly different. Preston was not the perfect man. Far from it.

I cannot marry you, ever. Is that clear enough for you?

Mortification scalded her insides, and her skin grew hot. "He certainly cleared up any illusions today. Trust me, I don't want anything more to do with him."

Chapter Three

❧

"I want to have an affair," Katherine blurted—just as a footman entered the drawing room with a tea tray.

She and Nellie were at the Meliora Club, their women's social club, for afternoon tea. The Meliora, named for the Latin word for "always better," was a place to advance the educational and professional pursuits of women. Katherine was here to plan an exhibition of her mother's paintings . . . except now she might never be able to show her face inside these walls again.

Mortified, she covered her mouth with a hand while Nellie just smiled at the young man, whose skin was now the color of a tomato.

"Thank you ever so much, Robbie," Nellie said. "You may put that on the table."

After the young man hurried out of the room, Katherine groaned. "Oh, my God. I cannot believe I said that."

"Forget it." Nellie waved her hand. "He's undoubtedly heard worse within these walls. Wasn't there a lecture on free love recently? Anyway, let's get back to this affair. Who are you considering?"

Katherine paused and thought about it. A dark cloud had settled over her ever since walking out of Preston's office three days ago. It still rankled that she'd waited for a year on Preston while he'd been out having fun, catering to a mistress, without a care in the world. Katherine wanted to have fun, too.

She was long overdue for some, in fact.

She'd spent four months in Spain last year with her aunt, and that experience changed her. It proved things were much different in other parts of the world, less restrictive. Not as judgmental. More accepting to other points of view. It was time to stop caring about what she was "supposed" to do and do what she wanted instead.

First item on the list? An affair.

Shrugging, she said, "I have no idea."

Nellie leaned in, brows raised in excitement. "Well, let's throw out some names, shall we? I met the pitcher for the Brooklyn Bridegrooms a few weeks back and he's very handsome. His mustache is a work of art. Or there is that young ambassador from Greece. He's gorgeous, Katie. Even better, he won't be staying long, so you don't have to worry about him getting attached."

Katherine chewed on the inside of her cheek. "Perhaps, though it sounds like a lot of work. Couldn't I just go to a ball or a club and find someone? Somewhere downtown, where no one would know me and I wouldn't have to worry about my reputation."

"If that's what you really want, then you're in

luck." Nellie's mouth curved into a knowing smirk. "There's a masquerade happening next week at Madison Square Garden."

"There is?"

"Yes, the French Ball. It's quite risqué."

"That sounds perfect. Have you ever been?"

"No, though it sounds like fun. Demimonde and theater types, along with High Society and Wall Street traders, all mingling in a late night bacchanal. I hear they sometimes toss the women from the dance floor up into the boxes above. But, Katie, I think that event might be too much for you. Perhaps wade in first before jumping into the deep water."

"No, that is exactly what I want. I've waited a year to have any fun whatsoever!"

Nellie held out her palms. "I'm all for women having fun whenever and however they wish. But do it for you—not as revenge on Preston Clarke, who certainly does not deserve one more moment of your time or ounce of your energy."

Katherine had recounted her meeting with Preston when Nellie first arrived today. Her friend had been properly outraged. "Nels, I *saved* myself for him. All the while he's seeing mistresses and cavorting around town. I'm such a dunce. No other woman on earth would've been so stupid."

"Stop disparaging yourself as if you did something wrong. You didn't." Nellie's face sharpened, her voice laced with irritation. "Your father arranged a marriage for you—something that occurs up and down Fifth Avenue nearly every day—and you honored the betrothal. All the blame lies with Preston Clarke."

It made sense, but Katherine knew most women wouldn't have waited a year to finalize wedding details. Nellie would have demanded answers after a few weeks. So, why had Katherine been so complacent, so willing to put her life on hold? Why was she so dashed *nice*? "Thank you, but I can't help but feel foolish."

"Would a fool have talked the Meliora Club into letting her host a showing of her mother's paintings? Would a fool be one of my very best friends, who makes lists and tries to help her friends find love? Stop being so hard on yourself, Katie."

Katherine reached over and grabbed Nellie's hand. "Thank you. I'll try. So back to the French Ball . . ."

"If you want to have fun, then I will help you have fun."

Of course Nellie would understand. She lived however she wished, seemingly uncaring that her invitations to the decent events dried up eons ago. It was quite admirable.

Grinning widely, Katherine exhaled a relieved breath. "Thank you. Will you come along? I don't think I can work up the nerve to go alone."

"I would love to go with you. Are you able to sneak out?"

"I'll manage it somehow. The bigger question is are we able to get tickets?"

"You're adorable, thinking I wouldn't be able to secure us tickets. Now, come to my house beforehand and we'll get ready and go together. What shall we wear?"

Katherine's heart began to pound. Were they

really planning this? "Something with a mask and a wig, so I'm unrecognizable. What do you think the other women will have on? We'll need to fit in."

Nellie gave her a bland stare. "Katie, they are not the kind of women worried about their reputations. They will wear tights or short skirts. A corset with no chemise."

"Then we should definitely follow suit." She raised her teacup in a toast. "To cavorting."

Nellie laughed and lifted her own cup. "To cavorting."

PRESTON TOSSED HIS derby onto the small sofa in Kit's office and threw himself into a chair. He rubbed his eyes.

Kit smirked and went back to his paperwork. "Hello, sunshine."

Preston grunted. It had been a miserable past few days. "Hello."

"Do you want a drink?"

"No, and you know why."

Kit held up his hands. "I won't force you, but you are not him. Furthermore, abstaining won't bring him back."

"I'm well aware." He hadn't consumed any alcohol whatsoever in three weeks. He was dashed tired of tea and lemonade, if he was being honest, but he wasn't ready.

"You look terrible," Kit said.

"Thank you."

Kit rolled his eyes. "With all seriousness, I'm worried about you. I've hardly seen you since the funeral, and when I do you're grumpier than usual."

"I'm . . . not over it, I suppose."

"I'd be shocked if you were, to be honest, and neither am I. Never thought one of us would actually *die*, not this young."

"I know." Preston scrubbed his face with his hands. Every time he closed his eyes at night, he saw the morgue, Forrest's mangled body on a cold metal slab. "Let's not talk about it."

"What should we talk about, then?"

"I had a visit from Miss Delafield last week."

"Lloyd's daughter?"

"Yes. Remember me telling you about a betrothal document our fathers arranged years ago? Turns out she took it seriously."

"You're engaged to Katherine Delafield?" Kit sat straighter in his chair. "I don't believe it."

"I'm not engaged," Preston said quickly. "I'm not honoring that agreement. Lloyd is out of his damn mind if he thinks I'll marry her."

Kit blinked a few times. "Is that an option? I mean, he could sue you for breach of contract."

"But he won't. It would embarrass her and the courts would tie up the proceedings for years. She'd be a spinster by then."

"That's cold, Pres. Even for you."

A familiar bitterness welled up in his throat. "I'm not doing it on purpose. But where was Lloyd's help when my father needed it? When we nearly lost the Fifth Avenue house? When my mother was forced to sell her jewelry and borrow money from her sister? When I had to quit school and come home?"

Kit held up his palms. "I understand, but Katherine is a sweet girl. She doesn't deserve to be caught up in this Capulet-Montague situation you have with her father."

"That's not my problem. I have enough on my plate as it is."

"Yes, I know. Preston Clarke's world domination. How's that coming along?"

"Slowly. I've only conquered half the world so far."

Kit huffed a laugh. "I have faith in you. How are things with Mrs. Russell?"

"*Things* ended two nights ago."

"I see. Want to talk about it?"

"No. Same old issues."

Arabella Russell, now his former mistress, had hated his demanding schedule, including frequent meetings and business dinners that often ran late. She hadn't understood his ambition or the day-to-day responsibilities of running a company so large, especially when he already possessed a lot of money. No amount of explaining about employees and shareholders and his father made a damn bit of difference, either. Arabella wanted to be the most important thing in his life, which was impossible. The company would *always* come first.

Still, while he wasn't in love with her, Arabella's parting words stung:

You are heartless, Preston Clarke.

It was becoming a recurring refrain in his life.

"Well, that's one problem easily fixed," Kit said. "You need another woman."

Preston doubted this was the answer, though he almost always kept a mistress. It was tidier. A neat, simple arrangement that suited his schedule and his appetites. A single partner was preferable to a string of random encounters with faceless women. But while he wouldn't mind losing himself in a woman for a few hours, the idea of finding someone he liked, someone with whom he was compatible, sounded exhausting.

"I'll get around to it," he muttered.

"There was the singer a few months ago, the one that asked about you. Want me to see if I can find her?"

"Definitely not. The last thing I need is for someone to get attached."

"Ah, allow me to guess? Arabella wanted more and you told her no."

"Yes, in very simple terms. Our arrangement was supposed to remain uncomplicated."

"You idiot. She's an actress. Everything about them is complicated." Kit would know. He dealt with singers and actors of all kinds for the supper club.

Preston stretched his legs out beside the desk and said, "I'll not make that mistake again."

"You aren't taking up celibacy, are you?"

"God, no. Bite your tongue."

Kit drummed his fingers on the desk, his expression pensive. "All right, so no singers or actresses. Well, there's that exclusive brothel over in the Village—"

"No—and I don't require help to find women, Kit."

"Clearly you do. What about the ballet? Dancers are very limber, and I think there is a traveling company from Russia in town."

Frustrated, Preston leaned his elbows on his

knees and studied the floor. "I'm in no mood to romance a woman into becoming my mistress right now. I want something . . . anonymous. Something fleeting. Not a permanent arrangement. Just harmless fun."

"Ah, I know what you mean. If I weren't married, we could go tear up the Bowery together."

"Those were the days," Preston said with a fond smile.

"You know, the French Ball is tomorrow night. Why not seek your harmless fun there?"

Hmm. This wasn't a terrible idea. "We used to love going to those. Too bad you're married or you could come with me."

Kit's expression softened as he shook his head. "I wouldn't trade Alice for any amount of debauchery. Someday you'll feel the same about your own wife."

"Doubtful." Especially as he didn't plan on marrying, not until he cleaned up Clarke Holdings into something more respectable. At the moment, that goal seemed as attainable as a trip around the sun.

"So, find a costume with a wig," Kit said. "No one will know it's you."

"It would be nice to escape my own head for a few hours. Be someone else for a change."

A heaviness settled between them, one that had been present since the funeral. Kit shifted in his seat and lined up the papers on his desk. "You know, you aren't responsible for what happened to him."

Fuck you, Preston. You ignored me for months. Don't try to act like you care.

Forrest's angry words, uttered during his short stay at Preston's Adirondack lodge, came roaring back. Preston would need to sell the lodge, because it was now just a bleak reminder of the entire awful experience, his failure to save his friend. "I should've tried harder," he said. "I tried to lock him in and clean him up, but I thought we had more time to get through to him."

Except there hadn't been more time. Forrest was too hell-bent on destroying himself, and Preston realized life was far more fleeting than he'd thought. It was fragile, an existence built on matchsticks that might collapse at any moment.

He, of all people, should've known this. Hadn't he spent the last five years rebuilding his father's lost empire?

"We all thought we had time," Kit said. "Christ, I was the last one to see him alive. Why did I leave him alone that night? Why didn't I take him out of that shithole boardinghouse?"

"You didn't know what was happening. I did. I knew and I still didn't try hard enough."

"Dash it, Pres." Kit rubbed his temples as if he had a blistering headache. "This is not helpful for either of us."

True, but Preston hadn't figured out how to ease the grief.

"I apologize," he said, rising. "I've ruined your night. I should've gone home after the office."

"Fuck off, you haven't ruined a thing. And I think you should stay. If drinking is off the table, we could, I don't know, raid the kitchen and finish off whatever Alice has left in there."

Preston collected his derby. "Take your wife

home, Kit. Enjoy the rest of your evening. Forget I came by."

"Preston—"

The concern in Kit's voice caused Preston to hold up a hand. "I'm fine. Honestly. I'll go to the French Ball, have a great time and everything will go back to exactly how it was before."

Chapter Four

❧

Katherine paused and pulled on the hem of her very short skirts. "Do I look ridiculous?"

"Will you stop? You look unbelievably gorgeous." Nellie grabbed Katherine's hand and looked her over from head to toe. "The men are going to swallow their tongues. Probably some women, too. Who knew you were hiding such a fabulous set of gams under your skirts?"

They resumed walking toward Madison Square Garden's entrance. To avoid recognition, they decided to powder their hair and wear masks. Katherine was Madame de Pompadour, with wide but very short skirts and white tights, while Nellie was supposed to be Marie Antoinette. Only, her friend looked more like a Bowery chorus girl with her corset and undergarments showing.

Nellie slipped her arm through Katherine's and locked their elbows. "How are the plans for the art exhibition coming?"

"Very well, actually. It's much easier than I thought."

"Only because you are the most organized

person I know. No doubt your love of art helps, as well."

"I've decided to include some unknown local artists, too. I had no idea there were so many."

"It's good that you're helping them. The galleries can be difficult and snooty. The owners generally only want to display the bigger names, the paintings they know will sell for a lot of money."

Surprised, Katherine glanced over at her friend. "You have a rather keen insight into a struggling artist's mind."

"I had an affair with one last year," Nellie answered. "He was gorgeous but couldn't paint to save his life. I bought six of his paintings, if you're interested in seeing them."

"Six! Goodness, he must have been worth it."

"He was, actually. Very tender. Had a poet's soul."

The crowds thickened as they approached the entrance. Katherine moved closer to Nellie. "I envy you. Most women would never dream of living the life you do."

A shadow passed over her friend's expression, a flash of what appeared like regret. "Not all of it has been fun. I've made mistakes, too."

"Still, what stories you'll have for when you get older."

Nellie gave their tickets to the man at the door. "Well, starting tonight, you'll also have stories for when you get older. Come on."

Music reverberated off the walls inside, a jaunty tune suited to a dance hall. Costumed revelers streamed every which way, many wearing revealing outfits, everything from court jesters and peacocks, to gods and goddesses. A nearly naked Cleopatra and Marc Antony brushed by her on their way to the main floor. Katherine tried not to gape at seeing so much skin on display in public.

"Stop gawking," Nellie murmured. "Besides, the good stuff supposedly doesn't happen until after midnight. Let's go this way."

They went into the main hall, which was packed with thousands of people, both on the floor and in the stands surrounding them. A one-hundred-piece orchestra was fashioned at the opposite end of the oval, while dancers covered the floor with their twirls and high kicks. Drawers were shown without hesitation, a flash of lace and thigh every way one turned.

"I feel overdressed," she shouted as her friend tugged her into the throng of dancers.

"See? And you were worried! Let's dance for a bit."

Nellie found an open spot and the two of them began to jump and spin, dancing until time blurred, one song after the next. Men came and went, stopping to whirl and chat before moving along. The atmosphere was friendly and loose, nothing like the uptight High Society balls. A scantily dressed woman showed them how to can-can, which drew a round of applause from those nearby—including some gentlemen sitting in the private boxes.

"Look over your right shoulder, in the box above," Nellie said over the music. "There's your king."

"What?" Katherine peeked at the private boxes hovering over the floor. A man dressed in the manner of a courtly French king—either Louis XV or XVI—was staring at her, his dark eyes glittering from behind a white mask. Atop his head sat a white wig, his shoulders and chest encased in a fine navy suit embroidered with silver thread. Her heart skipped once as their gazes locked, the intensity of him causing the breath to catch in her lungs. How long had he been watching her?

Facing Nellie once more, she said, "How funny. Should I go say bonsoir?"

"Definitely not. There are too many men here to settle for a despot hiding behind a mask and wig."

"He's probably married."

"Probably," Nellie agreed, then pointed to the wine gallery. "Let's go up and get a drink."

Absolutely parched, Katherine nodded. "Lead the way, your majesty."

The second-floor corridor was dark but crowded. Faceless couples lurked in the shadows, clearly engaged in scandalous activity. They passed a man with his head buried under a woman's skirts, while beyond, a woman was on her knees, a man's hips rocking toward her face. Neptune, complete with gold tights and a trident, was kissing one of the founding fathers against a pillar. A second later a young woman with her breasts bared ran past, laughing, as a pirate chased her down the hall.

Nellie's attention never wavered, seemingly taking it all in stride, while Katherine couldn't help but stare. She'd never seen intimacy firsthand, in public or in private.

It did look fun, though.

Once in the wine gallery, they settled in with champagne. The first glass disappeared quickly, so Katherine grabbed them refills. Then they took their drinks into the stands to watch the action below. The hour had grown late and the crowd was growing rowdy. Gents tossed women into the air, catching them, and people climbed in and out of the boxes freely. The straps of many a costume had slipped and bosoms were exposed without any apparent hesitation. Shirtless men were there, as well, rubbing against other dancers.

"This is unbelievable," Katherine said. "What a night."

"It's not over yet," Nellie said. "You still need to find your affair."

Katherine's gaze drifted back toward King Louis, who was alone in his box, drinking something clear out of a crystal tumbler. Her stomach fluttered, which was a ridiculous reaction to a complete stranger. The man was probably cheating on his wife. "It's fine if I don't find him tonight." She turned to the crowd. "This has given me inspiration, certainly."

Nellie finished her glass of champagne. "If by inspiration you mean fantasies for when you touch yourself, then I agree."

Before Katherine could reprimand her friend for saying such an outrageous thing, a woman in red tights and a corset leaned in, albeit unsteadily. "Hear, hear!" she slurred loudly. "They're always much better lovers in our minds than they are in real life, ain't they?"

"Indeed," Nellie said with a chuckle. "Unless you tell them precisely what to do!"

Their new friend found that humorous, and she passed Nellie the bottle of wine from her hand. "I like you, Queen Elizabeth."

"Thank you," Nellie said, even though it was the wrong monarch. "And I you, madam."

"Madam!" The woman snorted. "Ain't that rich." Her companion, a man in a black domino, wrapped his arms around her and began tugging her away. Their friend waved goodbye, giggling the entire time.

Nellie held up her empty coupe. "I'm ready for another drink."

A man approached them while they were waiting in line. He was fit, slightly older, with an elegant silk mask tied around his head. "Bonsoir, Marie," he said in a heavily accented French voice as he bowed in Nellie's direction. "I have been searching everywhere for you, mon petit chou."

"Adrian, hello." Nellie moved in to kiss both his cheeks. "May I introduce my friend?"

"Madame de Pompadour," Katherine said and held out her hand. "It is nice to meet you."

He kissed Katherine's knuckles. "I understand. We must hold up these pretenses in your restrictive society, non? I am Adrian."

"This is my fencing instructor," Nellie said.

"Ah. It's nice to meet you."

After receiving their champagne, the trio moved into the corridor, where Adrian and Nellie began flirting shamelessly. Katherine not only felt a bit superfluous but also like she was hindering her friend's fun.

"I'm going to walk around for a bit," she told Nellie. "I'll find you later."

"Are you certain?" Nellie stepped away from Adrian and pulled Katherine aside. "Are we making you uncomfortable? I can send Adrian away."

"No, don't be silly. Have fun. I'm perfectly capable of amusing myself for a little bit."

"I will stay in this general area so you'll know where to find me later on. In the meantime, do not wander into dark corners and only get your drinks from the attendant in the wine gallery."

She loved Nellie's protective streak. She kissed the other woman's cheek. "I promise. No corners and no strange drinks."

"Good. Now, go have fun, madame." Nellie playfully slapped Katherine's bottom with her palm. "And do everything I would do."

Chuckling, Katherine carried her coupe and strolled along the corridor. The music continued below but it was quieter up here, and she could hear moans and grunts coming from the private rooms. One woman reached her peak right as Katherine walked by, the loud chants of "Oh, God, yes!" echoing off the walls. Unexpected heat blossomed in her lower half. Whatever was happening in that room sounded pleasurable, much more so than when she used her fingers between her legs. Was this what she had to look forward to with a lover?

"Fuck me harder!" the same woman demanded. "Give me that big cock."

Ducking her head, Katherine darted past and tried to cool her flaming face with a long drink of champagne—and almost ran right into a wall of blue velvet.

Only, it wasn't a wall. It was a man coming out of the gentleman's retiring room. King Louis. She gave a swift intake of breath. Goodness, he was absurdly tall up close, his shoulders wider than the Brooklyn Bridge. She couldn't see much of his face, just his mouth and jaw surrounded by a long white wig, yet her insides heated as if a match had been struck.

"It is you," he murmured, then the edge of his mouth hitched in an arrogantly attractive move. "C'est impossible, madame."

He spoke French perfectly yet she could hear the Upper Fifth Avenue in his speech. Perhaps it was the two and a half glasses of champagne, but she returned in French, as well, making certain to adopt a saucy attitude. "And why is it impossible, your majesty?"

"Because I have been looking for you everywhere on the dance floor."

"Is this true?"

He placed a hand on the wall above her head and leaned in, his frame creating an intimate space for just the two of them. Her heart began pounding in her ears. "Indeed," he said. "I quite liked your high kicks."

Katherine would have blushed at such a compliment, but Madame de Pompadour accepted it as her due. "Thank you. A king's mistress must flaunt her joie de vivre."

"And is that what you are—a king's mistress?"

The words were loaded with meaning, a question that could easily lead her down a path of depravity. Nerves and excitement bubbled like the champagne in her glass. Still, it seemed surreal.

Who was this woman, talking so brazenly with a man she'd never met before?

He doesn't know you. Stop worrying.

Precisely. This was why she'd come tonight, to have anonymous fun. Nellie wasn't afraid to go after what she wanted, so why should Katherine second-guess herself?

Boldly, she moved a bit closer to the king. "I don't know. Am I?"

He took her elbow. "Come with me to my box and we shall discuss it."

PRESTON COULD NOT believe his luck.

He'd somehow found Madame de Pompadour in the corridor after watching her for the better part of the night on the dance floor. The French Ball was impossibly crowded, and he'd held little hope of meeting her after losing sight of her long legs and tall white hair. Yet, here she was.

He suspected her an actress or chorus girl out for a bit of fun. Bold and adventurous, she was exactly the type of woman he'd hoped to meet tonight. Her costume was risqué but she hadn't shown her tits or lifted her leg to reveal the part in her drawers, which made her all the more tantalizing. He wanted to peel back those layers of cloth to see what lay underneath and, based on her décolletage, he had very high hopes, indeed.

Honestly, she was the only woman to pique his interest since he arrived. Sitting in his box alone, he'd brooded, watching the rest of the revelers enjoy themselves. Even whiskey hadn't helped his dark mood.

A distraction in the form of Madame de Pompadour was exactly what he needed.

He opened the door to the box he'd reserved for the event. "Here you go, ma chérie."

The salon in the back of the box contained a sofa, two chairs and a small table. An ice bucket and a bottle of champagne had been delivered earlier, so he offered her some. "More bubbly?"

She arranged herself on the sofa, taking great care with her short skirts, and eyed the unopened bottle. Was she checking the label to ensure it was quality champagne? He didn't mind. It was the most expensive bottle available tonight.

"Yes, please."

He popped the cork and poured her a glass, then settled next to her, reclining to give her more space. Hopefully his size wouldn't intimidate her, as it often did with strangers. The last thing he wished was to make her uncomfortable.

"You're not imbibing?" she asked in English, nodding to his empty hands.

"I had a glass of whiskey earlier. That was enough."

"I'm surprised to find you up here all alone, without any loyal subjects to amuse you."

"What is the line? Uneasy is the head that wears the crown."

"I sense we are discussing more than your costume this evening."

"Costume?" He tried to appear affronted. "Je ne vois pas de quoi vous parlez."

She laughed, a musical sound. "Oh, you don't know what I mean?"

"Your French is excellent, by the way."

"As is yours. Though I'm better with Spanish and Italian."

A cultured woman who was this uninhibited? He could practically salivate at the possibilities. "Impressive. Tell me, what is your favorite French word?"

Sipping her champagne, she stared at him over the rim of her glass, her light brown eyes dancing. "Pamplemousse."

"A fine choice."

"But I also like étoile."

What a strange combination, grapefruit and star. The two words were some sort of insight into her mind, but he wasn't certain what it meant. Yet.

"And which are your favorites, King Louis?"

He had many, but he decided to see how deep her knowledge of the language ran. "Embrasse-moi is certainly one." Her gaze dipped to his mouth, so she clearly understood the words. He tried again. "Baiser is another."

Her lips pursed. "Basically the same word, no?"

"Not quite. As a verb, baiser takes on a more vulgar meaning."

"Oh." She took a sip of champagne, her throat working as she swallowed. "Do you mean . . . ?"

"To fuck."

"Oh," she repeated, a hand flying to her throat.

He chuckled. The innocent reaction was adorable. An act, of course, because no innocent woman would dare to step foot inside the French Ball. Regardless, the angelic response sent waves of heat through his blood, twisting and turning, tingling along his skin. There was something so pure, so honest, about her. He hadn't been this intrigued by a woman in ages.

He gave her his best seductive grin. "A king's mistress is no doubt familiar with these things."

That relaxed her, tucking them firmly back into their roles for the evening. "Of course, though I'm certain your majesty could teach me all sorts of interesting things."

Yes, he liked the sound of that. Probably too much. "What is it you wish to learn, mon chou?"

She was quiet for so long that he worried she wouldn't answer, her fingernail tapping on the side of the coupe as she stared at him. "Tell me about you," she finally said. "Are you married?"

He sensed she wanted to know about him, Preston, so he answered honestly. "No."

Her shoulders eased slightly. "Children?"

"No."

"How old are you?"

He draped an arm over the back of the sofa. "Twenty-five."

"Oh. You seem older."

"Do I?" Was that a compliment or an insult? He couldn't tell. Damn these masks. "Most women are actually pleased when they learn my age."

"Why?"

He dropped his voice to a seductive whisper. "Stamina."

She laughed, her face softening as it had below on the dance floor. She looked young and carefree, a bright-eyed ingenue, but that impression was dashed when a flirtatious smile twisted her lips. "And here I thought kings made their mistresses do all the work."

"Not this monarch. I have a very hands-on approach."

"They are nice-looking hands." She tilted her chin to where his hands rested on the back of the sofa. "Strong and competent."

He flexed his fingers. "They are, indeed. Would you care for a demonstration?"

"Not yet," she said and sipped more champagne. "I'm enjoying our conversation—and I haven't decided if you've earned more yet."

His skin crawled with anticipation. Madame de Pompadour's shyness had Preston's mouth watering for the tiniest taste of her. "I'll have to see what I can do to convince you. How old are you?"

"Twenty as of a few months ago."

"And what do you do when not attending scandalous balls?"

"Attend to my king, obviously."

The words were a blast of electricity to his insides, veins sizzling like he'd touched a live wire. "And what if your king needs attention here? Right now?"

"Then I would tell him to wait."

"You're adorable."

"Adorable?"

She seemed surprised, so he elaborated. "So adorable that I'm dying to kiss you."

She bit her lip, the plump flesh disappearing between straight white teeth. He couldn't read her expression, not with the mask, but she seemed uncertain. "We've only just arrived. I'm not certain . . ."

"A kiss, madam—and I'm able to wait until you decide. Just know that I'm thinking about it."

"If I kiss you, will you keep your hands there?" She nodded toward his arms, one on the sofa back, the other on the armrest. Was she nervous he would accost her?

Of course she is, you idiot. She has no idea who you are and has likely seen many women groped or accosted tonight.

He gave a regal incline of his head. "I swear it. I'll not touch you unless you ask me."

"Thank you." She put her glass down and scooted closer, near enough that her leg met his thigh. Her scent, sweet and dark with a hint of citrus, filled his head, and he dragged in a deep breath. The perfume wasn't overpowering, which he appreciated. He wondered if she applied it behind her ears and to the tops of her breasts. Perhaps he'd soon find out.

One small palm landed on his chest, the warmth of her skin sinking through the layers of silk and cotton, into his flesh, and goose bumps broke out all over his torso. He had no idea what she would do, but he was eager for it.

"I am curious," she said quietly, "if you feel as solid and impregnable as you look."

He clenched his hands into fists to keep from touching her as she traced the embroidery adorning his vest. She embarked on a slow, torturous examination of his upper half, and he watched her face, looking to see how his proximity affected her, ensuring there was no fear. She was flushed, pulse pounding at the base of her throat, as she explored with gentle sweeps of her fingers, testing the shape of him. As if she'd never touched a man before.

God almighty, that fantasy would send him right over the edge. He pushed it firmly aside.

Bolder, she slipped her hands under his jacket, up to his shoulders, with her head hovering perilously close to his. She concentrated on her task, and he was aching to kiss her, to taste her. To make some discoveries of his own. With a strength of will he hadn't known he possessed, he remained perfectly still and let her catalogue him—even when she returned to his chest and moved lower, over his stomach.

"Are you ticklish?" she asked, her voice a ragged whisper.

"No. Are you?"

"Very—not that you'll ever find out."

"You might change your mind."

She hummed in the back of her throat and slid a hand over his ribs. "I think I have my answer."

"To what?" he rasped, resisting the urge to lean into her touch.

She sighed dramatically and plucked at one of the silver buttons on his vest. "About whether you feel as strong as you look."

"And what is your conclusion?" He smiled at the top of her head, feeling like a young boy about to kiss a girl for the first time. When was the last time he'd felt so free, so *light*? In no hurry to rush things along and make them both come? It had been ages.

"I don't wish to say. Kings aren't known for humility as it is."

"Meaning, you're about to compliment me."

She tilted her face toward his, their lips so close that her breath warmed his skin. "Except mistresses are the ones who require compliments and presents, not kings."

Was she fishing? Because he had a long string of things he found both enticing and arousing about this woman. "I'm happy to shower you with compliments. I have a rather lengthy list in my head, if you like."

"A long list? Truly?" Her eyes sparkled behind the mask. "But you haven't even seen my face."

"I've seen enough to know you are beautiful, with a bright and mischievous smile. Brown eyes that resemble a fine ale. Legs so long they make a man crave feeling them around his hips. Skin like pale cream, especially the tops of your breasts." He nodded to where the plush mounds were nearly slipping out of her corset. "In fact, every single part of you is so damn lovely that I've been half-hard since the moment I spotted you in the crowd."

The lines of her face slackened and she blinked at him a few times. "Really?"

"Would you like to move your hand lower and find out?"

"I believe you." She slowly dragged a finger along the bare skin of his throat, above his cravat. "But I would like something else."

"Whatever you wish, madam."

"Embrasse-moi, my king."

Chapter Five

❧

Katherine could not believe the words coming out of her mouth, like the devil had taken root in her mind and forced her to say the most outrageous things. Though the true cause was more likely the anonymity and champagne. Whatever the reason, she was now lost in a sea of lust and longing for this man, one she'd just groped like a side of beef at an auction.

He felt magnificent, too. All lean muscle and solid bone, with wide shoulders and a tapered waist. He sat perfectly still, reclined, like the king he pretended to be, and allowed her to paw at him, never breaking his promise to keep his hands to himself.

It wasn't enough. She needed more.

The mask and costume allowed a sense of freedom she'd never experienced before, a loosening of the morals ingrained in her for the last twenty years. Louis didn't seem to mind the role-play, either, his eyes going dark after she called him "my king." His chest rose and fell with the force of his rapid breathing, and she noticed the bulge in his trousers when her fingers had traveled lower.

"You want me to kiss you?" he asked, leaning forward to press his nose into her powdered hair. Was he smelling her?

"Yes, but you may not touch me."

It was silly, this dictate, but he was large and . . . intense. Even through his mask and wig, she could tell this was a man with whom one did not trifle. And she didn't know him, not really. He could be a masher or a thug. They were alone in a salon in a crowded amphitheater where anything could happen and no one would hear her calls for help.

Thus far, he'd kept his word and respected her wishes, though they were both perfectly aware he had the upper hand between them. The muscles lurking beneath his clothing were not padding.

"Fine," he said. "May I remove your mask?"

For a beat she considered it, but recognition was too great a risk, given his age and cultured accent. There was every possibility they knew some of the same people or traveled the same High Society circles. "No—and leave yours on, as well."

"I see. Then we plan to stay in character."

She caught his gaze, mesmerized by the light flecks of green in his dark brown irises. At this close range, she could see the dark whiskers along his jaw and above his lip, the thick lashes framing his lids. Her belly dipped and swooped, the moisture between her legs evident. Never had she imagined a man could cause her to feel this reckless, this daring. It was like he'd lifted something heavy off her shoulders and she was finally floating free. "Is that a problem, my king?"

His mouth parted as hooded eyes, intense and hungry, locked on her mouth, causing a shiver to work through her. "Not at all. Now, kiss me, reinette."

Like he'd pulled her with a string, she started to close in, her face drifting toward his. She put a hand on his chest, steadying herself as the room narrowed to just the two of them. They were speaking in hushed whispers, as if they weren't alone. "Little queen?"

"Indeed." Dipping his head, he waited with his mouth poised above hers. "It was Madame de Pompadour's nickname and quite fitting for you, I think."

Heavens, this man was hazardous to a girl's innocence. He should come with some sort of warning, like in the pamphlets the teetotalers circulated about alcohol. *Caution: may cause you to lose your inhibitions and your virginity.* But this was no time for caution; this was a time for bold action, warning be damned.

I'm tired of waiting. I want to live my life.

And what better way than with a man she'd never see ever again?

Easing forward, she pressed soft kisses to the edge of his mouth, then the other side, while his breath ghosted over her skin, a hint of whiskey and cigar that reminded her of dark paneling and secret rooms. His heart pounded under her palm but he let her lead, grunting softly when she shifted closer and sealed their lips together. He tilted his head, making it easier for her, and their mouths moved, cautious at first, then stronger. More insistent, as if they'd waded into the shallows, decided they liked the water and then plunged into the depths.

In a flash, he took over. He kissed her hard, not letting up, and slipped his tongue in her mouth to stroke against hers. Her body melted against him, her fingers sinking into the plush fabrics he wore, to the muscle below, while her head spun. Who knew that kisses could be so consuming, so wonderful? He was a stranger, which made this all the more baffling, yet he was respectful of her, aware of his intimidating size. He'd done everything possible to put her at ease.

He broke off and dotted open-mouthed kisses under her jaw, then scraped his teeth across the sensitive tendons. "You're so damn perfect," he whispered. "I could devour you."

Each word and caress echoed in the tips of her breasts and between her legs. She couldn't think, could only *feel*. All that was left in her brain was the throbbing of pure lust, the pleasure created by his lips, tongue and teeth.

So . . . what would his hands feel like on her body?

When his teeth sank into the place where her shoulder met her neck, she gasped. This wasn't enough. She was drowning in need and longing. "Touch me. Please."

"Are you certain?"

Was she? This was what she'd wanted, an

encounter no one would ever know about. An experience she'd never forget, one most women her age couldn't even imagine.

You came here to have an affair. He doesn't know you, and you'll never see him again.

He'd proven trustworthy and she was attracted to him. A lot. So, what was she waiting for?

Scooting closer, she hid her nervousness behind Madame de Pompadour's bravado. "Do you doubt your mistress's mind?"

He chuckled, the sound rich and deep, and a large palm glided along the outside of her thigh, under her skirts, directly to her bottom. He squeezed one buttock through the thin cloth of her drawers. "I serve at your pleasure, mon chaton."

My kitten.

With his free hand on the side of her neck, he angled her head and took her mouth once more, devouring her, his lips slanting across hers again and again, without respite. It was as if her request had unleashed something in him, turning their kiss from a steady fire into a roaring inferno. While his tongue mastered her mouth, his hand caressed her thigh, teasing the bare skin above her garter, until she squirmed in desperation.

"Do you want me to touch between your legs?"

Did she?

She was pulsing there, wet and needy. The ache was unbearable. She nodded.

His fingers danced closer to where she craved them. "The words, if you please. Just so we are clear."

"Please, touch me. I am burning alive."

In a swift motion, he scooped her up and placed her on his lap, her legs dangling to one side. Ignoring the hard length under her bottom, she wrapped her arms around his neck as his fingers moved to her inner thigh, into the part of her drawers. There was no hesitation or fumbling; this was a man familiar with females and their clothing. Gently, he dipped a finger into her folds, near her entrance, and she sucked in a breath, surprised at how good it felt.

He kissed behind her ear. "Your pussy is hot and soaking. Is it all for me?"

Sweet mercy. Did he expect an answer? Because she was incapable of speech at the moment. Not only from his crude words but the intimate caresses between her legs. It was delicious, but not quite where she ached the most, the place she touched to bring herself relief.

The wicked man teased and stroked, the wetness from her core easing the glide across her skin. She sank her fingers into his muscles, urging him, as her hips began to rock, seeking. Finally— *finally*—he brushed her clitoris with the pad of his finger. The simple touch sent waves of pleasure through her, heat singing along every tendon and nerve, leaving a trail of bliss like she'd died and gone to heaven.

Why hadn't anyone told her it would feel so extraordinary?

"Ah, you like that, don't you?" he whispered. "You're so slick and soft, absolute perfection. Relax and let me make you feel good, beautiful."

He kissed her again, surrounding her and overwhelming her senses, and her body grew lax against him. She was floating, spinning, her mind dizzy, as the pressure built. He focused his attention in that one spot where all her nerves seemed to be centered, and as her muscles tightened, she pulled him closer, tensing in anticipation. It wouldn't be long, the final crest so very close . . .

His hand stilled. "Would you like more?" he asked, his voice like smoke, curling inside her, filling her.

"Yes."

"Then how do you ask me, reinette?"

What did he want? "Please."

"Please, who?"

She shook her head. This was too much thinking when all she wanted was for him to continue, to give her the orgasm hovering just out of reach.

He stroked her clitoris once and her eyes nearly rolled back in her head. "I want to hear you beg properly. Then I might let you come."

It fell out of her mouth without thinking. "Please, my king. Give me more."

One long finger pushed into her channel. "Christ, you are tight. Has it been a while, sweetheart?"

She nodded. Better to lie than have him find out she was an innocent.

"I will take good care of you, then." He withdrew a fraction, then pressed forward once more. The friction was unbelievable, the fullness a revelation. It was like he was inside and outside and all around her. Everywhere at once.

She threw her head back, eyes screwed shut,

and let out a long moan. It was too much, especially when he used his thumb on her bud again, and the peak quickly found her, her limbs shuddering as her muscles contracted. White heat consumed her, the rush of it dragging her into the heavens.

When she finally regained her senses, he was already placing her on the sofa and shifting to his knees. He shoved her skirts to her waist and wedged between her thighs. Wait, was this . . . was he . . . ? Right *here*? Katherine tensed and automatically tried to move away.

He clasped her thigh, holding her still, his dark eyes glittering in the gaslight behind his mask. "May I taste you?"

Taste her? Did he mean kiss her? If so, then why move to the floor? Perhaps he meant the skin of her legs

You are supposed to be a woman of experience.

Nodding, she forced herself to sink into the cushions. "I'd like that."

"You definitely will, if your reaction to my fingers is any indication."

Arrogant man. Though she had to admit, his fingers were talented. His touch felt even better than when she touched herself down there—

He folded in half, his tall frame bent at an awkward angle, and pressed his face to her center. What was he doing? He planned to kiss her . . . *there*? Good Lord. Was this something people—?

His tongue swiped across her most intimate flesh and her brain shut down. Took a holiday. Went on strike. Every bit of her intelligence disappeared when he began licking slowly, as if savoring her taste. She heard him growl, the sound soaking into her skin. "God, it's even better than I imagined," he said.

Clutching the sofa, she tried not to shout as pleasure rocketed through her. His tongue was thorough, his lips adding suction, and soon she was a quivering mess, on the brink of losing her mind. When he sucked her clitoris into his mouth, applying the best kind of pressure, she rapidly exploded into a million pieces of light, her limbs shaking like leaves in the wind.

Boneless, she sagged into the cushions and struggled to catch her breath. He rose and adjusted his mask, which had slipped slightly during his ministrations. His eyes were wild as he studied her sprawled form. "You are so beautiful and delicious. Licking your cunt got my cock so hard."

She shivered at his naughty words. Had he truly enjoyed it that much? Had he enjoyed *her* that much? The ridge in his trousers bulged obscenely, so clearly, yes, he had. So, should she reciprocate in some kind?

And how would you do that? You haven't the first clue on what to do.

Damn her lack of education on bedroom activities. Her naiveté was going to ruin this. Why hadn't she asked Nellie more questions as they were getting ready tonight?

He blew out a long breath and then reached for a coupe, downing a mouthful of champagne. Was he miserable, then?

The old Katherine would've waited patiently,

let the moment pass without doing anything. But she wasn't the old Katherine anymore. She was someone new, someone daring. Someone who was taking charge of her life.

Then take charge already.

Perhaps her lack of experience could work to her advantage. Perhaps she could gain an education without tipping her hand. She knew from hearing maids talk that men also pleasured themselves. Would he show her, if she encouraged him?

She blurted the words. "You could give yourself relief."

He paused in pouring more champagne. "I could," he said slowly, examining her expression. "Is that something you'd like to see?"

Absolutely. How else was she to learn about the male anatomy? "I would. Very much." When he seemed to hesitate, she added, "Please."

"Please, is it?" He ran his palm over the thick bulge in his trousers, then shuddered, his breath sawing out of his chest. "How could I refuse?"

Fascinated, she watched as he unbuttoned his clothes to reveal his erection. Katherine had seen genitalia in paintings and sculptures, but absolutely none of those had looked like this. This was thick and smooth, the mushroom-shaped head flushed red, with veins running along the side. How beautiful he was . . .

"Spread your legs wider," he rasped as he began to pump the shaft. Standing directly above her, he kept his gaze locked on her lower half.

Oh. The idea of him staring at her bare sex while he touched himself should have embarrassed her, but it did the opposite. Bumps broke out along her skin as heat bloomed in her belly, and she slowly widened her thighs, revealing herself, still swollen and wet from his mouth. A raw, desperate sound rumbled out of his chest, almost as if seeing her was too much, and she put the reaction to memory, to replay in her mind later when she was alone.

Reaching up, he placed his free hand on the ceiling to steady himself as he continued to work, fist flying over the head of his cock. Goodness, he was tall. Though most of him was covered, she couldn't tear her eyes away. He was riveting, glorious, the long planes of his body straining with his pleasure. His chest heaved, his movements slowing slightly—and then his hips jerked unsteadily, thick white ropes of spend erupting from the head of his shaft to land onto her drawers and stomach. It went on and on, the release coating her, like he was marking her.

"Oh, fuck," he shouted, his back bowing. "*Goddamn it.*"

Finally his shoulders slumped and his strokes grew gentler, until he gave a final twitch and finished. Sakes alive, what an astounding performance. Women should line up and pay to watch him do that. She bit her lip and stared at his softening erection, amazed at what she'd seen. What did the skin feel like?

"Wait," he said through his labored breathing. "Don't move. I'll clean you up."

HE'D LOST HIS mind. This woman made him more aroused, more desperate, than he'd been in years. In recent memory Preston couldn't recall a time when he had come so fast and with such enthusiasm. The woman's stomach was drenched with it, in fact—a primitive display he had no business enjoying as much as he did.

With shaking hands, he tucked himself away and closed the breeches of his costume. Finding a handkerchief in his coat pocket, he went to wet it at the water pitcher, reluctantly tearing his gaze away from his reclining companion. Everything about the moment was truly debauched, from her posture and the spend coating her body, to the uninhibited noises coming from the ball around them. He loved it.

She was surprising, this woman. It was perfect, her insistence to keep up their little ruse with no pressure or hint at more. Christ, it had been ages since he was with a woman without the trappings of his name dragging along behind him. Those of gentle breeding hoped for a match, while the rest hoped for access to his bank accounts.

Yet this sweet creature hadn't wanted anything more than his hands and mouth, her response so eager and genuine, almost innocent, that he'd become lost in the moment, delirious with desire. He'd tugged himself off right in front of her, for God's sake, unable to deny her request. He hadn't been so frantic, so *ravenous*, in quite a while, the taste of her driving him absolutely mad.

Kneeling between her legs, he cleaned her off, the scent of the encounter hanging heavily in the air, and he knew once would never be enough. He needed her undressed, naked and spread out beneath him, those big brown eyes looking up at him as he thrust inside her slick channel, riding her until they both came.

Merely imagining it was enough to get him hard again.

Would it be so terrible to see her after this? If he could keep their encounters casual, away from his real life?

When he finished his task, he tossed the handkerchief away and helped her sit up. Her fingers were slender and delicate in his own, and he was reluctant to let her go. He dropped onto the sofa and kept hold of her hand. "Did you enjoy that?"

"I did, actually. Twice."

He chuckled. Yes, he'd felt her climax each time, her body locking up, then quivering uncontrollably. He loved women and loved pleasuring them even more. "I enjoyed it, too. Very much." He plunged ahead, the need to have her again overriding all his good sense. "Would you be interested in a repeat performance, then? At a hotel, perhaps?"

"Tonight?"

"If you wish."

She chewed her lip, her gaze serious. Unfortunately, thanks to her mask, he couldn't truly judge her expression. Finally, his reinette shook her head. "I can't. I'm here with a friend."

"Another night, then. We can arrange to meet somewhere private."

"Without masks and costumes, you mean."

He brought her hand to his mouth and kissed her knuckles. "I think we are familiar enough, no?"

"I suppose that's true. Where did you have in mind?"

He had an apartment downtown, one he rarely used but had purchased for late nights and trysts. Arabella had hated it, declaring the place too shabby, but Preston liked the simplicity of it, a working-class neighborhood too busy to bother with anyone's comings and goings. He wasn't a Clarke there; he could be anyone he wished.

"My place on Jane Street. I'll write the address for you. Would tomorrow afternoon or evening work best?" He'd rearrange any appointment or obligation to suit her schedule.

"Evening. Late, like eleven."

"Perfect." He could attend his dinner meeting, get some work in, then come meet her. They could fuck all night, if the mood struck.

"How will I recognize you?" She was teasing, her light brown gaze dancing.

"Shall I wear my mask?"

"I rather like you in those breeches. They're very . . . tight."

He laughed, feeling lighter than he had in weeks. "Now you know why King Louis had so many mistresses."

"A man of many talents, clearly."

"Let us not forget his excellent taste in women."

"Are we discussing you or the king?"

"Both." He kissed her hand again. "So, tomorrow night. You'll meet me?"

She hesitated, then nodded. "I will meet you."

Was she nervous? "I'll not ask for anything you are unprepared to give. I know there are men who make such requests with expectations, but I promise I have none. I merely wish to see you again."

"Thank you. That does ease my trepidation. Believe it or not, I don't—"

"You don't, what?"

The lines bracketing her mouth deepened. "I do not visit strange men in their homes like that."

That much was obvious, and he was grateful she would consider it for him. "I believe it."

She angled to study him. "You do? Because I'm less than—"

"Stop right there. You're not less—you're *more*. You're real and genuine in a sea of falsehoods and deception." He dragged a finger along her jaw, desperate to touch her. "I watched you on the floor for a long time. You danced only with your friend and not the dozens of men who tried to engage with you. You asked me to refrain from touching you until you felt comfortable with me. And you've never once tried to find out my address or the amount of money in my bank account."

"But you barely know me."

"I know enough."

"Hmm. I'm not certain if that says something about me or the friends you usually keep."

"Both, I think. Now, I'll write down my address for you." Rising, he found a program for the evening—a useless piece of paper, really—and wrote the direction for his downtown apartment. "Here you are, mon chaton."

She folded and tucked the program deep into her bodice. "I should go. My friend is probably worried about me."

A sharp pang went through him, a reminder of what he'd recently lost, but he pushed it aside. "It's good to have friends who care. Here, let me help you." He pulled her to her feet, then rested a hand on her hip. With his other hand, he cradled her jaw. Her skin was so soft, so delicate. "Thank you for tonight. I'm very glad we met."

"Me, too. I suppose our costumes mean we were destined to meet tonight."

He didn't believe in fate, but no need to get into that now. Instead, he bent and captured her mouth in another kiss, the contact sending a jolt down to his toes. She was eager and sweet, kissing him back with abandon, without guile, and he drank it in like fine wine. The curves of her body fit perfectly with his, even given his height. How lucky he'd been to meet her here—an event with thousands of women.

When they broke apart, she was clutching his coat, her eyes unfocused. He felt a little dizzy himself, actually. Pressing a final kiss to her forehead, he said, "You should go before we lose our heads again. Shall I take you to find your friend?"

Stepping back, she righted her clothing. "That isn't necessary. I know exactly where she's waiting. Do you plan to stay longer?"

He shook his head. "No, I've had enough. I found what I want."

"Me?"

"You."

She moved in to kiss his chin. "Good. Unlike Madame de Pompadour, I don't fancy sharing.

I'll see you tomorrow night, then." She patted his chest, then walked out of the salon and into the corridor. He watched until she disappeared, already counting down the hours until tomorrow evening.

Chapter Six

❦

There you are! Where have you been?" Nellie rushed forward to take Katherine's hand. "You had me worried sick." She searched Katherine's face. "Did something bad happen? You're all flushed. And your mouth is . . . oh, my God. You've been kissing someone."

Katherine tried to suppress a grin—and failed. She held up a hand. "Give me a moment to breathe, will you? Where is Adrian?"

"He went to fetch champagne and look for you. I didn't want to leave in case you came back."

That made Katherine feel guilty. "Was I truly gone that long?"

Nellie's eyes went wide. "Katie, it's been an hour and a half."

It had? "Oh, I'm so sorry. I wasn't keeping track of the time."

"Obviously," Nellie said dryly. "So, who was he?"

Was she ready to talk about this here? She would tell Nellie all the details, but not now. Besides, it was fun having this little secret. Katherine shook her head. "Just a man I met."

"That is not going to do it, young lady. I want to hear what you were up to and with whom."

"I don't know him—and it was just a harmless bit of fun." Her skin grew hotter at the memory. She hoped the lights were low enough in the corridor that Nellie couldn't see her blush.

"You are turning bright red. Katherine Eloise Delafield, did you sleep with a man here at the French Ball?"

"No! Of course not. I told you, it was harmless fun."

"Because if you are thinking of sleeping with a man, you and I should talk first. I doubt your aunt has prepared you for what happens or how to prevent complications."

Oh, right. Katherine stared at the wall. Aunt Dahlia, her father's sister and Katherine's chaperone, certainly hadn't mentioned those things. Any knowledge Katherine possessed of intimate acts had been gleaned through paintings and drawings. "Good thing I'm staying at your house tonight. You can tell me everything you know."

"That would take longer than one measly night, unfortunately, so we'll just start with the basics. Cover the major points."

"You sound as if you're about to give a lecture."

Nellie threaded her arm through Katherine's and began towing them toward the wine gallery. "You'll definitely need to take notes. And there might be an exam, as well. Come, let's find Adrian."

The fencing instructor was still in line for champagne. Nellie and Katherine started toward him—but Nellie suddenly froze, her gaze locked on a familiar man leaning against the wall, his body angled toward a scantily dressed woman. Katherine squinted. "Is that the Duke of Lockwood?"

"Of all the nerve," Nellie hissed. "Has he no shame?"

"Well, he isn't married or attached. Though it's a bit strange that he's not wearing a costume or mask."

"Arrogant bastard. Never mind that he is supposed to be wooing a bride before sailing for England. Hard to imagine tonight helps toward that goal."

Apparently abandoning the refreshment line, Adrian arrived and immediately hauled Nellie to his chest. He bent to kiss her, but Nellie turned her face at the last moment and gave him her cheek. "I think it's time to go," she said. "This crowd has grown exceedingly dull."

That suited Katherine. She'd had her fill of excitement this evening. Adrian led Nellie toward the door, and Katherine was left to follow. Which meant she caught the expression on the duke's face as Nellie passed. His gaze tracked her departure, his expression shocked. Then it turned dark, almost angry.

Had Lockwood recognized Nellie despite her costume? Keeping her head down, Katherine hurried into the corridor and trailed Nellie to the ground floor. When they stepped outside, Adrian hailed them a hansom. "I will see the two of you home."

"No, thank you," Nellie said and kissed his cheek. "I'm tired and the two of us will be fine alone."

The fencing instructor appeared uneasy, his gaze taking in the drunken revelers spilling out onto the streets. "Are you certain?"

"Quite. I'll see you tomorrow afternoon."

When they were settled in the carriage, Nellie said, "Now, let's discuss your secret lover."

"There is no secret lover." The word implied a romantic entanglement. This had been a stranger, someone with whom she shared no emotional connection whatsoever. "He is a man I met that happens to kiss exceedingly well."

"And you have no idea who he was?"

"No. But . . ." She hesitated, unsure how her friend would react.

"But?"

"I agreed to meet him tomorrow night downtown."

"Katherine!" Nellie was horrified. "Absolutely not. You mustn't do something so unsafe. He could be a murderer for all you know."

"He is not a murderer. At least, I'm fairly certain he isn't a murderer."

"Fairly certain is not certain. This is a terrible idea. You cannot go."

"Why not? I would think you'd encourage such recklessness."

Nellie huffed, sounding annoyed. "I am all for being reckless if you are safe. That means knowing the person with whom you are meeting. Trust me, a stranger will not have your best interest—"

She clamped her mouth shut, the words dying abruptly.

Oh, this was interesting. "You are speaking from experience, obviously."

"It doesn't matter. Right now we are discussing *you*. Going to a strange man's house tomorrow is out of the question."

"But I want to go."

"Of course you do. You're still drunk on orgasms and champagne. It'll pass."

"I'm not, and it won't."

Nellie shook her head. "You will think more clearly in the morning, I promise."

"And if I don't?"

"Then I'll tie you down and refuse to let you out of my sight."

Katherine chuckled, part amusement and part exasperation. "This is ridiculous. You should be helping me, not telling me I cannot go."

"Katie, you are innocent and sweet. You make lists and dream about art. You try to help your friends find love, just as you hope to one day. I, on the other hand, trust no one because I know how awful people can be, especially men. As such, it is my duty to try and save you from poor decisions."

Katherine laid her head on Nellie's shoulder and sighed. She didn't want to argue. "Thank you for looking out for me. You are a good friend."

"You're still planning to go, aren't you?"

"Yes." When Nellie made a disbelieving noise, Katherine sat up. "How about this? I will tell you where I'm going. That way, if I disappear, you may give the police my last whereabouts."

"This is not making me feel better."

"Well, you could come with me. Meet him to ensure he knows someone is aware of my presence there."

"That's not a bad idea. Of course, he'll likely assume you brought a friend to join in the fun."

Katherine mulled this over, uncertain she'd heard this correctly. "Wait, two women at once? This is a thing people do?"

Nellie patted Katherine's knee. "Good thing we're having our talk tonight. You have a lot to learn."

At the knock, Preston looked up from his paperwork. "Yes?"

His secretary stood in the doorway. "Your permit to take down that building on Twenty-Third Street was rejected."

Mouth dropping open, he tossed his pen onto the desk. "That's impossible."

This project had been over a year in the making. The insurance company entrusted him with the development and architects were already bidding for the job, for Christ's sake. It was to be the tallest building in the world when completed, thirty floors high, a structure unlike anything the city or the world had ever seen. In fact, he'd bribed the buildings department official just last week to speed the permit along. The demolition of the existing structure should have been a foregone conclusion, considering Preston *owned the land*.

"They say someone else holds the deed."

"Who?"

"They wouldn't tell me, so I made some calls."

Of course she did. Mrs. Cohen was resourceful and smart. She always knew which rocks to overturn to find the snakes. "And?"

"It's Lloyd Delafield."

Ice settled in his veins as his hands curled into fists. What the ever-loving fucking hell? "I don't believe it."

"When the business dissolved that land went with Delafield, apparently."

"I have a deed that states otherwise."

Mrs. Cohen shrugged, her colorful aqua dress rustling. She liked to say bright colors made the dreary workday go faster. "Shall I search for another piece of available property?"

"I don't want another piece of land. There isn't another like this one, not at such a prominent intersection. Damn it!" He slapped a hand on top of his desk. "I already told Manhattan Surety we have that corner. What are they going to think if I tell them we don't?"

"I'll ring your lawyer if you agree to stop cursing."

"No need," he said, rising. "I'm going to see Delafield."

Once in a hack, he dug into his coat pocket for a cigarette. While he didn't often smoke, only three or four cigarettes in a given week, he needed one at the moment. He needed a clear head to deal with Lloyd.

After the Clarke/Delafield business dissolved, Lloyd Delafield continued buying and selling land throughout Queens, Staten Island, Manhattan and Brooklyn. In recent years, Preston had battled with him many times over various plots, so it didn't surprise him to learn that Delafield wanted this particular slice. It was one of the best locations in New York, right at Fifth Avenue and Broadway, along the southern edge of Madison Square.

But it belonged to Preston.

Henry Clarke had been a gambler, using the rent he collected from a few properties to fuel his love of cards. Unfortunately, Henry spent more than he earned, and debts were left all over the city. No one suspected a thing until the bank manager visited the house to tell Preston's mother they were in danger of foreclosure.

At that point, Preston immediately withdrew from school, came home and assumed control of everything. Henry died not long after, and his estate was quickly settled. The deed from the Twenty-Third Street property had still been in the Clarke safe.

Preston had seen the deed with his own two eyes. Any claims to the contrary were a lie. This was a ruse on Lloyd's part. It had to be. Was this a retaliation for Preston's refusal to marry Katherine? Or had his success threatened Lloyd?

Well, Preston wasn't as trusting as his late father. Lloyd had no idea who he was up against.

Once Preston arrived at Delafield's building, he felt marginally calmer. He went straight up to the office. "Mr. Clarke to see Mr. Delafield."

The young secretary's eyes went wide. She rose and hurried into Delafield's office, closing the door behind her. Preston examined the anteroom, noting the fine art and expensive furniture. Trappings of wealth that hadn't been used to help Henry Clarke when he'd so desperately needed it.

Bitterness scratched in the back of his throat.

The door opened and the secretary waved him in. "Mr. Delafield will see you now."

"Thank you," Preston said and entered Lloyd's office.

"Preston." Lloyd rose from behind his desk, his gold watch fob glinting in the afternoon sun. "This is unexpected."

Preston waited for the door to close before asking, "Is it?"

"Yes, of course." The other man drew closer, his hand extended. "It's good to see you again."

Preston ignored Lloyd's hand. "I wish I could say the same, Lloyd."

Lloyd's arm dropped and he frowned. "Shall we sit?"

"I'd rather stand, actually, and this isn't a friendly visit. You see, there seems to be a discrepancy with my land on Twenty-Third Street. I'm set to demolish that small office building Henry built in '75, but the buildings department has rejected my permit. They say the land doesn't belong to me."

"That's correct. It belongs to me."

The assertion was made with no hint of malice whatsoever, but Preston sneered all the same. "That is a lie. It's always been Clarke land."

"No, it was part of the joint business, then it became mine."

"I have paperwork that states otherwise."

"Then it's outdated."

"And how is that possible? When my father

died I inventoried every asset, every piece of property, every piece of *lint* that belonged to the Clarkes." He remembered it well, seeing as how he had to decide what to sell in order to keep the bank from taking the house. "I'm not wrong about who holds the deed."

"He sold me that land outright before he died."

"Horseshit."

If the foul language bothered him, Lloyd gave no sign of it. Instead, he looked almost smug, like he was enjoying the interaction. "There's no reason for me to lie. I have the signed revised deed and it's been filed."

"Then how much did you give him for it? And where did the money go?"

Lloyd lifted his shoulders in a small helpless shrug. "I'm afraid the details of that transaction must remain confidential. Rest assured I gave him fair market value."

"I want to see the paperwork. I want to verify that it's my father's signature."

"You think I forged a deed?"

Preston would absolutely forge a deed or any other paperwork, if necessary. Weren't they all playing by the same rules? "Convenient this happened right after your daughter came to see me about the supposed betrothal."

Lloyd's expression remained unchanged, as if he were unsurprised by the accusation. "You think this is in retaliation for your rejection of my daughter."

"Rejection?" Preston narrowed his eyes and folded his arms across his chest. He towered over Lloyd and he wasn't above using his size to intimidate the other man. "You telling her about that betrothal as if it were real was beyond cruel—even for you, Lloyd."

"I suspected you held a grudge over my dealings with your father, but that was no reason to hurt Katherine. She did not deserve your cruelty."

Cruelty? Preston had explained it carefully and calmly to her. "I went as gently as possible. It wasn't my fault her father filled her head with lies."

"Hardly lies when Henry and I had the betrothal paperwork drawn up and signed."

Preston had seen the contract. He was aware that it was perfectly legal, if one cared about the law. Which he didn't.

He said, "I don't care who signed it. All I know is that I didn't agree, and I wouldn't marry your daughter for all the money and land in Manhattan."

Lloyd's face remained inscrutable. "You're off the hook, then, because my daughter wants nothing to do with you. Why would I force her into a marriage with a man she despises?"

That was not an answer, not really. "At least I told her the truth. You should try it sometime."

"Do not presume to know how I have raised my daughter."

"I know she sees the world through rose-tinted glasses, thinking people are fair and kind when we both know they aren't. Don't we, Lloyd?"

"Again, you presume to know what happened with your father, but you do not."

"What I know is that I was left to pick up the pieces afterward. Alone. I suppose I have you to thank for that." This meeting was a waste of time. Why had he even bothered? He should've gone straight to his lawyers instead of coming here to reason with a man who was beyond reason.

As he started for the door, Preston said, "I want to verify the deed."

Lloyd said, "If you like. I'll have it sent to your office."

"Do that. I haven't any idea how you managed it, but I will task my people with finding out."

"It's not forged, Preston, but do what you must."

Preston put his hand on the knob, pausing to glare over his shoulder. If he could have incinerated Lloyd with his gaze, only a pile of ash would remain on the carpet. "Tread lightly, Delafield. You may have found my father easy to manipulate and ignore, but I promise you, I am not."

Chapter Seven

❧

$\mathcal{P}$reston prowled the tiny apartment, the worn floorboards squeaking beneath his boots. His mood was decidedly black after his shit-filled day.

After the news about Twenty-Third Street and the visit with Delafield, things hadn't improved. The unions on his twelve-story Wall Street project were grumbling, and materials for the nine-story office building in midtown were delayed. There hadn't been time for dinner, except a quick bite from a street cart.

He blew out a long breath and forced himself to relax. His glorious reinette would arrive soon and he didn't wish to take his terrible mood out on her. No, tonight he planned to charm her—and if that led to a vigorous bout of fucking, then he would not complain.

She'd completely undone him last night at the French Ball. Had knocked him sideways. He hadn't planned for that. He intended to find a woman there, share some mutual pleasure and never see her again. Neat and organized, just how he preferred.

But everything had changed after the pure and passionate way she'd responded to him. It was unlike anything in recent memory. There was a joyous innocence, a wide-eyed curiosity to her, that was so damn appealing. She hadn't even touched his cock and he'd shot off in his hand like a teenage boy.

He couldn't wait to take his time with her tonight, see where the evening took them. If she was amenable, he'd meet her here on a schedule. Twice a week should do it. Saturday night, of course, because he was usually free, and whatever night during the week he could manage.

A soft knock broke into his thoughts just as the clock on the mantel began to chime eleven o'clock. His reinette was right on time. Muscles clenching in anticipation, he strode to the door. The knob turned easily and he swung the wood panel open—

His body jolted. What on earth?

Katherine Delafield was on his doorstep. What was she doing here? Was she lost?

Something flickered in her eyes, something familiar. He'd seen it last night, as well as the surprised curve of her lips when they bumped into one another in the corridor.

Wait, had it been . . . ?

No, that was impossible.

Absolutely ludicrous.

And yet, what other explanation was there? Why else would this uptown princess come to an apartment building on Jane Street at this hour, if not to meet her lover from last night?

Goddamn it.

Ice sank into the marrow of his bones, freezing him over, as his mind raced. Had she known it was him the entire time? Had she thought to trick him? But to what end?

Was she trying to force him to marry her? Had her father put her up to this?

"You," he snarled.

She stared up at him, looking as bewildered as he felt. "You," she breathed.

Still gripping the door, he stepped aside. His voice was low and even. "Get inside. Right now."

She stiffened and leaned away from him. "Do not order me about, Preston Clarke. You have no such right, not with me."

"Get inside this apartment now, Katherine. Otherwise I'll happily have this conversation in the hall."

That did the trick. Head high, she pushed past him and entered the apartment. He shut the door with a snap. "I think you'd best explain yourself."

She whirled and lowered the hood of her cloak. "Me? You'd best explain yourself first."

The ice in his veins was quickly replaced by a white-hot anger so fierce that it was a wonder his skin didn't burst into flames. He wished for a drink, to dull the feeling, but that was the very worst reason to have one. "I have naught to explain, Katherine. You, on the other hand, have much to justify. Starting with why you, an unmarried lady, went to the French Ball."

"May I have a drink first?"

"Suit yourself." He gestured toward the sideboard and took a seat, rudely sitting while she stood. He was no gentleman. Better she learned it now.

Approaching the sideboard, she selected an empty tumbler and studied the bottles. After settling on one, she poured three fingers of rye and gingerly lowered herself into an armchair. She took a sip, made a face and set the glass down. "I thought I was ready for that, but indeed, I'm not. It's terrible."

Under any other circumstances he might've smiled. While she was adorable, she'd also tricked and lied to him at the behest of her father.

Preston forced his eyes to the floor and struggled to keep his focus. "Well?"

"I went to the French Ball to have fun. Same as you, apparently."

"Actually, I went to the French Ball to find a woman to screw. Convenient we found one another, wouldn't you say?"

"Are you implying I did this on purpose?" She blinked, her brows pulling together. "That I knew you were attending and set out to lure you into, what? Some sort of liaison? You already have a mistress. The entire city knows about her, in fact."

"Mrs. Russell and I have parted ways, not that it matters. And yes, I do believe you did this on purpose."

"That is absolutely ridiculous. And insulting. Why would I do something so devious?"

"Katherine, we both know the rules of society. Do you not understand what happened last night?"

She blinked at him innocently. A ruse or true confusion? He couldn't tell. Nothing made sense any longer. "We had fun," she said. "That was all."

"Wrong. I kissed you, fingered you. Licked your pussy. In short, I ruined you."

Waving her hand, she gave a dismissive sound. "No, you didn't," she said. "No one has been ruined."

Was she serious? "I assure you, I have. Therefore, I must ask myself if it was planned, as a way to force the marriage between us."

"Don't flatter yourself," she snapped, her gaze narrowing. "I went there to start living my life. To have fun after waiting on you for *a year*. I definitely am not trying to trap you into marriage."

"Did your father know you were attending last night?"

"My *father*?" She gaped at him, her eyes round and big. "He would lock me in my bedroom until my hair turned gray if he even suspected I planned to go."

Preston didn't believe her. Not after Lloyd's shenanigans with the Twenty-Third Street property. This was manipulation, pure and simple. "Oh, of course. This was coincidence, merely a chance meeting at the most lurid event of the year, with us in complementary costumes."

"Sarcasm doesn't become you, Preston."

"Lies don't become you, Katherine."

Roiling with fury and frustration, he studied her through his lashes. Brown hair was elegantly styled atop her head, showing off that creamy column of throat he'd kissed last night. He could almost remember the taste of her, the smell of lilacs on her skin. Her cries in his ear. The way her fingers clung to him when she found her release.

He no longer wanted that knowledge, didn't care to know what she sounded and looked like when she climaxed. Didn't want to see that delicate bone structure and luscious mouth sitting across from him, as if she hadn't ridden his tongue last night. Everything was now tainted, stained with the knowledge of what he'd done.

He could not allow himself to be attracted to Lloyd's daughter.

Dipping into his pocket, he withdrew his cigarette case and lighter. He lit a cigarette and inhaled a lungful of smoke, the ritual infusing some much-needed calm into him.

Scowling, she shook her head and reached for her drink once more. "I am not lying, no matter what you believe. This is a horrible mistake, nothing more. We're both going to forget last night and act like it never happened."

"Until you get home and inform your father of what you learned tonight. I suspect he'll be at my doorstep in an hour." Preston almost smiled. He couldn't wait to see the look on Lloyd's face when Preston refused to marry the girl.

Her lips parted, disbelief coasting over her expression. "You think I want to marry you, after all you've done? I'd rather die a shriveled-up spinster." She set the glass on the side table with a snap and stood. "You are impossible and absolutely the worst man I've ever met. I've told you the truth. If you refuse to listen, then that is your problem. I'm leaving."

Oh, no. She was not allowed to go now. He would have answers if it killed him. "Sit down, reinette," he said in a silky and commanding tone. "I'm not nearly done with you yet."

THAT DEEP SEDUCTIVE voice . . .

As much as Katherine didn't want his words to affect her, she couldn't resist his tone, the one he'd used last night.

I want to hear you beg properly. Then I might let you come.

She suppressed a shiver. Preston Clarke was her King Louis. It seemed impossible that the man who'd kissed her so sweetly and so passionately, the one who'd done all manner of wicked things both to her and in front of her, were one and the same.

I saw his cock.

Her skin warmed, like she was standing in front of a roaring fire. Granted, it had been a very nice cock, but she never would have guessed it belonged to Preston.

He masturbated and spent on me last night.

He'd been beautiful while doing it, too, with his head thrown back, the tendons in his neck standing out in sharp relief. Everything about their encounter had been lovely and perfect. How could such a generous and playful man be the same one sitting in front of her now, so cold and remote?

He continued to smoke, watching her with those intense dark eyes. Where had her teasing king gone?

He wanted to talk? Fine. He owed her answers, as well.

She lowered herself back into the chair. "Start explaining, then, because you watched me on the dance floor. You invited me to your box. This is your fault. Is this a jest to you, another way to control my life, as you've been doing for the last year?"

He exhaled a thin stream of cigarette smoke and it curled through the air to surround his face. Tingles ran up the backs of Katherine's legs. She'd never seen a man smoke before, not up close, and why was that so appealing? Because it called attention to his mouth?

He is the very last man to whom I should be attracted.

She had to stop thinking of last night, of the fantasy, and remember the real man sitting across from her now. The one who hadn't wanted to marry her. The one who'd been keeping her on the shelf for a full year. Granted, he hadn't known Katherine was honoring the betrothal, which made her feel even *more* foolish.

But as her aunt liked to say, a woman had to know her worth—and Katherine would not allow him to make her feel small ever again.

"Katherine, I was dressed as your lover. It's impossible to think we wouldn't have noticed the other. And you're so—"

He closed his mouth abruptly, biting off the words. Because he didn't wish to offend her? Too late for that.

She straightened and said in a rush, "I'm, what? Naive? Silly? Desperate? It must have given you quite a laugh that I came so willingly—"

"Gorgeous." He blew out another plume of white smoke. "I was going to say gorgeous."

Mouth suddenly dry, she swallowed. The unexpected compliment dulled her anger somewhat.

"So it only stands to reason that we were attracted to one another," he finished.

"I counted three other Madames de Pompadour last night. You could've ended up with any of those women."

"I never noticed any of them. Only you."

Ignoring the giddiness that fluttered in her chest at the revelation, she said, "Which means this was a coincidence. Nothing more than a terrible coincidence."

"Terrible? As I recall you quite enjoyed yourself."

He looked so smug, so positively righteous sitting in that chair, that she couldn't resist serving it back to him. "You quite enjoyed yourself, too. My clothing bears the stains to prove it."

His nostrils flared in response, and he leaned forward to stab out his cigarette in the crystal ashtray on the table. "Fine, we've established we are compatible in our desires. It means nothing because I still won't marry you."

"Nor I you."

He gave her a disbelieving look, like she was lying, and her skin prickled, irritation mounting again. She shot to her feet and gripped the chair back. "It's true. I don't wish to marry you any longer. I only allowed myself to consider it before I knew where things stood between us, but you settled that straight quick. *Twelve months too late.*"

He held up his hands, palms out, looking almost contrite for a moment. "This has not been easy on you and I sincerely apologize for it. I never for one minute thought you were waiting on me. I never thought anyone even remembered that betrothal agreement once my father died, let alone planned to honor it. Your father never said a word in all the years since."

"Perhaps we were thinking you were a man of honor. A man of your word."

Now it was his turn to appear irritated as he stood up. "First of all, I am a man of my word. It was never *my* word given on that agreement, it was my father's. Second, I'm not an honorable man, which is why I ejaculated all over you last night and then invited you here. I had every intention of seducing you again in the hopes that I might engage you as my mistress."

"Mistress!" She clenched her jaw so hard it was a miracle it didn't pop. "You have some nerve, assuming I would ever agree."

"As I said, I'm entirely dishonorable—which is why I'm doing you a favor by refusing that betrothal contract. You would hate being married to a man like me."

Sakes alive, the absolute delusion of this selfish man. "A favor." She nodded, her lips twisted in a mocking smile. "Indeed, thank you for allowing me to endure a second season, where everyone will be wondering why I'm not already married. Indeed, what a gift. I can hardly wait."

"As I said, I didn't know. But interesting that your father didn't push the betrothal until recently, when I turned Clarke Holdings around and began making a nice profit. Wouldn't you agree?"

"You're saying this is motivated by money?"

"Isn't everything?" His tone implied she was a fool if she thought otherwise.

"I feel sorry for you," she blurted. "You think everyone is out to get you or trying to steal from you. What a cynical, sad and awful way to live."

A muscle moved in his jaw, and his eyes burned as he stared at her. Still, he said nothing.

Her hands flopped uselessly at her sides. This was a disaster. Arguing with him accomplished nothing, and she needed to put distance between them. "Obviously we must pretend as if last night never happened."

The infuriating man had the nerve to shrug. "I told you, I'm dishonorable. I won't marry you to save your reputation, so I don't care whether you tell your father or not."

"Well, rest assured I have no intention of telling him—or anyone else. Last night was a mistake. Tonight was a mistake. I never should have come here."

"Yet you did." His intense gaze did a slow sweep of her body, one that made her feel exposed. Like her clothes were too tight, but in the very best way. "You were hoping for more of the same."

Now she was thinking of last night, too, memories of his feverish kisses and rough hands. The naughty words and the confident manner in which he'd pleasured her. She had hoped for more of the same, but it couldn't happen, not after learning King Louis was *him*.

"I need to go." She turned and bumped into a chair in her haste to get to the door.

"Say hello to your father for me."

She paused, curiosity getting the better of her. "What happened between you two? It's clear you don't like him. Did a business deal go bad?"

The lines of his face sharpened, and she knew there was something he wasn't telling her. "Ask your father. No doubt he'll be more than happy to fill you in—right after you tell him about last night."

An awful suspicion prickled over her skin. Had his surprise been a ruse tonight? Was this part of some grander plan? "Did you . . . seek me out last night as some sort of revenge against my father?"

"No," he said instantly. "I honestly didn't know who you were. If I had, I would've avoided you. My quarrel is with your father, not with you. I'm dishonorable, yes, but I'm not a monster."

She believed him. Her shoulders relaxed a fraction. "Good. Rest assured I won't breathe a word about this to anyone—and I suggest you keep it quiet, as well."

"You don't need to worry. I won't be the one who tells."

Implying she would? God, he was delusional. "I cannot believe I ever found you the least bit attractive." She lunged for the doorknob. "This was a huge mistake."

As she slammed the door behind her, she heard him say, "That is an understatement."

Chapter Eight

❦

$\mathcal{K}$atherine never thought she'd pity a duke, but seeing the Asher twins accost the Duke of Lockwood tonight was too horrifying to ignore. Lily and Millie Asher were terrors in silk and lace, following the duke around and interrupting any conversation he dared to start with anyone else. How Lockwood hadn't run screaming from the room was a miracle in itself.

She and Lockwood had met in June, at Maddie Webster's house party in Newport. She'd found him polite and decent, and certainly easy on the eyes. He was classically handsome, as if he'd stepped out of an advert for evening wear. His posture was impeccable, and he had a wealth of pride and confidence in his bright blue steady gaze.

Right now, Lily and Millie took turns shoving each other out of the way to get Lockwood's attention, and he was glancing around, looking helpless and uncomfortable. Katherine could not leave him to suffer.

Besides, it was a good distraction from her own

problems, which included far too much brooding over Preston Clarke and what happened at Jane Street three nights ago.

She approached the trio, then pretended to trip and bump into Lockwood, spilling a bit of her champagne on his sleeve. She straightened and tried to appear appropriately apologetic. "Oh, Your Grace, I beg your pardon. I'm so clumsy."

Millie and Lily stared in horror at the duke's wet sleeve, aghast at the faux pas, which gave Katherine the chance to wink at Lockwood. He relaxed and gave her a private smile.

"Miss Delafield," Millie whispered. "You've ruined the duke's evening suit."

Nonsense. A little bit of champagne wouldn't hurt the fabric. Still, Katherine kept up the pretense. "Your Grace, I must escort you to the retiring rooms straightaway. The stain must be dealt with promptly."

"Thank you, Miss Delafield," he drawled in his proper Mayfair accent. "I would be grateful. Excuse me, ladies."

The Asher twins promised to find him later as Katherine took his arm and quickly led him away. "I apologize, but you looked miserable. I couldn't think of anything else to do."

"I owe you a debt of gratitude," he said as they threaded through the crowd. "I've been trying to shake those two for the better part of an hour."

"I could tell. They can be overwhelming at the best of times." She gestured to the door near the back. "The retiring rooms are there, if you'd care to clean your coat."

"My coat is fine. I'd rather escape the room for a moment, if you're amenable."

"How about the card room? Most of the mothers and unmarried ladies avoid it."

"Sounds heavenly."

They drifted toward the corridor and into the card room, where a dozen or so men were sitting around tables. "See? Not a woman in sight."

"You are a genius." He drew in a deep breath and let it out slowly. "This never gets easier."

"The hunt for a bride? No doubt you're besieged."

"Yes, well. The title and all that. I imagine it's the same for you, besieged by suitors."

"Not really. It's almost my second season, so I'm no longer new and shiny. Instead, everyone's wondering what's wrong with me."

Understanding lit his blue gaze. "Considering I've courted two ladies who ended up with other men, I'm fairly certain they're wondering the same about me."

"We are a pair, then. No wonder we're both avoiding the crowd and hiding out in the card room."

He leaned in, as if sharing a secret. "Is it wrong if we stand here for the rest of the night?"

"Not in my opinion." She smiled up at him. Part of her wanted to mention the French Ball, confess how she'd seen him there, but that would mean admitting her own presence at the scandalous event. Instead, she held up her hand in promise. "I swear to protect you from any wandering debutantes with ducal aspirations in their eyes."

"Thank you. And who or what am I protecting you from?"

"Boredom?"

He laughed, drawing the attention of several card players. "I don't believe that for a moment. You don't strike me as a woman who sits around and waits for excitement to find her."

Actually, I did sit around and wait. For one whole year.

"I'm not, at least not any longer. It's harder for unmarried ladies, though. You gents get to have all the fun."

"Yes, fun," he said, his tone implying the opposite as he swiped two coupes of champagne off a passing tray. "I am relieved to see a friendly face tonight, though."

A small smidgeon of guilt worked its way under her ribs. She couldn't help but feel partially responsible for his predicament. "I hope you don't hold the past against me."

"You mean how you schemed to break up my betrothal to Maddie?" he finished dryly. "No, I don't hold it against you. Nor do I begrudge Alice for choosing another instead of me."

"I apologize. I never meant to hurt anyone. I just wanted my friend to be happy."

"Understandable. But perhaps you and I could become friends and then you'd be on my side for a change?"

"I'd like that. I—"

"Katherine!"

She spun at the booming voice and found her father approaching. "Hello, Daddy. Were you looking for me?"

"Yes, I've been searching everywhere." He leaned to kiss her cheek, then addressed the duke. "Your Grace."

"Mr. Delafield." They shook hands. "I apologize for monopolizing your daughter's time."

"Nonsense. I'm pleased to see the two of you getting along."

Uneasiness settled in Katherine's belly. She would need to set her father straight on her friendship with Lockwood. There was nothing romantic happening, so Daddy shouldn't get his hopes up for a duchess in the family. "We're hiding out in here. The pitying stares in the ballroom were a bit much."

Her father's face fell. "Oh, Kat. Forgive me for asking you to attend tonight."

"It's all right. I'm tougher than I look."

"Yes, you most definitely are." He suddenly snapped his fingers and shifted toward the duke. "Say, Your Grace. I'd like to discuss a business item, if you're amenable. I wonder if you'd join my daughter and I for dinner tomorrow night. Nine o'clock at Sherry's?"

"Uh." Lockwood glanced at Katherine, unsure.

She understood. Her father could be a force of nature when he set his mind to something. He wouldn't let this drop until they all three dined together. But this could also show her father that she and the duke were merely friends.

She gave Lockwood an encouraging smile. "That sounds like a grand time. Will you come?"

The duke nodded once, all politeness and grace. "It would be my pleasure."

"Excellent," her father said. "Tomorrow night, it is. Katherine, are you ready to leave?"

God, yes. She'd reached her limit on polite conversation.

They said goodbye to the duke and Katherine went with her father to the front door. Once they were outside, safely tucked away in a carriage, she said, "You know, the duke and I are merely friends."

Her father's expression made it clear he didn't believe her. "And you know the very best marriages are between friends, correct?"

"Do not try and make a match between us. He nearly married one of my closest friends and courted another. The duke is off-limits, Daddy."

"We'll see."

"I'm serious."

He tapped his fingers on the silk evening hat in his lap. "It's important for you to start your own life, Kitty Kat. Have your own family. I won't always be around, you know."

"Daddy! Don't be so morbid." The words came out strangled due to the emotion lodged in her throat. "It's bad enough that you're working and traveling more often these days. I don't want to think about losing you, too."

Her father was all she had left. Someday she might marry, but she wasn't in any hurry—especially after waiting for Preston for a whole year. There were more important things to do first before she settled down with a husband and family.

"You're not losing me, but we never know what the future holds."

"Well, I don't wish to hear it. You're going to live a long time, and we'll ramble around in that big house together—you, me and Aunt Dahlia."

He hummed but didn't answer, and Katherine was left to worry over what tomorrow night would bring.

THE DINING ROOM inside Sherry's was packed with New York's elite, popular actors and businessmen. Preston had a table along the wall, where he preferred to sit for privacy. This also allowed him to see everyone in the room.

Which was precisely how he spotted Katherine Delafield the instant she walked in—with her father and the Duke of Lockwood.

What in the goddamn hell?

Preston tracked the trio's progress to a table by the windows. Katherine's cream silk dress, embellished with tiny crystals that winked in the soft electric lighting, hugged her elegant form while maintaining propriety. The candles on each table brought out the faint golden strands in her brown hair, as well as the cream of her flawless skin. The duke helped Katherine get settled, his hand lingering a touch too long on the back of her chair before he took the seat across from her, with Lloyd between them.

Preston's own hand curled into an unwitting fist.

"Just don't tell my wife we ate here," Kit said from across the table, his attention entirely on the menu. "She's still angry that Louis Sherry stole one of Franconi's assistants away and offered him a head chef position."

Kit and Preston were enjoying a rare night out between the two of them. In the past, they would have been joined by his former mistress, Arabella, and one of her beautiful friends. But times had changed. Kit was married and Preston hadn't yet secured another mistress.

His gaze returned to Katherine. She was smiling at Lockwood, and Madame de Pompadour's teasing grin flashed through Preston's mind. The encounter had been scorching, one of the best of his life.

Please, my king. Give me more.

Heat licked through his veins at the memory. She'd driven him past the point of reason, to where he'd have done nearly anything in that tiny salon. Did she think he pulled his cock out and stroked it in front of just anyone?

It turned out that Katherine hadn't told her father about the ball. Lloyd most definitely would've demanded a wedding straightaway if she had, which meant Preston had been . . . wrong about her. She hadn't set out to seduce him into marriage at the French Ball. Their meeting was a coincidence, as improbable as that sounded, based on nothing more than simple attraction. He'd noticed her smile and her long legs, not to mention the naughty innocence in her gaze. She'd seemed both delighted and shocked at the revelers on the dance floor, and that combination had lured him in like a moth to a flame.

Now he couldn't get that night out of his head, specifically the image of her with her legs spread, her pussy glistening and swollen from two orgasms. It was the most arousing sight he'd ever witnessed and that it had been this girl—the innocent and gently bred, list making Katherine Delafield—was driving him absolutely mad.

And she was here tonight with another man.

"Everything all right over there?" Kit put down his menu. "You seem more intense than usual all of a sudden."

"I'm fine."

"Really?" The waiter delivered another round of drinks and Kit waited until the man departed before speaking. "Should I be worried?"

"Of course not." Preston took a long gulp of scotch, the burn a pleasant distraction from all that was happening by the windows.

Kit folded his hands on the table and leaned forward. "I see you're drinking again. Quite a lot, if tonight is anything to go by."

Sighing, Preston carefully placed his glass on the table. "I'm not Forrest, but point taken."

"Tell me what's wrong."

It was hard to let the words out, but the reminder sat not even twenty feet away, unrelenting and beautiful, and smiling at another man. No way could Preston enjoy a relaxing dinner while Katherine and Lockwood were on the other side of the room. Besides, he had to get this weight off his chest somehow.

Taking a deep breath, he faced his friend. "I did something terrible."

"For you, that could mean any number of things. Did you cheat a lumber company? Bribe the wrong politician?"

"Nothing business related."

"Is there anything in your life that isn't business related?"

"Sometimes, yes. But you'll never find out what it is unless you stop teasing me."

"Ah, so it's a woman. Let me be clear: if you made a pass at my wife, I'm going to stab you in the balls with my butter knife right here in the dining room."

"What did I just say about teasing?"

Kit drummed his fingers on the table, his expression somber. "Who said I was teasing?"

Preston barely resisted the urge to roll his eyes. "I seduced an unmarried debutante."

Kit's eyebrows flew up. "I wasn't aware you knew any debutantes. You're firmly anti-debutante."

"Yes, I'm aware." Preston filled Kit in on the broad strokes of what happened at the French Ball and Jane Street, not mentioning the girl's name.

"So you ruined her," Kit said flatly.

Preston shifted in his chair, his eyes flicking toward Katherine once more. The trio were toasting with champagne, all smiles, and Preston gnashed his teeth. What was she doing? Lockwood was trolling New York for an heiress like an angler on the open seas. Was she seriously interested in becoming a duchess? Or had Lloyd orchestrated the dinner to push his daughter into Lockwood's path?

Whatever the reason, Preston didn't like it. Four nights ago she was ready to have an affair with *him*. Now she was letting Lockwood court her?

"Christ, what's Lockwood doing here?" Kit's voice dripped with loathing. "Why does every woman in Gotham look at him like he's a chocolate bonbon and Tiffany's diamond bracelet rolled into one?"

Indeed, Katherine was grinning at Lockwood like a lovesick fool. A muscle ticked in the corner of Preston's right eye.

"You must be kidding."

Preston whipped his head toward Kit. "What?"

"Her?" He mouthed, "The debutante?"

There was no use denying it. Kit knew him too well. "I was unaware it was her at the time."

"I bet. But now you have to marry her, considering."

"No, I don't. It didn't go quite that far."

Kit gave a harsh laugh. "You know such things don't matter, not in our world."

"I told you, it didn't go that far—and you're supposed to be on my side."

"Oh, there are sides now?" Kit leaned in, his mouth a thin, white angry line. "She's friends with my *wife*, Preston. Harrison's wife, as well. What were you thinking?"

"I don't see how that matters. It's no one else's concern what occurs between Miss Delafield and me."

"Sure, until it blows up and then I have to choose between your friendship and keeping my wife happy. Can you guess which I'll choose?"

Definitely not Preston. Kit was madly in love with Alice.

"It's not going to blow up. She wants nothing to do with me."

Kit went back to studying his menu. "Good. Leave her the hell alone."

Leg bouncing under the table, Preston continued to stare at Katherine and Lockwood. The two were appallingly cozy, talking easily with no awkward silences, while Lloyd looked on proudly. The urge to disrupt their charming little group was nearly unbearable.

He imagined charging over there and informing Lloyd and the duke how thoroughly acquainted he was with Katherine, how he'd felt her orgasm on his fingers and his tongue. How he'd been the first man to give her pleasure.

How she belonged to him.

Shit.

Dragging a hand through his hair, he tried to pull himself together. This was not good. He was not impulsive or hotheaded. He was careful and logical, which meant he couldn't be jealous of Lockwood. Or any other man. Whomever Katherine married was none of his concern. Preston had no right to interfere.

Please, my king. Give me more.

Damn it.

Preston was tossing his napkin on the table before he even knew what he was doing. "Excuse me."

"Where are you going?" Kit snapped. "I sincerely hope you aren't intending to cause trouble for her. Lockwood, fine. Cause him all the trouble you like. But leave her alone, Preston."

"I'm not going to cause a scene. Relax and enjoy your drink. I'll be back before you know it."

Rising from the table, he went to the front and located the maître d'hôtel. Preston slipped the other man a fifty-dollar bill. "I need a favor."

Chapter Nine

༄

"Thank you for agreeing to dine with us tonight," Katherine's father said to the duke as their drinks were poured. "I haven't been here in ages, and I do miss their lamb chops."

Lockwood was perfectly situated in his chair, every inch a duke. "I'm quite fond of their oysters myself."

Katherine lifted her coupe and waited for the other two to do the same. "Cheers."

They drank and carried on with small talk for a moment. On the way over, Katherine had warned her father—again—about not trying to match her with Lockwood. She liked the duke well enough, but as a friend. She had no designs on being a duchess or moving to England.

So she held her breath when her father said, "I must admit, I had an ulterior motive in inviting you here tonight, Lockwood."

The duke's face remained bland. "Oh?"

Please, don't let this be about me.

"I have a piece of land on Twenty-Third Street," her father began.

She paused, uncertain she'd heard him correctly. This was about land?

Daddy continued, looking at her. "I was thinking of gifting it to you, Katherine."

"To me? Why?"

"Independence. I'll ensure it's yours and that it stays yours, even after you marry."

The enormity of such a gesture caused her throat to tighten. Of course he was trying to take care of her. "Thank you, but what would I do with it?"

"Whatever you like, though I do have an idea."

"Yes?"

"This showing of your mother's paintings, the one you're organizing at your social club? Why not do it on a permanent scale?"

"Like a museum?" Lockwood asked.

Her father lifted his glass in confirmation. "Exactly. Katherine came home from Spain going on and on about the museums there, and she knows quite a bit about art. Just as her mother did."

Katherine couldn't speak. The prospect of opening an art museum felt daunting. Yet it also felt . . . right. Could she do it?

"Excuse me, Your Grace, Mr. Delafield."

The restaurant's maître d'hôtel now stood by their table. "Yes?" Lockwood asked, one brow lifted in arrogant annoyance.

"I have a telephone call at the front for Miss Delafield."

A telephone call? This made no sense. No one knew she was here, other than her aunt and their butler. "For me? Are you certain?"

"Yes, miss. Shall I tell them you are unavailable?"

"No, I'll take it." She smiled at her father, who was scowling. "I'm sure it's nothing, Daddy. It's probably Aunt Dahlia. I'll return momentarily."

Lockwood rose, as well. "Shall I come with you?"

So considerate. He would make a fine husband to some lucky woman one day. "No, that's all right. You both enjoy the champagne. Order the Blue Point oysters and I'll be back before they arrive."

She followed the maître d'hôtel to the front. Instead of handing her the telephone, however, he motioned toward the small coat closet. "Please, forgive me, miss. He was insistent on speaking with you."

What on earth? She tamped down her growing alarm and stepped to the closet. "Hello?"

A hand shot out and dragged her into the darkness. The aroma of tobacco and spice filled the small space—and instantly she knew who'd orchestrated this ruse.

Jerking her hand out of Preston's grip, she shoved blindly and hit his chest, which was like trying to move a brick wall. She hissed, "What on earth! Have you gone mad?"

"I could ask you the same thing," Preston said, his voice loaded with unwarranted accusation. "Why are you here with Lockwood?"

Her jaw fell open, not that he could see it. "How is that any of your concern?"

"Katherine, tell me what you're doing."

"I'm dining out, the same as you." Undoubtedly

he was here with a woman. Had he found a new mistress already? "Now let me go before my father begins to worry. This is unseemly."

Her eyes had adjusted enough to see him dart ahead to block her path. "As if you care about unseemly, reinette."

Unwelcome heat unspooled in her belly, and she resented him for it. "Do not remind me. I prefer to forget my lapses in judgment. Now, move."

"Is he courting you?"

Impossible. He was utterly impossible.

Instead of answering, she asked a question of her own. "Why do you care?"

"I don't, but you can't seriously believe it's a good idea."

"He's my friend, which is more than I can say for you. Get out of my way."

His huff of derision, like she was a fool, filled the darkness. "Unattached men are not friends with unattached women. He wants your family's money and to get under your skirts."

"No, he doesn't. Not everyone is as crass as you."

A fingertip glided slowly across her bare collarbone. "You don't mind crass. At least, you didn't at the French Ball."

Tingles cascaded down her spine at his touch, so she moved out of his reach. "Don't remind me. I'm trying to forget."

This wasn't entirely true. She allowed herself to think about him late at night as she stroked between her legs. This included a very detailed list of everything she wanted him to do to her.

Number one was very filthy, very arousing and not something she'd ever admit out loud.

Into her silence, he said, "You can do better than Lockwood, Kat."

Everything fell into place. His comments, his anger. The way he'd called her away from the table. "I cannot believe it. You're *jealous*."

Preston rocked back on his heels, as if the accusation surprised him. "Hardly. I've never been jealous in my life. I just cannot understand what you and your father are playing at."

Of course he would make this about her father.

"*We* are having dinner, Preston. Same as you. Return to your actress or singer and forget you know me."

Considering he still blocked the exit, she had no choice but to push past him. He didn't move, the scoundrel, and their shoulders brushed, while her skirts pressed to his legs. She sucked in a quick breath when his arm bumped her hip. The tiny space wasn't built for a man of his size, let alone two people, and it felt like he surrounded her in the very best way.

Without warning, his fingers stroked the edge of her ear, his voice a seductive whisper. "But I do know you, mon chaton. I know what it is like to kiss you, to bite you. I even know the taste of your slick arousal and the feel of your orgasm on my tongue."

The words sent a lick of wicked heat through her, turning her insides to molten wax, and her knees actually wobbled. Why was he torturing her like this?

Torture him back.

Without second-guessing the impulse, she placed her palm on his stomach, directly on the silk of his vest, and it had the desired effect. Muscles jumped beneath her hand and air hissed through his teeth. Emboldened, she moved in and lowered her voice to a husky rasp. "I do hope you've stored those memories in a safe, safe place, my king, because they're all you'll ever have of me."

"Fuck," he said on a long whisper, sounding pained.

Dropping her hand, she reached to move the curtain aside.

"Wait." He grabbed on to her arm. "I wanted to apologize. It's clear you didn't tell your father about the ball, so I'm sorry for insisting you would."

The unexpected words scrambled her brain for a moment. Preston Clarke, apologizing? "Thank you."

Then he had to go and ruin it when he said, "Now, tell me you aren't seriously considering Lockwood."

She tried to pull free. "That is none of your dashed business. Now, let go of my arm or I'll scream bloody murder."

"You wouldn't dare."

"I might, if only to humiliate you."

He let her go, so she darted through the curtain and back into the restaurant. The maître d'hôtel avoided her eye as she passed, the coward.

She didn't have time for Preston or his nonsense. Lockwood and her father were waiting, probably worried over her disappearance. As she walked, she deliberately did not look around to see where Preston was sitting or with whom.

Now who's jealous?

Oh, how she hated that inner voice of hers.

The duke and her father were talking and laughing like old pals as she approached. She tried to smooth her features as Lockwood pulled her chair out. "Is everything all right, Miss Delafield?" he asked.

"Yes, thank you. It turned out the phone call was not for me after all," she lied and retook her seat. "Did you two discuss the museum idea while I was away?"

"We did," her father answered. "The duke possesses a large art collection, and we negotiated a price to allow you to borrow it."

Katherine blinked. "That is fantastic. Thank you, both of you."

"It is my pleasure," Lockwood said. "Once I marry and renovations begin on the country house, I would need to put them into storage anyway. This saves me the trouble."

Excitement fizzed in her chest like champagne bubbles. An art museum. She absolutely loved the idea. Could she really do it? "It's an enormous project to undertake."

Her father smiled fondly at her. "I'll help you, if you need it, of course. But you adore art and you're clever. I can't think of a better person to oversee it, actually."

She flushed with his praise. "You are biased."

"Of course I am—you're my daughter and my favorite person in the entire world. But that doesn't mean I also can't see how wonderfully capable you are."

"Thank you, Daddy. I'm very touched."

"Excuse me." Their waiter had returned, this time with a bottle of wine. "This is compliments of the gentleman over there." He gestured toward the back wall, where Preston sat with Kit Ward. Preston's dark eyes locked on hers before sliding to her father, a brow raising in silent challenge.

Unbelievable.

She dug deep for composure, shoving aside her irritation so Lockwood wouldn't notice anything amiss. Serenely, she said to the waiter, "No, thank you—and please tell Mr. Clarke we require nothing whatsoever from him."

THE WIND WHIPPED along Broadway as Preston approached Twenty-Third Street, his overcoat flapping behind him. Dashed traffic put him behind schedule, and he'd been forced to travel on foot for the last block and a half. "Mr. Kimball," he said loud enough to be heard over the city noise. "Forgive my tardiness."

The president of Manhattan Surety turned to the sound of Preston's voice, his eyes colder than the East River in January. "I don't have much time, Clarke."

They shook hands, and Kimball performed the necessary introductions to the others in the group, all executives and lawyers of Manhattan Surety. The insurance company had engaged Preston to put up their new office building here, on land that Preston would sell to them. For slightly more than fair market value, of course.

This wasn't Preston's only development project—far from it—but it was his most prestigious.

The only problem was straightening out the issue of land ownership with Lloyd Delafield . . . but Preston wasn't worried. The parcel had belonged to the Clarke family going back decades. His lawyers would soon sort it out.

"Thank you for meeting with us," Kimball said. "The board is asking for a report on where things stand, so walk us through the footprint."

Preston swept out his arm. "Then let's not waste any time."

As he led them around the perimeter, he told them how the building would loom over the entire city, the tallest inhabitable structure in the world. He explained about the steel frame, the elevators and the bedrock, even the shape of the building. "Everyone across the globe will soon know the name Manhattan Surety," he added.

"We hear another group of investors is looking to develop the tallest building down on Park Row," Kimball said.

Preston also heard those rumors. "You'll beat them, if we can get underway in the next three months."

"They're planning on thirty-one floors."

"I'll believe it when I see it," Preston said, then held out his palms. "Listen, the city isn't keen on granting many permits for towering steel buildings. Half the residents are scared of structures that tall and the other half are outraged over changes to the skyline."

Another Surety employee asked, "And what makes you think you can get the permits?"

Because Preston had the money to bribe the buildings department. Slipping his hands into his pockets, he said arrogantly, "Your permits won't be an issue."

"That all sounds well and good," Kimball said, "but I haven't yet seen the deed. We need to settle on a price and then decide on the architect."

"You needn't worry about the deed. I'll get it to you soon, along with my price. And we should have all the bids from the architecture firms in the next two weeks."

"Good, good. I want the building here, by the park. It's too crowded downtown."

Preston nodded. The land was the main reason Kimball had given him the job. "I agree. It'll be a building to last hundreds of—"

Suddenly, his gaze snagged on a tall woman on the opposite corner. Brown hair, long legs. Big eyes that drew you in like the warmth of the sun. *Katherine.*

He felt a familiar tug, the one in the pit of his stomach whenever he thought of her, a mixture of fascination, regret and lust. Three days had passed since he saw her at Sherry's with Lockwood, and Preston had been unsuccessful in purging her from his brain. The harder he tried to forget her, the more she haunted him.

At the moment she was standing next to a man, and they were both examining and pointing at the same lot where Preston and the Surety group were gathered. What the hell was she doing here?

"I think we have enough," Kimball said, regaining Preston's attention. "I need to get back for a meeting. Thank you, Clarke."

"You're welcome. We'll be in touch regarding the architects."

"I expect to hear from you regarding the deed sooner than that."

"Of course." Preston nodded and gave half-hearted goodbyes, his mind stuck on the woman over on the far corner. He needed to find out what she was up to.

As soon as he was alone, he strode over. "Miss Delafield."

She started and pressed a hand to her heart. "What on earth? You scared me."

Preston didn't answer. Instead, he turned to the man at Katherine's side. "I need a moment with Miss Delafield."

The man glanced at Katherine, unsure, and she gave him a small nod. "I won't be long, Mr. Jennis."

When they were alone, Preston asked, "Why are you here? Are you following me?"

Her chin lifted regally, like the little queen he'd once dubbed her. "Believe it or not, I have better things to do than to follow you around the city. And not that it's any of your concern, but I'm meeting with my father's architect to discuss the art museum I'm building on this block."

The words hung in the air as he tried to piece them together, like tiny lines and shapes that combined to complete a drawing.

When he could speak, he said, "Art museum? Here? Right here? You can't do that."

Her lips flattened. "No doubt you believe buildings should only be designed and built by men. I hate to inform you, but—"

"No," he said. "This is my land. I own it. And no matter what your father says, I'm keeping it."

Seconds ticked by as she stared up at him, distrust swirling in her light brown eyes. "My father said this land is his."

"It has always been Clarke land. It's mine."

"This doesn't make any sense. Why would he lie to me?" Implying that Preston was clearly the dishonest one.

"I couldn't say. He claims my father sold him the land when their company dissolved, but I don't believe it."

"Well, have you seen the deed or the paperwork?"

"Yes."

"And?"

He clenched his teeth together and forced out, "My father's signature is still being verified." She relaxed and let out an amused huff, and he didn't care for the smirk on her face.

"I see what's happening. Someone has something you want, but won't give it to you. So you're acting like a child, thinking you are entitled to it, regardless."

Irritation crawled along his spine and settled between his shoulder blades. "You have quite a low opinion of me."

"Let's just say I have some experience with what happens when Preston Clarke doesn't get his way."

God, this woman. "Meaning, I'm acting like a child when it comes to you?"

"You dragged me into the coat closet at Sherry's."

"I was trying to help you. Lockwood is the last man you should marry, Katherine."

"The *last* man? Really? Are you certain of that? Because I can think of one or two others who rate higher on that list."

Him, in other words. Shoving apart the sides of his overcoat, he put his hands on his hips. "Kat," he said, sternly. "You should know that I do, eventually, always get my way. No one is more determined than me. There is no limit to what I will do in order to win, no line I won't cross."

He remembered what it was like to lose almost everything. To have one's entire life nearly stripped away. He'd be damned if he ever let it happen again.

She didn't appear swayed, seemingly staring down her nose at him, though he was several inches taller. "This is a ridiculous conversation to have right now. I'm in the midst of a meeting."

"A meeting that is a waste of everyone's time, because you won't be building anything here. I'm putting up an office building."

"How original," she drawled. "The city doesn't need another office building, Preston. It needs more art, more greenery. More public spaces."

"Then I suggest you start looking elsewhere for available land."

Her smile was all teeth. "Why, when my father has given me the perfect block right here?"

The moment stretched as the midday traffic carried on around them. He was both frustrated and aroused, an odd combination for him. The urge to yell at her was equal with his urge to kiss her.

Color rose on her cheeks and he could see the pulse beating at the base of her throat. Anger, or was she contemplating a kiss, as well?

Wishful thinking on my part, no doubt.

Clenching his hands into fists, he stared at the foot traffic and carriages as they passed. This was absurd. As if everything that transpired between them wasn't bad enough, now Lloyd was lying to her, building up her hopes regarding an art museum here. The project would never come to fruition because this block belonged to Preston. Her father was beyond cruel.

Preston let out the breath he'd been holding. What was he doing? Lloyd deserved Preston's animosity, not Katherine. The two of them had been more than compatible at the ball without Lloyd Delafield between them. If not for her last name, Preston certainly would've tried to seduce her.

She was caught in a struggle she didn't understand, with her father pulling the strings, and Preston wouldn't do that to her. He liked her, if he was being honest—and he didn't like many people. She was funny and smart, unafraid to stand up to him. Decent and kind and everything he *wasn't* . . . yet naughty enough to come to the French Ball and turn his world upside down.

But she didn't fit into the life he'd built for himself. She wasn't a mistress or a friend. That was all he had time for, probably all he'd *ever* have time for, and this woman would never fill one of those two boxes. Which meant he had no idea what the hell this was about.

It was time to stop interfering in her life.

He put up his hands in surrender. "I'll leave

you to your meeting, then. Please, heed my advice and look elsewhere. I wish you luck."

Turning, he started to walk away. He needed to return to the office and the mountain of work and meetings awaiting him. There was no time for a beautiful brunette with plump, kissable lips and a gorgeous smile.

"Wait," she called from behind him.

Pausing, he glanced over his shoulder, surprised to find she'd caught up to him. "Preston, I want to hear why you think my father is plotting against you. I want to know . . ."

"What?" he prompted when she fell silent.

"I want to know why you hate my father. Why you hate me."

A weight settled in his chest, one he suspected was guilt, which he deserved. He'd treated her abominably. "I don't hate you," he said quietly, staring down into her big brown gaze. "Far from it, actually. Furthermore, I'm sorry. For everything I've said and accused you of, and that you're being dragged into my history with your father."

"Thank you." She searched his face, perhaps to ensure he was telling the truth. "I'd still like to know what happened, though."

"Why? You can't change it, and you might not like the answer." It would certainly alter her opinion of her father. "It's best if you ask him instead."

"Oh, I will, but I'd also like to hear your side."

Side? He nearly snarled in response to the word. There were no fucking *sides*. There were clear winners and losers in this world, and Lloyd thought he had Preston beat, but he didn't. In the next few days, Preston's lawyers would discover how Lloyd had perpetuated this flimflam and get the proper rights back.

Tamping down his irritation, Preston reminded himself that she didn't deserve it. "Perhaps someday I'll tell you," he hedged.

She struck out her hand. "In the meantime, truce?"

He accepted her hand, engulfing it in his larger grip as they shook. "Truce."

The busy Twenty-Third Street traffic carried on around them, but he didn't let go of her hand. He stood perfectly still and watched her, fascinated, enjoying the different emotions that played out on her face. Katherine wore her every thought, as transparent as glass, and her suspicion and relief transformed into a nervous blush. The slim column of her throat worked as she swallowed.

Was she thinking about the French Ball? About their kisses and heated breaths? The whispered words and naughty games? Because he was very much thinking about it, about how he craved more of the same. She brought out something in him that no one else ever had, a playful and impulsive side he'd long thought buried.

In that moment, he didn't care about her last name or her father. He only wanted to spend more time with her, however he could get it.

Before he could change his mind, he said, "May I buy you a drink, reinette?"

Chapter Ten

❧

$\mathscr{B}$iting the inside of her cheek, Katherine stared up at him. A drink? In the middle of the day? The old Katherine would never have agreed to something so scandalous.

But she was the new Katherine, the girl who'd found adventure and a lover—and that man was standing across from her, hidden under layers of bitterness and ambition. Did she dare try to coax him out again?

I even know the taste of your slick arousal and the feel of your orgasm on my tongue.

Was he obsessed with memories of the ball, as well? Because Katherine couldn't stop remembering, couldn't stop replaying that short time in her head. He'd been so different, so relaxed. Mischievous and sweet. The opposite of how she knew him as Preston Clarke.

Something new lurked in his mahogany gaze, however—a softness that hadn't been there before. Like he saw her, really *saw* her, and appreciated what he noticed. It caused her skin to pebble and her breath to catch. She wanted to lean into it, let it surround and consume her.

She wanted to say yes.

Shoving aside her misgivings, she said, "Let me finish with my meeting first."

"Of course."

He released her hand and stepped back. "I need to cable Mrs. Cohen to reschedule my afternoon appointments." One dark brow quirked. "And perhaps my dinner engagement."

Always striving for more, this man.

"Don't get ahead of yourself, Mr. Clarke."

"I wouldn't dream of it, Miss Delafield." Shoving his hands into the pockets of his overcoat, he said, "Wait here for me. I'll return in ten minutes with a carriage and fetch you."

She nodded once, her head spinning with what she'd just agreed to.

It's merely a drink. Nothing more.

"Miss?"

Dragging in a deep breath, she tried to appear calm and collected. Intelligent, a woman capable of overseeing the construction and development of the Madison Square Art Museum, or so she'd been calling it in her head. Walking over to the architect, she said, "I apologize, sir. Shall we continue?"

"Is everything all right? Do you know that man?"

"Yes, that's Mr. Clarke, an associate of my father's. Apparently there's some dispute over who owns this land."

Mr. Jennis made a face. "Mr. Clarke isn't exactly known for being on the up-and-up, you

know what I mean? You'd be wise to stay away
from the likes of him. Let your father deal with
Mr. Clarke."

That was an ominous warning.

"I will. Are you ready to return to our discus-
sions?"

For the next five minutes, she and Mr. Jennis
discussed her idea on the building design, and
it quickly became clear they didn't see eye to eye
on the look of the museum. She preferred a more
Beaux Arts style, which was all the rage, while
Mr. Jennis insisted a classic Empire style would
be more pleasing.

She frowned at him. "But this is a modern art
museum, so it should reflect a modern style."

Mr. Jennis's expression turned patronizing.
"Well, if you want to hire McKim, Mead and
White to design it—"

"No, I'm not saying that, but if you've seen the
Metropolitan or Harvard Club, that's what I'm
after."

"That is not my style, Miss Delafield. I design
in a classic Empire style for your father. If you
don't like it . . ."

He let the sentence trail, and she could fill in
the rest. *If you don't like it, then that is too damn bad.*

The familiar urge to apologize, to retreat, rose
up in her chest—but she beat it back. This was
her project, not Jennis's, and she would not compromise. "Perhaps you could try it this once, as
a favor to my father. He's told me such wonderful things about you, and I would hate to have to
explore other options." *But I will, if you don't agree.*

His upper lip curled into the hint of a sneer.

"Miss, I'm a busy man with many prestigious projects. I don't need to compromise my aesthetic for you. I think you should leave this to the experienced men who know design and buildings, the people who do it professionally."

Uncertainty burned in the back of her throat. Perhaps she was out of her depth with this endeavor. She didn't know the first thing about what it took to get a project of this scope off the ground. All she'd wanted was to honor her mother and her mother's love of art by sharing it with the entire city.

Should she trust Jennis's vision, shoving aside her own?

The idea didn't sit well. It felt like compromising, just as she'd done for the last year while believing herself betrothed. She was tired of waiting and compromising, of not putting herself first.

Know your worth. Wasn't that what Aunt Dahlia always said?

Preston stood by his carriage, arms crossed over his chest, watching her from under the brim of his derby. He was too far away to overhear, so she lifted her hand, beckoning him. "Mr. Clarke?"

His long legs carried him over, eating up the pavement beneath his feet. Then he towered beside Mr. Jennis as he inclined his head. "Yes, Miss Delafield?"

"What do you do when you and your architect disagree on a building's design?"

Preston's mouth curved in an annoyingly arrogant way. "We don't, because I pay his salary."

"Meaning, he agrees with your vision for the project."

"Yes."

"And if he refused?"

"Then I would find a new architect."

She lifted her chin and regarded Mr. Jennis. "You're fired."

Mr. Jennis's mouth dropped open, his mustache drooping dramatically. "I beg your pardon."

"I'll find another architect to work on the museum with me. Your services are no longer needed."

Disbelief quickly morphed into anger, his voice growing tight. "*You* are firing *me*? Because this"—he gestured toward Preston—"hoodlum told you to?"

"No, he only confirmed what I was thinking. I don't appreciate how you've treated me, Mr. Jennis. It's clear you don't wish to work on this project, and I'd rather find an architect who does."

Jennis snorted. "This is a mistake, Miss Delafield, but I won't argue, as I was only doing this as a favor, anyway. Good luck finding someone willing to take on your little museum."

"I can think of at least three architects I'd recommend," Preston said, giving Katherine a sly, conspiratorial grin.

She grinned back. "Excellent. I'll take those names, Mr. Clarke."

Jennis threw up his hands and started to walk away. Then he looked over his shoulder and gestured to Preston. "Oh, and I will be telling your father about this. Good day, miss."

That dimmed a bit of her enthusiasm. Daddy would ask questions about her relationship with Preston, and she wasn't ready to answer them.

I don't have a relationship with Preston.

True. They weren't even friends. According to Preston, unmarried men were incapable of friendships with unmarried ladies. So, why had he asked to buy her a drink today?

"How did that feel?" Preston asked when they were alone, his dark eyes dancing. "Good, I assume?"

She pushed aside the worry over her father and Preston's motivation. "Very, very good."

"I take it he was condescending and patronizing."

"How did you know?"

"Because I could see your reactions to whatever he was saying. He deserved to be fired. You might not have done this before, but you can do it. If you know what you want, don't waver from what you can see in your head, no matter what anyone else says. Never compromise."

Hope bloomed in her chest like a flower in the rain. Still, the doubt lingered. "Are you just saying what you think I wish to hear?"

He put a hand over his heart, his tone quiet and solemn. "I may be a dishonest man, but I promise to always be honest with you."

"Thank you," she said, just as quietly. "I'm glad you were here."

"You mean on my property, where I'm about to build the Manhattan Surety office tower?"

"Are you already breaking our truce, Preston Clarke? It hasn't even been an hour."

He let out a deep chuckle. "Fair enough. No more building or property talk today. All right?"

"All right."

"Good." He held out his arm. "Let's go to a little spot I know and share a drink."

PULLING OUT A key, Preston unlocked the door to the supper club. "After you."

Katherine slipped through the opening and went in. "This is exciting. I've wanted to come here since it opened."

"So, why didn't you?" He closed the door and relocked it. The supper club wasn't open this early in the day, but he thought it might be fun for her to see the place without the risk of ruination.

And they could talk here without interruption.

"You know why," she said, waiting for him in the dark corridor. "But that was the old me. The new me is ready to see and do and explore."

I went there to start living my life. To have fun after waiting on you for a year.

The truth of it pricked at his insides like the sharp end of a nail. But he hadn't known. Rather, he'd pushed it aside, another task for which he didn't have time when trying to save his family from rack and ruin. He'd assumed Lloyd took the hint after Henry's death, when it had been quite clear that Preston hated anything with the Delafield name attached to it.

But I don't hate her. Not anymore.

He honestly didn't. Katherine's cheerful personality and her infectious curiosity appealed to him, perhaps because it was so different from his own. Still, he wasn't certain why they were here, why he wanted to spend time with a woman he couldn't fuck . . . and yet, he was leading her into the club he'd built, ready to show it off in the hopes of gaining her approval.

He shook his head, disgusted with himself. Idiot.

Flicking a few switches, he illuminated the dining room and stage. Katherine gasped and clapped her hands. "Oh, it's gorgeous. The perfect mix of gaudy and tasteful. It's naughty, but not *too* naughty."

Precisely what he and Kit had been trying to achieve with the decor. Preston found himself smiling. "I'm glad you like it. Take a seat and I'll mix us a couple of drinks. Any preferences?"

"No. I'll have whatever you're having."

He went to the bar and studied the bottles. The sight reminded him of Forrest, and Preston's failed effort to save him. It had only caused Forrest to run away and slip deeper into a bottle. Preston would live with that regret for the rest of his life.

You have to learn to relax, his mother often told him. *You cannot bend the world by sheer will alone.*

And why not? Preston couldn't see any other way to do it, actually.

He chose a sweet lemon liquor and fixed up a drink for Katherine, then poured water for himself. The memories of Forrest were too raw, the grief too strong, and drinking didn't exactly help.

When he sat, she frowned at his plain glass. "You aren't having one?"

"I will, just not at the moment. Enjoy." He gestured toward her coupe. "I think you'll like it."

Carefully, she brought the glass to her lips and took a sip. Her brows flew up. "It's delicious. What's in here?"

"That is my secret."

"It tastes like lemonade but with a kick."

"It's one of my favorites for the summertime." Or it was. He leaned back in his chair and stretched out his legs. The nape of his neck ached, his body exhausted. The pace of the last few months was catching up with him.

"You seem tired," she said, propping her elbows on the table so she could rest her chin in her hands. "Working or playing too hard?"

"I haven't played hard since Harvard."

"What was that like, the four of you off at college?"

She meant him, Kit, Harrison and Forrest. "We had some wild times. I was forced to leave early, but before that was a lot of fun."

"It must've been hard to leave your friends behind at school," she said, taking another sip. "Did you miss them?"

"I was too busy, frankly. And they made a point of coming to New York often. We still managed to get into some trouble here."

"I bet." She sighed dramatically. "Men have it so much easier than women."

"Because we may visit saloons and have affairs?"

"Yes. You have freedoms women only dream of. Women are taught to think about marriage from the time they're in short dresses until the moment they walk down the aisle. It's a singular obsession, and a girl's entire worth depends on it."

She'd removed her gloves while she was speaking, and the sight of her delicate fingers distracted him. Briefly, he wondered what they would feel like on his bare skin. He forced his gaze back to her face. "You've proven that isn't true. So has your friend Nellie. And certainly there are other women who don't aspire to land a husband."

"Not many, and Nellie has been ostracized for it. It's also worth noting that I believed I was betrothed for the last year."

"I still find it mind-boggling. I'm sorry, but I can't understand how you agreed. Didn't you wish to get to know me, to decide if you desired the match?"

She quickly reached for her drink, almost desperately, lifting it to her mouth and taking a swallow. Preston cocked his head and studied her. "What are you hiding, reinette?"

"Stop calling me that," she said, the edges of her mouth curling, as if she were smothering a smile.

"Why? I know you like the nickname."

"It's inappropriate. We're *friends*."

She emphasized the last word, and he nearly laughed. "That's not what I would call it, but fine."

"What would you call our relationship, then?"

He stroked his jaw and considered this. There was no good word for his thoughts regarding her, the myriad feelings that erupted in her presence. He was a man of measured action, not impulsive words, and all he knew was the need to taste her again, to hear the sound of her cries in his ears.

Angling toward her, he said, "Unfinished."

She dragged her bottom lip between her teeth, while color dotted her cheeks. "Then I would have to call you delusional."

He let that go, instead returning to the question she hadn't answered. "Why didn't you feel the need to meet me before you agreed to the betrothal? Have a dinner or a drive in the park? Something?"

"I did meet you."

Was she joking? "We met? When?"

"We were introduced during my debut. I—"

When she didn't finish her sentence, he edged forward, curious. "You, what?"

"I need another drink." She pushed her empty coupe toward him. "Please?"

She was clearly trying to distract him, but avoidance wouldn't work, not with him. He'd negotiated with criminals and lawyers and politicians; one beautiful woman wasn't going to outwit him. Rising, he took her glass to the bar and fixed another drink.

When he sat the full coupe on the table, he didn't let go, not even when she reached for it. "Tell me."

She chuckled and rolled her eyes to the ceiling. "It's ridiculous, but I had a tiny crush on you."

His hand fell off the glass and flopped onto the table as he struggled to make sense of this. A crush? On him? She picked up the coupe and drank, her eyes glittering with amusement over the rim of the glass. The only thing he could think to say was, "You're pulling my leg."

"Oh, I can't believe I'm telling you this." She took a hasty gulp of the alcohol. "I'm making a fool of myself again."

Hardly. They'd met and he didn't remember. At all. And this gorgeous creature had planned her whole future as his wife because of it? The knowledge made him feel two inches tall.

Rubbing the back of his neck, he said, "Believe me, I'm the fool, Kat."

Her smile turned teasing. Flirtatious, like they shared a secret. "Well, perhaps if I had been in short skirts and a wig the night we met you would've remembered."

Lust sparked in his groin at the memory of her costume. Hard to say what he'd liked more: the tight bodice thrusting her tits up or the short skirts showing off her spectacular legs. Luckily, he didn't have to choose.

He shifted closer, much closer than was proper for a friend, and lowered his voice. "I can't get the image of you in that costume out of my head. I think about it often. Every morning, in fact." When he pleasured himself before he got out of bed, but he didn't tell her that.

"I think of you and the things you did, too. At night. When I'm alone."

His body jolted and his mouth went dry. Was she implying she touched herself to thoughts of him? The possibility was pure torture and, for once, he couldn't think of a witty or flirtatious rejoinder. "Is this the sort of thing friends share?"

Her long lashes fluttered as she blinked at him innocently. He didn't buy it. She knew exactly what she was doing—tormenting him, as she'd done in the coat closet. "So, you're allowed to tease me and I can't do the same?"

"You're allowed to tease, but be prepared. If you bite me, sweetheart, I'll bite back."

"Is that supposed to be a threat?" Her gaze darted to his mouth. "Because I don't think I'd mind that."

Oh, Jesus, this girl. Without thinking, he reached for her, desperate to touch her, to pull her closer, but she stood and edged out of his reach. "May I go up on the stage?"

An evasion? Or was this another of her games? He couldn't tell. "Of course."

She threaded through the tables and stepped up onto the small stage. When she turned around, he couldn't drag his eyes away. The yellow cast from the overhead bulbs brought out the golden strands in her brown hair, as well as the glow of her skin, and he was mesmerized. Even in a small jacket, shirtwaist and long skirts, he found her utterly enticing. Arousal thrummed in his veins, an increasing pressure that echoed in every cell, causing his skin to feel too tight for his bones.

Walking the length of the stage, she glanced around, then faced the audience as if ready to begin a performance. Preston called out, "Can you sing?"

Katherine shook her head. "Sadly, no. I'm not musically inclined." Striking a dramatic pose, she recited, "To be or not to be. That is the dashed dilemma."

He burst out laughing. "Question," he said, grinning. "That is the question."

She shrugged. "Shakespeare is boring. It could use some reworking."

"Well, I know you can dance." Indeed, those high kicks and short skirts fueled his erotic dreams.

Lifting her hands for an imaginary partner, she performed a basic waltzing box step.

"Try again," he said.

Then she barely raised her skirts and did an Irish step dance.

He tapped his fingers on the table, fighting amusement. She was adorable, but also maddening. They both knew what he was asking for, and she liked denying him. It was swiftly becoming a recurring theme between them. Lacing his voice with doubt, he said, "Maybe it was Nellie I was watching. Now that I think of it . . ."

A huff of amused indignation escaped her mouth. "How dare you? We both know you couldn't take your eyes off me on that dance floor."

"Hmm, I can't recall. Too bad you'll never show me and prove it."

"You are so transparent. You think I won't do it unless you trick me."

He waved his hand, like a king to his royal subjects. "Please, Katherine. Dance for me."

"You think you deserve it?"

"No, but I told you I never play fair. And it's clear you're too shy. I understand."

With a smirk, she hiked her skirts to her

thighs—and every single one of Preston's muscles clenched. He sat perfectly still, transfixed, as she began to move, kicking those long legs into the air like a can-can dancer. Any amusement died, swiftly replaced with a fever that blanketed him from head to toe. The flash of her drawers and bare skin caused his cock to thicken in his trousers, her movements exactly like the scandalous girls in the dance halls. Christ almighty, she was good at this.

These same graceful movements and lithe limbs had drawn his eye at the French Ball, and instantly filled him with a longing he barely understood. Now that he knew her, his longing was a hundred times worse. This was Katherine in all her innocent and alluring glory, and he wanted her all to himself.

When she turned and bent over, flicking her skirts up the back of her thighs, he struggled to remain seated and not rush the stage in eagerness. He began contemplating the back room and the furniture the two of them could use—

"What in the hell is going on in my club?"

Chapter Eleven

❧

$\mathcal{K}$it's angry voice echoed off the walls, the sound causing Katherine to drop her skirts quickly and spin around. Preston glanced over his shoulder to see his friend's furious face, along with his wife's shocked expression from where she stood at Kit's side. Shit.

"Katherine!" Alice exclaimed, hurrying forward toward the stage. "I had no idea that was you. Hello!" The two women embraced, but Kit suddenly filled Preston's line of sight, preventing him from seeing more.

Lips thin with fury, his friend pointed toward the back of the club. "My office. Right now."

Preston sighed. There was no avoiding this conversation, not if he didn't want Kit making a scene. No doubt his friend planned to berate him, but Preston was co-owner of this supper club. He didn't need to ask Kit's permission to bring women here.

He rose and buttoned his coat, hoping to cover his semi-erection for propriety's sake. "Katherine, I'll return in a moment."

She nodded and began whispering with Alice, and the two of them headed in the direction of the kitchen. Kit had already started for the back, so Preston followed to the office. When he entered, Kit was already behind the desk, glaring in his direction. "Hello, Kit."

"Shut the door."

Preston closed them in and settled on the sofa against the wall, putting as much distance as possible between him and his friend lest this turn ugly. They hadn't come to blows in years, but Preston was not about to cower like a schoolboy caught cheating on a test.

"What was that?" Kit asked, gesturing toward the club. "Seriously, have you lost your mind?"

"I haven't a clue what you mean. I brought Katherine here for a drink and she wanted to get on the stage for a moment."

Kit pressed the heels of his hands into his eyes. "Preston. You cannot bring women here in the middle of the day. It's a business and we have a hundred things to do before—"

"Wait a minute. I don't need a lecture from you about responsibility. Between the two of us, I think we both know who has the proven record there. Also, I'm co-owner of this place. If I want to use it to entertain women, then I damn well will."

"Is that what you were doing? 'Entertaining' Katherine Delafield? Because to me, it looked more like she was entertaining you. And what the hell, Preston? She's a goddamn debutante. Innocent and pure."

Not so innocent and pure, not really. Katherine

had a naughty streak, one she was just discovering, and Preston was more than happy to join her on that path of enlightenment. "If you must know, it was harmless fun. Moreover, it's none of your concern."

"Right, none of my concern." Kit drummed his fingers on the wooden desk. "She is friends with my wife. Now Alice will be asking questions and interfering. You have just bought yourself a world of trouble, my friend."

"What does that mean?"

Kit rolled his eyes. "You don't understand, do you? Alice, Maddie and Katherine—these women are obsessed with matchmaking. I saw it firsthand in Newport."

"Kat and I were matched once. It won't happen again. Neither of us are interested in it."

His friend's brows shot up. "Kat, is it? How cute. What does she call you?"

Please, my king. Give me more.

He shifted on the sofa, not liking this inquisition one bit. These things were private between him and Katherine. "I don't see why you're so angry," Preston said. "You've caught me in more compromising situations."

"Not with one of my wife's friends, who happens to be the unmarried daughter from a good family."

"Good family," Preston sneered. "Please."

"You know what I mean," Kit snapped. "Jesus, are you purposely ruining her?" Suddenly, Kit straightened as fear flashed over his normally cool expression. "Fucking hell, you are. You are purposely ruining that sweet girl as revenge against her father. Have you gone mad?"

Preston blew out a long breath and dragged a hand through his hair. "I swear, I'm not."

"I don't believe you."

"I'm not lying. We ran into one another today on Twenty-Third Street. I asked her to have a drink with me."

"Twenty-Third Street? Where you're building the Surety office tower?"

"Yes. Except Lloyd has told Katherine she can put an art museum there."

Kit shook his head as if clearing it. "Wait, what?"

Preston quickly explained the dispute over the land. "Lloyd somehow cheated my father out of that property. I just need to figure out how."

"So, you're seducing her as leverage against Lloyd? Or you're seducing her into dropping the art museum and letting you have the land instead?"

That leap in logic had Preston glowering at his friend. "I'm doing neither. For Christ's sake, why do you immediately assume the worst of me?"

"How about a decade of friendship? No one knows you better than I do. And this is something you would absolutely do."

"You make me sound Machiavellian."

Kit held out his hands as if to say, *That's because you are.*

"Fuck off," Preston said. "I'm not trying to hurt her."

"Except you've somehow convinced her to can-can on my stage and flash you her quim."

Darkness slithered under Preston's skin, a barely restrained violence that threatened to burst free. He leaned forward to snarl, "You better not have looked at her. If I find out you did, I'll blacken both your eyes until you can't see a goddamn thing."

Kit rocked back in his chair. "I don't believe it. You're territorial and jealous over this woman."

"Don't be ridiculous. I merely don't want her humiliated."

His friend tilted his face toward the ceiling and shouted, "What the fuck is happening here?"

Preston shot to his feet. "This is a waste of time. I should collect Katherine and take her home."

"Are you going to see her home?" Kit rose and put his hands on his hips. "Or are you taking her to a hotel? Because I won't allow you to use her as a pawn against her father. Alice will never let me hear the end of it and I'll be forced to buy out your half of the club."

"I'm not using her as a pawn—and you may buy me out whenever you wish. You can certainly afford it."

Kit scowled like he was unhappy at the prospect, even though he'd been the first to raise it. "I don't want to buy you out. This was supposed to be something for us to do together."

"Then don't lecture me about using the club."

"Fine, but can you warn me the next time you have a woman here performing for you? Perhaps put a necktie or a glove on the front door. That way I won't have to worry about what Alice may or may not see."

"Fair enough, but this won't happen again."

Kit approached, his eyes grave as he pressed

his hands together as if in prayer. "Listen, losing Forrest made me realize I don't want to lose anyone else I care about. Please, Pres. Choose another woman. I'm begging you. This is not going to turn out well."

An uncomfortable silence stretched where Preston grappled with the logic of what Kit was saying, versus the desire he felt for his reinette. Damn it. Of course Kit was right, and nothing about this made sense. Lloyd's daughter was the last person Preston should entangle himself with, even if she was a delight in every way.

Even he could see this had the chance to turn messy. It was why Preston kept mistresses, arrangements that suited them both where the rules were clearly defined. He didn't want an unpredictable affair where his partner might grow attached, then turn bitter when he didn't return her sentiment. There was no telling what could happen then. It could send his whole life spinning out of control—and he'd lived through that once already, unfortunately. He had no desire to ever experience that uncertainty again.

Pressing his lips together, he stared at the wall and forced himself to do the right thing. "I promise I'll leave her alone."

"Thank fuck. Now, let's go. I've got employees arriving in a few minutes."

ALICE KEPT SLIDING Katherine curious looks. Moments ago, Kit dragged Preston off into the depths of the club, and Katherine, while embarrassed, was enjoying watching Alice prepare for the evening's dinner service. Her friend was the head chef of the supper club and extremely talented in the kitchen.

Finally, Katherine couldn't take it any longer. "You may ask me, you know."

"It's really none of my business." Alice continued chopping onions. Her cuts were perfect and quick, like she'd done it a thousand times before. "Whatever is happening between you and Mr. Clarke is your concern."

"Alice, it's clear you have something to say. Just say it."

"I don't want to meddle."

"We're friends. Meddling is allowed. I meddled with you, trying to warn you away from Kit. I'm sorry about that, by the way. I was clearly wrong."

"You told me to be cautious, and I was glad you did, actually. It's nice to have friends who care."

"Well, you don't need to warn me away from Preston. I already know he's a terrible choice. I have no serious designs on him, but there is something about him that temporarily makes me lose my head."

Alice put down her knife and wiped her hands on a towel. "I like Mr. Clarke. He would do anything for those he cares about. He's intense and intelligent, and I'm a little afraid of him, to be quite honest."

"But?"

"But nothing. If you like him, then don't waste another moment."

"I don't like him, not like that. I don't want to marry him. That ship has sailed."

"What does that mean?"

Katherine filled Alice in on the betrothal agreement and meeting Preston at the French Ball. Alice's eyes grew wider with each word. By the time Katherine finished, Alice's jaw was nearly on the floor. "This is the most remarkable tale I've ever heard," Alice said. "And here I thought the way Kit and I fell in love was unusual. You have me beat."

"Preston and I are not falling in love," Katherine rushed to say. "I just want to have fun. I feel as if my life has been on hold for an entire year."

"So, you're with Preston because he's convenient?"

"I'm not *with* him. We saw each other today and he invited me here to have a drink. That's all."

"You're not attracted to him?"

Katherine could feel her skin growing hot again. "Oh, I'm definitely attracted to him—but nothing will come of it. We had fun at the ball, and I like teasing him. Which you probably noticed when you came in."

"Why do you say nothing will come of it? If you want to have fun and you're attracted to him, then he's a good choice for something temporary."

That was an excellent point. Preston wasn't the type of husband she wanted, but she wouldn't mind more of what happened at the French Ball. "You wouldn't judge me if I had an affair with him?"

Alice reached for another onion. "I once asked Kit to teach me how to seduce a man, then ended up seducing him. I could hardly judge you, Katherine."

"Do you think I'll regret it?"

"Only you can answer that. I regret so much about my life up until now, all the things I should have done but never had the courage. So, just ask yourself, will you regret it if you don't?"

Katherine thought it over. Would she regret an affair with Preston? Was Preston even interested?

You're allowed to tease, but be prepared. If you bite me, sweetheart, I'll bite back.

Something told her Preston wouldn't need much cajoling.

She smiled at her friend. "Here I thought you'd be the one to talk me out of an affair, and Nellie would be the one to encourage it."

Alice kept chopping, her hand flying to produce neat squares of onion. "Nellie would probably tell you one man is as good as another. She'd encourage an affair, but not with Preston. I'm pretty sure Kit is the only one of those three men she actually likes."

Yes, that sounded about right, based on Nellie's reaction to the betrothal. Katherine picked at one of her fingernails and confessed, "I've been avoiding her because I don't want to tell her any of it."

Which made Katherine feel guilty because Nellie was her best friend. Their last interaction was days ago, when Nellie wrote the morning after Katherine was to meet her French Ball lover. Katherine quickly sent back a note saying the evening didn't happen and there was nothing to worry about. At the time, it had been true.

Now things had changed and it seemed like a betrayal not to tell her friend.

"She's the most understanding person I know," Alice said. "I was terrified to tell her about Lockwood courting me, because she seems to hate him. She said he would be lucky to have me."

"Any man would've been lucky to have you."

"You're being very kind, but enough about me. I want to talk about why you were dancing for Preston Clarke in the dining room."

"God, I'm so embarrassed about that, Alice. Forgive me."

"Don't be embarrassed. It's Preston's fault for not warning us he was bringing a guest here today. And it's clear the two of you were having fun. He seemed incredibly annoyed at the interruption, in fact."

Katherine bit her lip and studied the tiled floor. Had Preston enjoyed watching her? There was something about having that man's undivided attention that made her bold. Reckless. One step away from shedding all her clothes and crawling onto his lap.

She tried to brush it aside. "We were just playing around."

"I believe it." Alice slid her diced onions into a bowl. "Goodness knows you deserve a little fun after waiting on him for a year. Before that, you were in mourning for your mother. This hasn't been easy for you. So whatever you decide, I'll support you."

"Thank you, Alice. You're a good friend."

Alice gave her a grateful smile. "As are you. And I know how it feels to have your life on hold, out of your control. I never thought I'd have my own kitchen, let alone a husband who adores me. Don't waste another second. Go out there and find your passion."

"I will. You give very good advice, Alice."

"I do? That's nice to hear, considering you're the one who gave me possibly the most important piece of advice I've ever received."

"I did?"

"Yes. You told me to know my own worth. I've never forgotten it."

Aunt Dahlia's words, but Katherine remembered passing them along at the house party. Had she forgotten her own advice? She'd nearly let Mr. Jennis talk her out of her dream design earlier today. Why was she so willing to let others direct the course of her life?

The kitchen door swung open and Kit walked in. Preston was directly behind him, his expression flat and distant, not at all like the man who'd teased her into dancing for him. Kit inclined his head toward Katherine. "Miss Delafield. My apologies for not greeting you properly earlier."

"Hello, Kit. And I should be the one to apologize for getting up on the stage—"

"Nope," he interrupted. "We are never going to discuss that, not ever. I'd like to keep all my teeth, if you please."

What on earth did that mean? Katherine's brow furrowed as she glanced at Preston. But he was no help, ignoring her to go over and greet Alice. The others chatted about food and the evening's reservations for a moment, giving Katherine the chance to examine Preston's strong profile, the broad expanse of his shoulders. The fabric of his suit stretched across his wide back, then down his long legs. He was the most compelling man in any room, like a beautiful summer storm, one you hurried outside to watch.

I serve at your pleasure, mon chaton.

Tingles streaked along her inner thighs, and she pressed her legs together tightly. She wanted more of Preston's playfulness. She liked teasing him and making him smile. She liked the way he touched and kissed her, as if he was starving for her. She even liked his arrogance.

Perhaps Alice was right. Katherine should go out and find her passion. Build a museum and have an affair, become the woman she was always meant to be.

And Preston could certainly help.

He swung toward her, so she dragged her gaze off his body and up to his face. The quirk of his brow said she'd been caught staring, but his voice and expression remained blank. "Miss Delafield, we should probably return you home."

The chance to sit in a closed carriage with him once more loomed like a thrilling drop on one of those rides at Coney Island. She pushed off the stool. "Yes, we probably should."

Chapter Twelve

❦

After saying their goodbyes and collecting their things, Preston led her out the door and toward his waiting carriage. He said nothing as he handed her up and climbed in after her. His long legs were tucked awkwardly in the interior and Katherine tried to angle hers to give him more room.

"Don't bother," he said. "I'm used to it."

"I could sit in your lap," she offered playfully, more than ready to get back to their easy teasing of before.

He drew in a sharp breath. "Christ, do not say that."

She waited for him to explain or flirt back. When he remained silent, she tried not to fidget. "Why not? I thought we were friends."

"Friends do not sit on my lap."

He was being evasive and she didn't like it. Perhaps she just needed to ask him. *I may be a dishonest man, but I promise to always be honest with you.* So if she wanted something, she merely needed to ask for it.

"What if I want to be more than friends with you?"

Preston rubbed his eyes with his fingers. "Kat, I'm sorry. As fun as that sounds, it's a terrible idea. I never should've encouraged it in the first place. Your instinct the other night was correct. It's better if we keep our distance."

Disappointment thumped in her ears in time with her heartbeat. "Why?"

"Because of your father. Because of this land on Twenty-Third Street. Because you're an innocent woman who is looking for a husband. Need I go on?"

"Yes, I think you'd better. None of that mattered an hour ago. What happened?"

"I've come to my senses. I thought you would be glad about it, honestly. The last time I saw you, that night at Sherry's, you told me to forget I knew you."

"And in response you recounted all of the indecent things you did know about me."

"Well, I shouldn't have said any of that."

"I liked hearing it. I wish you'd tell me more." When he didn't respond, she kept going. "Don't you ever do anything impulsive?"

"Not if I can help it."

That sounded boring to Katherine's ears. Perhaps he merely needed a little *push*. "Earlier in the club you said you still think about it. Being with me, I mean."

He shifted on the seat, his gloveless fingers gripping his knees so tightly that his knuckles turned white. "We should not discuss this. I vote for riding uptown in silence."

She was having fun needling him, so much that she could hardly contain a devious grin. "Overruled. Tell me what you think about specifically when you wake up in the morning. Then tell me what you do about it."

"No."

"Why not? Are you embarrassed?"

"Christ, no. You've seen me do it up close, Kat. So there's no need to go into great detail."

"But details are my favorite thing."

A muscle in his jaw jumped. "I won't do this anymore. It's not fair to you."

Not fair to her?

She pushed that comment aside for now, too focused on getting past that impenetrable wall of determination that surrounded him. "Shall I give you my details instead, the ten items I think about late at night and what I do after?"

His throat worked as he swallowed, but he didn't look at her or speak. She wondered if he truly was done playing with her. Just when she was about to give up he gave a small nod.

Emboldened by her victory, she angled toward him and rested her head against the carriage wall. She focused on his shoulder and said quietly, "Number ten on the list is your costume, the way it fit your body. You looked very strong and tall. Nine is your thighs in said costume, which were so spectacular as to deserve their own number. Eight, your huge hands and how they felt on my skin, all rough and eager." She shivered at the memory. "Seven, the filthy way you talk when you're being intimate with a woman.

Six, the little growls and grunts you made when you were pleasuring yourself."

He hadn't reacted thus far to her list, other than the rapid rise and fall of his chest. So, she asked, "Shall I go on?"

"Please."

It was an anguished rasp, as if he both loved and hated what she was saying, and the air in the carriage grew thick and heavy. Her next words were softer. "Five, your lips and tongue and how they teased mine. The fourth thing I think about is your erection, with its veins and smooth-looking skin. It seemed so very hard that night. I wish I had touched it and kissed it."

Preston's head dropped back, his eyelids sweeping closed. "Fuck," he whispered, adjusting the bulge in his trousers.

The words were affecting her, as well. Between her legs throbbed with excitement and longing, and she rubbed her thighs together to seek a small bit of relief. There was no reason not to tell him the rest of it, she supposed.

"Three, when you spoke to me in French, but especially when you called me 'mon chaton' and 'reinette.' I liked that very much. I spend quite a lot of time thinking about number two, which was when you kissed and licked between my legs. It's like the very best secret no one told me about, unless this is a special skill only you've developed."

He rolled his head toward her and the heat in his gaze scorched her. It was the intense, hot stare she remembered from the French Ball, the one that curled her toes. "I loved licking your pussy. I'd do it every day, if I could."

"If it's like that every time, I would definitely let you."

The edge of his mouth hitched, like her comment satisfied him. Their heads were inches apart in the enclosed space and it felt as if the entire world had distilled down to this carriage and this man. They weren't Katherine and Preston, struggling against expectations and rules. In here, they were two people lost in lust and longing, with shared breaths and secrets that might lead to more.

Please, she thought. *Let it lead to more.*

Finally, he asked, "What is number one, reinette?"

She moistened her dry lips and whispered, "When you were licking between my legs, you put a finger inside me. I loved the fullness. I liked knowing you were inside my body. I can't help but wonder what two fingers would feel like . . . or maybe three."

Almost before she finished speaking, he closed the distance and took her mouth with his own, his lips rough and hungry. Unapologetic and demanding, and every bit as arousing as she remembered from the night of the ball. His large hand cupped her jaw, angling her where he liked, and the kiss turned deeper, until she couldn't breathe, couldn't think. It didn't matter. She didn't need air and her brain was welcome to nod off for the time being. She wanted to drown in the feelings rioting through her, the desire burning in her blood.

It felt so good, like she'd had too much champagne. Her head swam with the smell of leather, musk and the hint of tobacco. That was pure Preston, her naughty hardworking king.

Hers?

His hand slid down to cup her breast and she lost her train of thought. Arching her back, she pressed the aching mound into his palm, cursing the cloth and whalebone that prevented a more thorough exploration. When he broke off from her mouth, his dark whisper filled the humid interior. "Will you show me?"

"Show you?"

His teeth captured her earlobe and bit down, sending a shower of sparks racing through her limbs. Sweet heavens, that felt amazing.

"Have you already forgotten?" he said against her skin. "You said you would tell me what you do while recounting that list late at night."

Oh, he wanted those details, as well? "You'd like to hear about how I slide my hand—"

"No," he interrupted. "I want you to show me. I need to see things with my own eyes to understand them."

"Liar. You're a developer, a visionary." She threaded her fingers through his thick hair, needing to hold on to him. "You merely wish for me to entertain you, as I did in the club."

"I told you I'm terrible."

"It doesn't matter, because I can't possibly do that here." In a moving carriage? In the daylight? In front of another person? She would die of embarrassment first.

"Why not? I pleasured myself in front of you at the ball. Come on, mon chaton. Show me."

True, but still. It was different for women, wasn't it? As if to prove her wrong, her clitoris throbbed, begging for attention, and her skin grew itchy and hot with unfulfilled desire. "Preston . . ." She let her voice trail off, not certain what to even say.

He quickly removed the glove from her right hand, then moved to the other seat and faced her. "It's just me, Kat, and I've already seen your gorgeous pussy. There's no reason not to give us both what we want. Won't it feel good to stroke yourself and come all over your fingers? Ease that terrible ache in your belly?"

Oh, God. Yes, it definitely would.

He didn't stop, the cad. "There's no reason to wait until you're alone tonight in your bedroom. You can pleasure yourself right here and I'll talk to you the entire time. Show me how you pet yourself, reinette. Please."

Was she considering this?

You wanted to be bold. You wanted to cavort.

True, and the way he was staring at her, with dark expectation and salacious hope, would've enticed the most pious woman to dance with the devil. As if whatever happened here was their secret, no one else's, and he needed this more than his next breath. The thought of holding his attention, of being what he needed, what he *craved*, caused her chest to flutter. Brazenness came over her, the same brash and bold sensation as when she followed him to his box at the ball or danced for him onstage.

It was the need to crack his hard exterior, dig past the mistrust and suspicion and see him undone once more.

Ever so slowly, her fingers twitched and curled, gathering layers of fabric in her hand.

PRESTON HELD HIS breath until his chest burned with the need for air. He didn't care. Katherine was actually going to do this, and he held still, not wanting to risk this performance by scaring her.

She was so beautiful, so natural and pure. The pressure in his groin was nearly unbearable from hearing her whisper the list of things she recollected at night. Yet he didn't move as her skirts drifted higher.

This was entirely about her.

Afternoon light slashed through the interior, across her fine features, revealing the tiny lines between her brows. That wouldn't do. He wanted her relaxed and totally engaged in the moment, with nothing on her mind but her own pleasure.

Licking his dry lips, he said, "That's it, just a bit higher. Get all that heavy fabric out of the way."

She complied, wriggling her hips a bit on the seat. The cotton and lace of her drawers emerged as more of her skirts gathered at her waist. Her breath came fast, chest rising and falling, clear evidence of her excitement. Was she wet? The desire to discover the answer, to see her glistening quim, had him panting like a schoolboy.

I promise I'll leave her alone.

He hadn't broken his promise to Kit, not really. Preston wasn't touching her at the moment. Yes, he'd kissed her moments ago, but that was as far as he'd take their physical interaction. He would keep to the opposite seat and watch, then drop her at home and forget all this ever happened.

Katherine's skirts finally reached her middle, revealing long legs covered in delicate fabric, her thighs tucked firmly closed. She waited, her gaze fixed on the empty seat in front of her, so Preston took this as his cue to give her an out. "Kat," he said gently. "If you don't want to do this, I'll understand."

"I want to," she breathed. "I just . . . well, I thought you were going to tell me what to do."

His blood ignited and fire raced to his balls. Christ, this woman and her games. He could easily become addicted to this.

He wrapped his fingers around the bench beneath him as he leaned in slightly. "Hold your skirts out of the way with one hand so I can see you. Now, slide your thighs open slowly. Show me how wet and swollen you are."

The gap between her knees widened as she moved them apart, and the slit between her drawers revealed her mound, the pale skin of her thighs. She kept going, opening her legs, until he could see the petals of her sex, glistening in the daylight.

He growled deep in his throat. "Oh, mon chaton. I can see how slick you are, you gorgeous creature. You liked telling me about your list, didn't you?"

She nodded, her bottom lip disappearing between her front teeth.

He could feel his cock leaking, eager to find her heat. God almighty, he might give his entire fortune in this moment to fuck her. But reality intruded once again. Anything more than this was impossible.

Instead, he said, "I'm going to help you find relief. We're going to take care of your pussy right now, aren't we?"

"Please," she whispered, her eyelids sweeping closed, as if the admission embarrassed her.

"Keep holding your skirts but use your free hand to slide over your mound, then along each inner thigh. Don't touch your clitoris yet."

Her long fingers glided through the crisp hair between her legs, then swept from one leg to the other, teasing. He heard the hitch in her breath as she coasted past where she ached the most, frustrated at being denied. Which meant he wasn't going to give her what she wanted yet.

"Again," he ordered.

"Pres," she said on a whine, but did as he asked.

The carriage turned a corner, but he hardly noticed. His focus remained on the heavenly place between her thighs and watching her hand as it drifted over her skin. "Good girl," he praised. "Now, with one finger, gather the moisture at your entrance."

Her middle finger dipped into her entrance and Preston ground his back teeth together, fighting the urge to touch himself. He could easily spend in seconds, her movements more arousing than anything he'd ever witnessed. "Use that moisture on your clit, reinette. Smear it across that little bud and make it wet."

The second she did as he asked, her back arched off the seat, a soft moan filling the carriage. "Oh, God," she said, her eyes remaining closed.

"Does it feel nice?"

"Yes."

"Keep going. Show me how you like to stroke yourself."

She used tight circles, faster than he would have used if he were touching her. The skin covering her pearl had retracted, giving him the perfect view of her clitoris, engorged and red, as she worked it. Fuck, that was a beautiful sight.

Her head dropped back to rest against the carriage, as if she was lost in the pleasure, her pants coming faster. Was she close to peaking? He didn't want this to be over so soon. He wanted to watch her do this all day. "Stop," he ordered.

"No, please." She paused, her brow creased. "I'm so close."

"Precisely why you must stop. I'm not ready to let you come."

"But why not?"

Because I want to torture us both.

Because I'll never have this chance again.

Because I need this to become number one on your list.

"Because you're my reinette and you'll do what I say. Aren't you?"

She visibly shivered. "Yes, my king."

The pleasure those words sent cascading through him should have embarrassed him. He pressed his palm against his erection, unable to help a quick stroke through his clothing. Jesus, he needed to come so badly.

Forcing his hand back to his side, he swallowed and returned his attention to her. "Do you feel empty, mon chaton?"

Her lips parted and she nodded once.

"I thought so," he said. "Put a finger inside you, exactly where you ache."

Her hand moved lower, then one finger extended to slowly disappear inside her channel. It took every ounce of his control not to move as he watched her walls suck the digit inside. "Fuck," he whispered. "I love how that looks. Does it feel good?"

"It does," she said on a gasp. "So very good."

He could imagine that tight heat, how it had clasped his finger the night of the ball. He wished he'd given her more, but there hadn't been time. "Would you like to try two?"

"Will it hurt?"

"It shouldn't but you may go slow."

She inhaled a deep breath, his brave reinette, and began working her index and middle fingers inside her. His pulse hammered in his ears as he watched the careful invasion, wishing he could touch or lick her, anything to bring her more pleasure. It wasn't in his nature to hold back and sit passively, and he knew how delicious she tasted. He was dying to get her flavor on his tongue once more.

"Do you like watching me?" she asked, still feeding her fingers into her channel, rocking them back and forth. She hadn't opened her eyes since lifting her skirts, so she didn't know how her actions were affecting him.

"God, yes. My cock is so hard it hurts, and my balls are tight and full of come. It would take about three pumps before I spent."

"Then why don't you?"

"Because this is about you. Keep going. Fill yourself with your fingers."

Finally, after another long second, the digits were seated inside. Her chest heaved, her body quivering. "Oh, goodness. I can't . . . it's so much."

But not as much as my cock.

He dug his nails into the leather, trying not to think about how tight she would be around him, how deep he could fill her. Now was not the time.

"You can," he said confidently. "Your body was made for pleasure, reinette. Pump your fingers like I would."

She obliged him, her hips lifting to meet the movement, chasing the pleasure just as she would if he were fucking her. A moan escaped her throat to join the slick sounds of her channel, an obscene sound that was music to his ears.

"Shall I open the windows?" he asked. "So that everyone on the street can hear your cries?"

"Oh, God," she squeaked, her fingers shoving in as she pressed her palm to her clit. "Please, I can't take it."

He took pity on her. "Now, my gorgeous girl. Stir your button with two fingers and make yourself come."

She didn't hesitate, too far gone to feel any reticence whatsoever. Fingers coated in her wetness flew to the top of her sex and worked, circling, brushing, while her face slackened in pure bliss. He needed to see the exact moment when the pleasure crested.

"Open your eyes. Look at me, Kat."

Her lids lifted, and her eyes met his. Her pupils were so wide that her gaze was nearly black. The lines of her face sharpened, her body tightening, and then it happened. She never looked away, instead letting him see every second of her orgasm as it washed over her, her limbs trembling against the leather. Soft moans enveloped them both, the sound of her climax like a caress to his balls, and he drank in the sight, committing it to memory.

This was definitely his number one.

Finally, she slumped into the upholstery, her hand moving to her knee but otherwise remaining perfectly still. Her eyes closed again, but he couldn't wait a second more. "Give me your fingers," he rasped.

She cracked one eyelid to peek at him. "What?"

Gesturing to the hand that had just been between her legs, he repeated, "Give me your fingers."

Her brows knitted but she lifted her hand. He leaned in and grasped her wrist, bringing her closer until he could suck her two fingers into his mouth. The taste of her arousal flooded his senses and coated his tongue, and his eyes closed in pure bliss. Christ, he loved it.

Thoroughly, he cleaned her skin, making sure to get every hint of her moisture. He longed to lick it straight from the source, but he'd promised. This would have to do.

The carriage slowed and he forced himself to release her. "I could watch you do that all day."

"I can't believe I actually did it," she whispered.

He would not allow her to regret it. "It was the most arousing thing I've ever witnessed."

"Honestly?"

He gestured to his crotch, where his erection bulged. A wet spot had formed on the cloth, thanks to the leaking currently occurring from the tip of his cock. "I've never been harder."

Her lips curled with satisfaction as her attention wandered to the street. "Wait, we're here already." She turned back to him and tilted her chin toward his groin. "What about . . . ?"

"Don't worry. I'll take care of it after you leave. Forgive me if I don't walk you to your door, however."

She arranged her skirts to cover her legs, much to his disappointment. Her tone turned teasing when she said, "But I might be set upon by a pickpocket or a murderer. You must keep me safe and see me to the door."

"I wouldn't be much help, not in the condition I'm in. You're better off taking on any pickpockets and murderers on your own."

The carriage drew to a halt, two houses down from the Delafield residence, exactly as he'd instructed his driver. Katherine smirked at him as she patted his knee, and his cock pulsed. "Poor man. You stay here and think about me after I'm gone."

As if he could do anything else.

Instead of squeezing by politely to get out onto the street, she was all flailing arms, brushing across his rigid cock and driving him out of his skull. Then she pretended to fall, and he widened his legs to catch her, which put her hip directly on top of his erection. "Fuck," he grunted.

"Oh, my. It is in a state, isn't it? Best of luck with that problem, Mr. Clarke."

He couldn't help but laugh. "Enjoying my pain, reinette? I'll not forget it for next time."

"I look forward to it, my king." Then she opened the carriage door and disappeared.

Shit. There wasn't supposed to be a next time. This woman made him forget everything but her.

Chapter Thirteen

❧

Katherine placed the paintings against the wall of the Meliora Club's salon, then stepped back to study the works. No, that wouldn't do. The styles clashed. She couldn't put a Sisley and a Renoir next to a Gérôme. They would have to find another impressionist painting—and fast. The art show was next week.

"Hello, Katie."

She turned to find Nellie entering the room. They hadn't seen each other since the night of the ball, and Katherine tried not to feel guilty about avoiding her friend. But Nellie saw too much, knew Katherine too well. She feared her secret tryst with Preston would be evident on her face.

It had been three days since her carriage ride with Preston, and Katherine couldn't stop thinking of it. The entire experience had been . . . incredible. Life-altering. Exactly the type of encounter she'd imagined when crafting her plan to start living boldly. Like Alice had said, Preston was a good choice for something temporary. She couldn't wait to see what he came up with next.

Returning her gaze to the paintings, she kept her voice light. "Hello, yourself. I hadn't expected to see you today, but I'm glad you're here. You can help me with these paintings."

"No offense, but that one on the right doesn't match."

"Exactly. I need to find another impressionist painting. Your father has that Monet, doesn't he?"

"Yes, we recently moved it to the upstairs hall. Would you like to borrow it, along with the Renoir we already discussed?"

"Please. We'd need them for three days next week, if possible."

"I'll have someone bring them over tomorrow." Nellie gestured to the table and chairs. "Can we sit? I haven't seen you in forever. Let's catch up."

The somber note in Nellie's voice caught Katherine's attention. Her friend wasn't usually so serious. "Of course. Shall I ring for tea?"

"Or whiskey. Whichever you prefer."

Katherine tugged on the bell rope. "Whiskey? Goodness, should I be worried?"

"I don't know." Nellie dropped onto the sofa and removed her gloves. "Probably."

An attendant arrived and Katherine ordered a tea service, then sat on the other end of the sofa. "Well, let's have it."

"I went to Alice's supper club last night."

A prickling sense of dread settled between Katherine's shoulder blades. "Oh?"

"Yes, and she told me something interesting."

"Is that so?"

"Why didn't you tell me you're having an affair with Preston Clarke?"

Katherine smothered a grimace. Not so much an affair as teasing him, letting him watch her pleasure herself. Her cheeks heated at the memory.

"You're blushing," Nellie exclaimed. "What happened between you two? Last I heard about Preston, you stormed out of his office after telling him off over the betrothal."

She let out a long breath. "I'll fill you in, but please don't judge me."

"Goodness, Katie." Nellie shook her head. "You know me better than that. I wouldn't dream of it."

"The whole thing is embarrassing. You're going to think I'm foolish."

"Well, now you must tell me everything."

Katherine started explaining, from the ball and Jane Street apartment, to Sherry's and the supper club. "It's harmless fun," she finished.

"You're attracted to Preston."

"Very."

"I assumed, otherwise you never would've gone to meet him that night, fully prepared to let him be the first man you slept with."

It was true. Katherine sighed. "I wish I could explain it. There's something about him. At the ball, he was intense but surprisingly sweet. And the things he says . . . It's like he flips a switch inside me that causes me to lose my mind."

"Hmm." Nellie frowned as the footman arrived with their tea service. It took a few minutes for the tea to be poured, and then they were alone again.

Katherine picked up where they left off, eager to get answers. "You sound disappointed that I'm attracted to Preston."

"No, but I can't understand why you were hiding it from me. It hurt my feelings, Katie."

Katherine hurried to put her cup down, then reached for Nellie's hand. "I'm so sorry. I never meant to hurt you."

"Then, why? You know the absolute worst about me, all the embarrassing and socially unacceptable things I've done. How could you possibly think I'd ever judge you?"

"Because I know you don't like him. I was worried you'd try to talk me out of it."

"I might have at first, but if it's something you want then I'll support you. I'll help in any way I can."

Guilt settled in Katherine's stomach like a lead weight. Her eyes started to tear up as she said, "I don't deserve you. I'm sorry."

Nellie's gaze grew glassy, as well. "Katie, I love you like a sister. I don't know what I would do without you. Even at my worst, you've stuck by me. So, don't think you're getting rid of me now."

Katherine leaned over and threw her arms around her friend. "I love you, too, and I wouldn't dream of getting rid of you."

They stayed that way for a long minute. When they'd both recovered enough, they pulled apart. Nellie dabbed at her eyes with her fingers. "Do not make me cry, Katherine Eloise Delafield."

"I wouldn't dream of it, Eleanor Lucinda Young."

"Now, I want to hear more about Preston. I'm assuming with all his experience he has skills you've put to good use."

Katherine thought about what happened in

the back of Preston's box and in the carriage. Honestly, she wouldn't change a thing. "Do you really want details?"

"From the queen of details? Of course I do. I bet you remember every naughty word and filthy kiss."

"I do, but it wouldn't be proper for me to share all of it, would it?"

"Maybe just one or two little morsels," Nellie said, reaching for a small tea cake. "You know I won't tell anyone."

Katherine knew this well. Nellie was not a gossip. "He's very . . . forceful. But playful, too."

"Preston Clarke, playful? I don't believe it."

"No, he is," Katherine said. "We have this thing we do where we—"

"Stop," Nellie interrupted. "I changed my mind. I don't want details."

Katherine chuckled. "It's your loss. They're very good details."

"I'm sure, my dear, but I may have to face that man again someday and I need to be able to keep a straight face. Just tell me, have you slept with him yet?"

"No, and I'm not certain there is a 'yet.'"

Nellie made a disbelieving sound in her throat. "I know Preston and you're obviously gorgeous and fun. A little ray of sunshine in his dreary life. He will try to get under your skirts again."

Katherine wasn't so certain. Three days had passed since the carriage and not a word from Preston. "Even if he tries, I might not let him."

"True, but based on what you've said, I think

you will. Which means we need to discuss practicalities."

"We had that talk already," Katherine reminded her. "After the ball, remember?"

"I'm not talking about disease and contraception, but I'm glad you haven't forgotten. Who knows where that man has been? For God's sake, make sure he uses a shield." Nellie finished her cake. "No, I mean your feelings. Keeping yourself from falling in love with him."

Katherine took a cookie off the tray. "There's absolutely no chance of that. He hates my family and has no interest in marriage. Not to mention he had his chance, and I'm not keen to give him another."

"Katie," Nellie said on a sigh. "Sometimes our feelings don't care about who is right for us, or who is interested in marrying us. The heart has a mind of its own, you know?"

"Are you speaking from experience?"

"This is about you at the moment. When are you supposed to see him next?"

"We have no plans."

"Hmm. For two planner-types of people, you are both hopeless."

"Maybe he's changed his mind about us. He did try and put me off in the carriage at first. I wonder if Mr. Ward said something."

"You can bet Kit tried, but something tells me Preston does as he wishes. He's not one to let another control him."

No, he'd much rather do the controlling, a trait Katherine didn't mind when it came to their games. "Perhaps I should send him a note."

Nellie considered this as she chewed on a macaron. "I think you're better off letting him come after you. Preston seems like the type to get off on the chase, like one of his property developments."

"What if he doesn't?"

"He will. Based on how he acted in the coat closet and the carriage, Preston won't be satisfied until he's had you. The question is, are you willing to let him?"

PRESTON WAS IN the midst of reviewing a contract when his office door opened. "Two things have arrived for you," Mrs. Cohen said.

Without looking up, he said, "Oh?"

"Yes. One is your lawyer. He's waiting out front."

Preston's lawyers had been reviewing the paperwork on the Twenty-Third Street property. A decision must have been made. Preston put down his pen, stood and reached for his coat. "Excellent. Does it look like he's carrying good news?"

She straightened her spectacles, and he could see a hint of amusement on her face, like she held a secret. "All lawyers look the same to me, so I couldn't say. However, in my experience, they never bring good news."

"Oh, ye of little faith."

"I have plenty of faith. Just not with lawyers."

When she didn't move, he prompted, "You may show him in now."

"Don't you want to hear about the second thing that's arrived?"

Rarely had Mrs. Cohen appeared so animated. Curious, he said, "Yes, if it moves things along."

"Miss Delafield has sent you a gift."

Preston blinked, positive he hadn't heard correctly. "A gift?" No one sent him gifts. He'd given plenty, mostly to mistresses, but he couldn't remember the last time he was on the receiving end.

He hadn't stopped thinking about her since their afternoon in the carriage. The sight of her pleasuring herself was burned into his brain for all eternity, the memory his favorite new masturbatory fantasy. She made everything so easy, so fun. He'd promised to leave her alone, though, and he was going to stick to that promise, even if it killed him.

"Yes, a gift," Mrs. Cohen said. "A thing one person gives to another person to show their regard."

"I know what a gift is," he said dryly. "What is it?"

"Paintings."

A thread of warmth pulled through his chest, like a string tightly wrapped around one's finger. He hadn't experienced this simple excitement in a long time, the flattery that someone cared enough to pick something out for him.

What had she sent?

"Where are they?" he asked, already on his way out the door. "By your desk?"

"Yes," Mrs. Cohen said, hurrying after him. "Wouldn't you like to see Mr. Strong first?"

No, he didn't. He needed to see what Katherine had sent him. Right this instant.

"Mr. Clarke," Strong said, coming to his feet when Preston emerged in the outer room.

Two wrapped parcels, their brown paper crisp and tied with strings, sat on Mrs. Cohen's desk. "Hello, Strong. Give me a moment."

Snatching up scissors from a drawer, he quickly snipped the string on the first painting. Tearing through the paper, he flipped the frame over to reveal soft pastel colors to form a beautiful countryside. It wasn't something he would have chosen for himself—his tastes ran bold and dark—but this was pretty. Soothing in a way.

"I like that," Mrs. Cohen said from over his shoulder.

Yes, so did he.

The second painting was a match to the first, same colors and style but a different landscape. They were the perfect pair. He stared down at them both, astounded. How had she known? Moreover, why had she bothered?

After what she did in the carriage, he should've sent *her* a gift. He should be bowing and scraping at her feet, grateful for the most erotic experience of his life.

"There's a card," Mrs. Cohen said, pointing.

He ripped it open, so eager it should have embarrassed him.

Neat loops and swirls filled a small piece of cream vellum.

For your office. A king should always be surrounded by pretty things.

Yours,
Kat

Yours.

Christ, the power that single word had over him. It was both deeply satisfying and absolutely terrifying. He'd consider it later, when he had more time.

Shoving the card into his coat pocket, he asked his secretary, "Have we a hammer and nails?"

"Yes. In the closet over there."

"Mr. Clarke," Strong tried again. "I have a very busy day ahead."

Preston waved his hand at the lawyer on the way to the closet. "Yes, as do I. But you'll allow me a few more minutes. I'm paying you for your time, after all."

It took a second or two to find the required materials and select the perfect spot on his office wall, just off to the side, right where he could see both paintings. He drove the nails into the plaster with ruthless efficiency, and soon both pictures were centered exactly. Standing back, he admired them.

Soothing, serene, quiet beauty.

"Those are precisely what you needed in here," Mrs. Cohen said. "She has a fine eye."

Pressure built in Preston's chest, as if that invisible string was pulling taut again, burrowing inside him. He cleared his throat. "Indeed, she does."

She turned for the door. "I'll bring in Mr. Strong."

Preston was still staring at the paintings when Strong entered. He forced himself to turn away and greet the lawyer. "Sorry to keep you waiting. Won't you have a seat?"

"Thank you."

When they were settled, Preston said, "Let's have it. What did Delafield do to con my father out of that property?"

"Unfortunately, it appears that paperwork is legitimate, signed by your father."

Frustration and fury peppered Preston's skin, undoing the tranquility of Katherine's gift, and his hands curled into fists. He stared at the paperweight on his desk and contemplated hurling it into the wall. "That is utter horseshit. Those documents were manipulated."

"Unless you can produce evidence to the contrary, there's nothing we can do. This appears to be on the up-and-up."

"What about the forging experts we asked to review the documents? What did they say?"

"Inconclusive."

Preston banged his fist on the desk, and Strong held up his hands. "I'm sorry, Clarke. I wish there was more I could do."

"I refuse to let him win."

"Who?"

"Delafield. Think, Strong. There has to be another expert. Or we take it to a judge. Let's get his lawyers on the record to admit what they've done."

"There has to be a reason for the lawsuit. Disagreeing with the signature isn't a reason."

Preston tapped his fingers on the armrest, thinking. He'd come too far to lose. Beyond all the time and money he'd invested on this property, he could not let Lloyd do this. If Delafield succeeded in stealing this block, Manhattan Surety would pull the project and give it to another developer. Someone else would erect the world's tallest building, and Preston's career would sink like a boulder in the East River.

A failure, just like his father.

He had to keep cool. Deal with this logically. Hmm, why not try to beat Lloyd at his own game?

Lips curling with devious satisfaction, he stifled the urge to rub his hands together. "What if we could produce paperwork to the contrary?"

Strong shifted in his chair and smoothed his silk vest. "That would certainly convince a judge, though I thought you said Lloyd had the only copy."

"What if I could produce a version? Bribe someone at the records department to backdate a more recent deed transfer? One that shows the property was given back to my father."

Strong's brow creased dramatically. "What you are suggesting is illegal. I cannot be involved in something like that."

Preston steepled his fingers and studied the other man. Strong's firm had worked for the Clarkes for ages, and Preston now questioned the wisdom of trusting this to them. After all, hadn't Strong and his cronies watched as Henry Clarke destroyed himself and nearly destroyed his family? Where were they six years ago when Preston had been mired in a mountain of debt and trying to piece together a crumbling empire?

And Lloyd Delafield had used Strong's firm, too, before the joint business was dissolved.

Preston felt like a fool. Hadn't he learned ages

ago not to trust anyone? Nothing would stop Lloyd Delafield from getting what he wanted—even if it meant breaking the law. After all, they were cut from the same cloth. Bribing Strong or forging documents would've been too easy.

There had to be another way. Preston was not about to give up on that property. By rights, it was his and the Manhattan Surety project was already underway.

"Whose side are you on here, Strong? I'm the one paying your fee."

"Which isn't enough to risk getting disbarred."

"Then I'll hire another lawyer, one who isn't so shortsighted."

"You are welcome to do so, of course," Strong said, rising. A flush worked its way above his collar. "But good luck finding one who is both talented and willing to risk his career for you."

Preston clenched his jaw. There had to be a clever lawyer in this corrupt cesspool of a city who was willing to make a quick buck. "We'll see about that. You're fired. Send your bill to Mrs. Cohen."

The lawyer left and Preston turned to the new paintings. His shoulders relaxed a tiny fraction, logic returning to replace the anger. He merely needed to think a bit more, find a way around this dilemma. Quickly.

But he had faith in himself, in his abilities. There was nothing he wouldn't do to beat Lloyd on this.

Absolutely nothing.

Chapter Fourteen

❧

The Duke of Lockwood handed Katherine up into the open-air carriage for their late-afternoon drive in the park. He settled next to her in a well-tailored navy suit, looking poised and graceful, comfortable in his own athletic skin. There was no pretense with him, and he was quite personable and funny. Little wonder why the ladies of Fifth Avenue were so taken with him.

She folded her hands on her lap. "Thank you for agreeing to do this. I've needed a break all week."

A break from her own thoughts. She'd begun to *miss* Preston, going as far as to send him gifts for his office. It was clear she'd lost her mind, especially considering she hadn't heard a word from him since their carriage ride. Were the paintings just a pathetic attempt at getting his attention once more? Why had she signed the card "yours"?

Did she want to belong to him?

No, she couldn't. Her pride wouldn't allow it. He hadn't wanted her—*still* didn't want her. This was merely light and fun, nothing more. A bit of cavorting until she felt ready to settle down.

"It's my pleasure," Lockwood said graciously as he smoothed his perfectly creased trousers.

Forgetting Preston for the time being, Katherine studied the hard edge of Lockwood's sculpted jaw. Why couldn't she have been attracted to the duke instead? He was available, interested in marriage, and a decent person. Everything would have been much simpler.

During the drive south to the park, they discussed the mild weather and the latest society gossip. As they turned onto Seventy-Ninth Street, she asked, "And how have you been since I last saw you? Busy wooing debutantes, I suppose."

He grimaced. "A bit, yes."

"I sense it's not going well."

"It's exhausting, to be honest. As well, I'll need to travel home soon to deal with some issues with the estate."

He didn't sound thrilled by his prospects. "Why don't I help you? Tell me who you've been eyeing and I'll guide you in the right direction."

"Are you certain? I'd hate to come across as cavalier, but I would like any insight you may provide. These aren't families with whom I'm acquainted."

"I would love to, Your Grace. Give me a name."

They entered the park, which was crowded thanks to the mild weather. She nodded to some acquaintances while she awaited his answer.

He asked, "Have you met Miss Beatrice Bend?"

Of course she had. Beatrice was a year younger than Katherine, and a member of prominent society. Beatrice had given Katherine a list of places to visit in Spain last year. "I know her well. She does like to travel, though Not fond of staying in one place for too long."

"Hmm."

Lockwood's fingers tapped on his knee, and Katherine had to think a duchess with wander-lust wasn't ideal. He asked, "What about Miss Edith Bishop?"

"Dedicated to her various causes and marches. There have been some rumors about socialism."

Lockwood nodded. "I see. I'm not certain I want a political duchess."

"Who else?"

"Perhaps we are going about this the wrong way," Lockwood said. "Why don't you offer up some suggestions on who might make a suitable match?"

"That's a good idea, but I'll need to think on it. Tell me what you're looking for in a duchess."

He cleared his throat. "I feel as though I should mention that I consider you a friend and only a friend."

Was he . . . ? Oh, goodness. "I'm not angling to become your duchess, Lockwood."

He visibly relaxed next to her. "That is a relief. As pleasant as I find your company, I've sworn off your little circle of friends."

Right, because of Maddie and Alice. "Totally understandable, and I should mention I abhor England. I'd never wish to live there. No, I'm good right here in New York."

"I apologize for misreading the situation. I merely needed to be certain."

Because he'd misread two situations recently. She understood. "You are the catch of the season, after all. It stands to reason that every available girl here is angling to get to you."

"Not every available girl," he murmured.

This was interesting. "Who?" Katherine couldn't help but ask. "Do I know her?"

"Let's move on from this boring topic," Lockwood said. "How go your plans for the museum?"

Fine, except there seemed to be the pesky issue of who actually owned the land.

Katherine began filling Lockwood in on firing the first architect and her search for another.

"There's a fellow Brit here," the duke said. "I've known her for years. She's an accomplished architect. I'd be more than happy to make the introduction for you."

"She?"

"Of course. You've heard of the Mansfield Hotel? His wife, Mrs. Phillip Mansfield, designed it. Along with other buildings on the East Coast."

A female architect? Katherine would love that. She wouldn't have to worry about any more condescending looks from men who thought she couldn't handle this project. And the Mansfield Hotel was one of the nicest in the city. "Would you? I would appreciate it."

"Consider it done."

"Thank you." She couldn't help but return to the subject of marriage. His situation was so unique and fascinating—and a bit sad. "Does it ever bother you that you cannot marry anyone you wish?"

A shadow passed behind his beautiful eyes. "It

doesn't matter. The title is greater than any one man."

"Sounds as if you've heard that line a time or two. Or ten."

"You'd be right. My father said it, and my grandfather before him."

"Well, I think it sounds lonely."

"No need to feel sorry for me. I have a life of unbelievable privilege. And I take the responsibilities very seriously."

Suddenly a familiar rider drew closer from the opposite direction. Was that . . . Daddy? Indeed, it was her father, perched atop his favorite stallion, riding next to Mrs. Whittier, Katherine's mother's best friend. Katherine sat up straighter, ready to get their attention.

"Is that your father?" Lockwood asked.

"Yes. The woman with him is Mrs. Whittier, my mother's closest friend while she was still alive."

"We should say hello."

Katherine opened her mouth to call out . . . just as her father picked up Mrs. Whittier's hand and brought it to his mouth. Eyelids sweeping closed, he kissed the inside of the other woman's wrist, and the gesture could only be described as loving and tender. Intimate.

Katherine blinked, thoroughly confused. Wait, was her father romantically involved with another woman? And Mama's best friend?

The couple continued along the path, unaware of anyone else around them, and Katherine's stomach cramped with uncertainty and confusion. This didn't make any sense. Mama and Mrs. Whittier had been extremely close. Katherine could remember their visits, the house ringing with their laughter, before her mother grew ill. The two women had gone to finishing school together, friends since before their debuts.

Her father . . . was seeing another woman.

How had this happened? More importantly, when? Had Mrs. Whittier accompanied him on his long trips recently? Had she gone to Scotland with Daddy last year? Then a sickening thought occurred. Had their relationship started before Mama died?

She stared off into the trees, not truly seeing them, while pain scalded her chest. She could hardly breathe. And here she thought he'd been spending time away from home because he was working too hard . . .

"I take it you weren't aware of their relationship." Lockwood's voice was soft, understanding threading the crisp, accented words.

Swallowing past the lump in her throat, she said, "No."

"I'm sorry. This is a terrible way to find out, though there's never really a good time to learn that one's parent has feelings directed toward another."

"Your mother?"

"No." He grimaced. "My father had a mistress for years. He made little effort at discretion and seemed to truly love her."

"That must have been hard. Was she a widow or another aristocrat?"

"Barmaid."

"Oh, goodness."

"Indeed."

The carriage rolled along but Katherine couldn't think of anything to say. She kept picturing her father with Mrs. Whittier. It seemed inconceivable. While Mama and Mr. Whittier were still alive, the two families had vacationed together in Newport and Bar Harbor nearly every summer.

Now her father was in a secret relationship with the woman?

The duke finally asked, "Will you speak to your father about her?"

"Most definitely."

"I wish you luck, then. Men can be cagey when matters of the heart are involved."

"Including you?"

"I've heard it said I have no heart."

"Nonsense. Perhaps you haven't found it yet."

"You are a hopeless romantic, Miss Delafield." He tipped his hat at a carriage rolling past them. "I hope some man doesn't take advantage of your good nature."

Too late, she wanted to say, thinking about the last year. But no one would take advantage of her ever again. She'd make certain of it.

And she was going to demand answers from her father as soon as possible.

HOURS LATER, WHEN her father walked into the dining room, Katherine studied him from under her lashes. He looked . . . happy. The lines on his face weren't as severe. Had he just finished up with his rendezvous?

Stomach roiling, she reached for her wineglass. "Evening, Daddy. You look well."

"Hello, ladies," he said to Katherine and his

sister, Dahlia, as he took his usual seat. "I apologize for running late."

"Yes, Lloyd," Aunt Dahlia said with suspicion in her voice. "What's got you smiling today?"

"Am I not allowed to smile every now and again?"

I would merely like a day or two when I walk by here and don't experience an awful knot in my stomach.

Had he meant those words? Or was he taking down the paintings because of his new relationship? God, had Mrs. Whittier visited his bed upstairs, the one he'd shared with Katherine's mother?

Katherine closed her eyes, her head throbbing from all the unanswered questions swirling around in it.

Her father served himself from the platters on the table. "And how was your day, Katherine? I hear you went out for a spell. Working on the exhibition again?"

She spoke slowly, carefully observing his reaction. "I went for a drive in the park."

Abruptly, he dropped the serving fork and it clattered to the porcelain. As if nothing happened, he picked it up and selected another slice of beef. "You did? With whom?"

"The Duke of Lockwood."

He still didn't look at her, his gaze focused on his plate. "That's excellent news. Perhaps Lockwood is serious about courting you after all."

I saw you. I saw you with her. How could you not tell me?

"Indeed, it is good news," Aunt Dahlia said. "The duke is a fine match."

"The duke is not serious about me," Katherine announced. "We're merely friends. You remember what that's like, Daddy. To have *friends*?"

He glanced at her then, his brows coming together in confusion. "Yes, I do."

"Are you saying you don't wish to marry the duke?" Aunt Dahlia sounded aghast at the idea of it. "He's the catch of the season."

"Who's been thrown over twice," Daddy said.

Katherine felt the need to rise to Lockwood's defense. "Those weren't his fault."

"Lloyd, I thought you'd be pleased," her aunt said. "A duchess in the family would be quite prestigious."

"I don't care about prestige. I care about my daughter's happiness."

"Do you?" Katherine couldn't help but ask. "Do you, really?"

He put his knife and fork on his plate and sat back. "Is there something you wish to say to me?"

Katherine stared at him, her mind churning. She didn't like secrets. They rotted and festered, ruining relationships and memories. She much preferred to have everything out in the open.

Exhaling slowly, she put an elbow on the table and leaned toward him. "I saw you with her."

He didn't move, his body perfectly still, as they looked at one another. After a long minute, he broke off and cleared the room of staff until the three of them were alone. "In the park, I suppose."

Well, at least he wasn't going to deny it. "How long?"

"Wait," Aunt Dahlia said, shaking her head slightly. "What are we discussing?"

Daddy pressed his lips together and smoothed his silk vest. "I've been seeing someone."

"Not just someone," Katherine said. "Her best friend."

Aunt Dahlia appeared confused. "Lloyd? Is this true?"

"Yes. Mrs. Whittier and I found solace in one another."

Bitterness clogged Katherine's throat as she asked again, "How long?"

"That is none of your concern," he said sternly.

Still, she pushed on. "I need to know. Was this—" She swallowed. "Was this going on while Mama was still alive?"

He winced. "No. For God's sake, Katherine. Rebecca and I have been seeing one another for a year and a half now."

The words tore at Katherine, jagged cuts to her heart. A year and a half! Before his mourning period ended, then. Why hadn't he told her? Why hide it and sneak around?

I'm not trying to hurt you or your mother's memory, but this will help both of us move forward.

Now she understood why the paintings were taken down. He'd been trying to help *himself* move forward. With Rebecca Whittier.

She forced herself to ask the question she dreaded. "Is it serious?"

"Yes."

It had seemed so, based on the way he'd kissed the other woman's hand, but hearing him admit it was like a punch to Katherine's sternum. Tears burned the backs of her eyelids and she drew in a ragged breath.

"Kitty Kat, this is why I didn't tell you," he said gently, gesturing to her face. "That expression. I knew this would upset you."

She tried to keep her voice even. "You are already trying to replace her."

Daddy closed his eyes briefly as he grimaced. "I could never replace her, but life marches on. I don't wish to spend the rest of my time here alone."

A tear slipped out of Katherine's eye and trailed down her cheek. "Then why didn't you tell me? Why keep this a secret? I thought you and I were close, and now I find out you've been keeping this from me for a year and a half! All these long hours at the office and business trips. Were they even real, or just excuses?"

"Now, Katherine," her aunt said. "Your father is allowed to find happiness again."

"Happiness he doesn't want me to share in, obviously."

"I didn't want to hurt you," he said. "I thought it might be easier for you to hear once you were married and settled."

"I suppose that's why you were eager to push me toward Preston Clarke."

"That's not fair, Katherine. I honestly believed the two of you would be compatible."

"It would've made things easier for you, if I was out of the house. Right?" He didn't answer so she braced herself. "Are you going to marry her?"

He didn't meet her eye, instead straightening his place setting. "I don't know."

Another lie? How was she to know what to

believe anymore? He'd only admitted to the relationship because he'd been caught. Otherwise, he would've continued to hide it from her, pretending and lying the whole time.

Pushing back from the table, she stood. "I've lost my appetite. Good night."

In the corridor, she passed a large bouquet of orange blossoms. When she used to dream of her wedding, it was a huge affair filled with these delicate flowers, which were supposedly good luck for brides and symbolized fertility.

Now the green leaves and yellow-white blooms seemed to mock her.

Katherine grabbed the entire bouquet and held it out to the first footman she found. "Please, get rid of these. Give them to a housemaid, the cook, a stable boy . . . whoever. Just get them out of the house."

"Of course, miss. Anything else?"

"Yes. I must send a cable, then I'll need a hansom." She couldn't stay in this house one second longer.

Chapter Fifteen

❧

$\mathcal{P}$reston paced back and forth, smoking his second cigarette. The worn floors creaked beneath his shoes, his worry mounting with each minute that passed. Katherine had cabled and asked to see him immediately downtown. He wasn't certain why the rush. Had something terrible happened?

Or was she tired of waiting to hear from him?

He should have reached out after their carriage ride, of course. Ignoring a problem didn't make it go away, and Preston was not known for avoidance. He preferred to confront issues directly. So, why was he dreading the moment she arrived?

I want to see her again. I shouldn't, but I do.

He wanted more of her smiles, more of her laughter. More of her teasing and definitely more of her kisses. He just plain wanted *more*.

He shouldn't, though. Not only had he promised Kit, but this was a terrible idea. For all Katherine's talk of living independently, she was an innocent from a High Society family. Nothing would ever change that, and her future included a husband and children and summers in Newport.

Her future definitely didn't include an affair with an unscrupulous bastard like him. But Christ, how he wished it did.

Thank her for the paintings and send her on her way.

Yes, that seemed like a fine idea. Anything else was impossible.

A knock sounded and he stabbed his cigarette out in a crystal dish. When he answered, Katherine stood on the threshold, and he drank in the sight of her. She was gorgeous, a natural beauty without cosmetics and embellishments, and her brown hair was pinned up to draw attention to the low neckline of her dress. The soft swell of her breasts teased from behind the cloth, and a lash of possessive need whipped through him, causing gooseflesh to erupt all over his skin.

Instead of waiting for an invitation, she slid past him, her body brushing over his in the most provocative way. The smell of her—lilacs and sunshine—trailed her into the tiny apartment. He closed his eyes, needing a second to collect himself. God, he was pathetic. Already he was on edge—and she'd barely arrived.

When he was ready, he closed the door and faced her. "I was surprised to get your note. Is there something—?"

One second she was across the room, the next she was in his arms, kissing him. He suddenly forgot what he was going to say.

Katherine's mouth was warm and insistent, almost desperate, as her lips moved over his again and again. He could barely think, his mind focused only on her, the taste of her mouth and the press of her body against his. He kissed her harder, sliding his tongue into her mouth, savoring the slick haven as desire unfurled in his belly.

He loved the way she kissed, the way she sighed into his mouth. The whimpers she gave when he started to pull away, like she couldn't bear for him to stop. She clutched his shoulders, holding him tight, her body trembling against him. It was as if she held nothing back, as if she totally and utterly belonged to him in that moment.

I want her to belong to me.

He wanted to have her every way he could take her. Make her beg and scream. Order her to do every little dirty thing he could think of . . .

Mine.

Determined fingertips shoved his coat off his shoulders, down his arms, then went to work on the buttons of his vest. His brain finally returned to working order, and he stayed her hands. "What are you doing?"

"Undressing you."

She tried to wriggle free, but he tightened his hold. "Katherine, wait. What's happening? Why are we here?"

A deep crease formed on her brow as she stepped back. There were shadows in her eyes he didn't like, as if something was troubling her. But she turned away, unfastened her cloak and tossed it over a chair. "I thought it would be obvious to a man as smart as yourself."

He went to the sideboard. As he poured her a glass of bourbon, he said, "While I may be smart, I'm also creative. I can imagine several reasons you might want me to undress. But shouldn't we discuss this first?"

"What is there to discuss?" She came over and grabbed the crystal tumbler out of his hand, and took a big gulp of the liquor. "I'm here, you're here. There's a bed."

A shocking amount of pleasure darted to his groin. His cock very much liked the idea, lengthening in his trousers in heady pulses, yet he knew there was more happening here than she was telling him. "Just like that? Out of the blue, you're ready to sleep with me?"

"Out of the blue? Have you been paying attention at all? I thought . . ." With a practiced flick of her wrist, she downed the rest of the bourbon and swallowed it. Then she set the glass on the table with a thunk. "Forget it. I shouldn't have come here tonight. I just needed—"

When she reached for her cloak, he sprang forward, grabbing her arm. "Kat, please. Give me a moment to catch up. Talk to me."

"Do you want to sleep with me, or not?"

He didn't like the wild desperation in her gaze, the recklessness he could almost taste in her kiss. Though it was likely idiotic, he gave her the truth. "Of course I do. I've been thinking of nothing else since our carriage ride."

The edges of her mouth curled slightly and she moved away from him. Then her fingers went to the fastenings on her bodice, popping them open one by one. He stared, transfixed, like the world had slowed down. "Stop," he said, weakly, unable to look away from her small fingers. "We should talk first."

"I don't want to talk, Preston. I want to *feel*."

"That isn't how this works."

The sides of her bodice hung loose and she shrugged out of the heavy piece, revealing bare arms and delicate shoulders. His fingers curled into fists, nails digging into his palms.

I need to put a stop to this. She's trying to seduce me.

Then she reached for the fastenings on her skirt. The movements were brisk, efficient, and soon layers of silk and cotton pooled at her feet. She stepped free, her form clad in just undergarments. "It has to be you, and it has to be tonight."

Why?

He certainly thought the question but couldn't get his brain to actually voice it, not when she undid the tiny buttons of her petticoat and shoved it over her hips, lowering the cloth to the ground. Her cream chemise and corset matched her silk drawers, and she was so exquisite that his teeth ached.

Instead of removing more, she stepped toward him, the mounds of her breasts bouncing with every step. His muscles were locked in place, the pounding of his heart echoing in his ears. Moving closer, she plucked at the buttons of his vest, opening them, then pushed the silk off his shoulders. His necktie soon joined the vest on the floor. His chest heaved as she removed his collar and worked on his shirt, the brush of her hands over his clothed skin the best kind of agony.

When she lowered his suspenders, his trousers slipped a bit on his hips. They both watched together as she unhooked the fastening at his waist, the ridge of his erection nearly obscene through the layers of fabric. When the wool slid down his legs, the thin undergarment did little to hide how much he wanted her. The head of his cock was already leaking, a small wet spot evident on the cotton.

She brushed the length of his shaft through the cloth with her knuckles. "You want me," she whispered.

Had she doubted it? "Very, very badly. But I think you'll regret it, Kat."

"Do you have any diseases?"

"No, but—"

"Will you take precautions so I don't conceive?"

"Yes, of course."

Her palm swept over his cock, pressing hard and making him see stars. "Then what could I possibly regret?"

Fuck. Goddamn it.

He could feel his resolve crumbling like dry plaster. "You'll regret giving away your innocence so impulsively."

She stroked him again. "When you eventually marry, will you care if your bride isn't a virgin?"

"Hell, no. But—"

"There is no *but*, then. I think it's the older ladies who care more about virginity than men do. Decent men, anyway. And I don't care, so why should you?"

He had no argument for that.

She wants me. She trusts me.

Damn that tiny voice rationalizing his insatiable hunger for her. Only, it wasn't tiny. It was growing louder and louder by the second.

No one will know.

Her hand didn't stop, slowly dragging over his erection, and he had to lock his knees to keep upright. The backs of his legs ached, the need for her doubling, tripling in his veins, until he arrived at the inevitable decision.

How could he possibly continue to fight when they wanted each other this badly?

"Oh, my beautiful reinette," he said, his voice nearly unrecognizable with lust. "The filthy things I am going to do to you."

If the promise worried her, she gave no indication. In fact, her mouth curved slightly. "When?"

"Right now. The bedroom is directly behind you."

As IF DRUGGED, Katherine made her way into the bedroom. Her body buzzed with excitement, the knowledge that her plan had worked. He'd agreed.

He'd agreed.

Soon they would be naked. In bed and touching one another. Nerves bubbled inside her at that realization, turning her palms damp. Yet she wouldn't turn back now. This was what she wanted, even if the prospect felt daunting at the moment.

The bed was large, the size of it taking up most of the small room. A wardrobe and side table comprised the rest of the furniture, and she stopped, unsure what to do. Preston went to the side table and turned on the lamp. He unfastened his cuff links, then shrugged out of his shirt. Only a thin undergarment remained, outlining every inch of his tall, powerful frame.

Then he removed the last piece of clothing.

She sucked in a breath when he stood, his body

on unapologetic full display. And really, what did he have to be sorry for? He was . . . magnificent. Michelangelo never sculpted so perfect a man. Wide shoulders and tapered hips. A powerful chest with dark hair that trailed down to a flat stomach and his groin. He was a towering slab of bone and tissue, every bit as imposing as the buildings he constructed all over the city.

His thick erection pointed at her, standing out from his body in primal demand, and she realized she had a new number one item on her nightly list.

"Change your mind yet?" his deep voice asked, as if he expected his naked body to send her running from the room.

Quite the opposite, actually.

Fingers itching to touch him, she eased around the side of the bed, all the while pulling the pins out of her hair. Long locks fell around her shoulders, and he watched this avidly, as if mesmerized by the sight.

When she finished, she lifted the heavy mass of hair and presented him with her back. "I won't change my mind. Now, remove the rest of my things and make good on your promise."

Anticipation hung heavy in the room, like a vapor clinging to the insides of her lungs. His warm breath gusted along the back of her neck as he loosened the corset's strings, and heat rolled off his large body to wrap around her, the sensation both soothing and exciting.

When the strings eased, he popped the corset fastenings with a dexterity that spoke of experience. Just how many times had he done this? She pushed the question far from her mind. His past hardly mattered. They weren't married—now or ever.

The heavy garment fell to the floor, and she blinked as he lowered to his knees, his face just above her breasts. "Jesus, Kat. You are lovely." Large palms swept over her ribs, to her breasts, cupping her through the thin chemise. As he lifted the mounds higher, he dropped his head and began pressing open-mouthed kisses to her exposed flesh. She sighed and placed her hands on his shoulders to steady herself. He was surprisingly gentle, worshiping her with his lips and mouth, little nips of his teeth that made her knees quiver. For all their frenzy at the French Ball, this was the exact opposite.

He treated her like he had all the time in the world. Like she was all that mattered.

It relaxed her, this unexpected tenderness and care, yet it also excited her. Everywhere he touched came alive, and the hard points of her nipples ached along with her core. After a few more minutes of his caresses, she dug her nails into the meat of his shoulders. This wasn't enough. She needed *more*.

"Preston," she whispered, the single word a plea.

He tugged her chemise to her chin, baring her to his dark gaze. As she removed the garment, his hands returned to her breasts, this time with no barrier between them, and he immediately drew her nipple into his mouth. Wet heat pressed on the tip of her breast and she sucked in a breath. He laved her with his tongue, suckling her, and she felt every tug and stroke between her legs, too, as if her breasts were directly connected to her sex.

"I've been dying to see these," he said, nuzzling her nipple. "I've spent quite a lot of time imagining the shape and taste of your breasts."

"And what have you discovered?"

"Perfection," he sighed, drawing her into his mouth once more.

Never had she expected this to feel so good, so all-consuming, like she was drunk on pleasure. Dimly, she was aware that he switched to the other nipple to give it the same attention, but she could only moan and close her eyes, her pulse pounding in her ears.

"Kiss me," he rasped, suddenly rising, and his mouth quickly claimed hers in a kiss that was far from gentle. It was all teeth and tongue and grasping hands, his hard shaft between them, pushing against her belly impatiently.

When he finally broke free, he said, "Get on the bed."

After she climbed onto the mattress, he stripped off her drawers and shoes. She started to remove her silk stockings, but he held up a hand, his eyes glittering. "Leave them. They make your legs look even longer."

He liked her legs? She eased back and let him see all of her, no longer afraid of any flaws or imperfections he might see.

"You are breathtaking." His gaze slowly traveled the length of her. "No man on earth could possibly deserve you, least of all me."

"You definitely don't deserve me, but you do

owe me for ignoring me for a year. I think pleasure is a fair trade."

The edge of his mouth curled, as if he liked the
idea. "We'd best get started on repayment, then.
Where should I begin?"

Instead of waiting for an answer, he crawled
onto the bed and slid his hands under her bottom
to push her higher the mattress. "Spread your
legs. Let me taste you again." She complied, making room for his shoulders between her thighs,
and his mouth descended. Without preamble, he
dragged the flat of his tongue directly over her
clitoris, causing her back to arch as her every
nerve tingled. A cry escaped her throat, a helpless sound of pleading, her body begging for
more. But he didn't let up, giving her soft flicks
and gentle nips, deep kisses and long licks.

He opened her wider and moved lower to swirl
his tongue at her entrance. "You're so wet and
delicious," he whispered. "God, I love the way
you taste."

Then he continued to worship her with his
mouth, and her thighs began shaking, her body
preparing for the release barreling down upon
her. She threaded her fingers into his hair, needing to touch him or hurry him along—she wasn't
sure which. Her breath caught in her throat,
lungs squeezed in anticipation, sensation rushing up too quickly. As if sensing her impending
climax, he slid one finger into her channel and
pleasure streaked through her instantly. Light
exploded in every corner of her being, with Preston's hands and mouth her only tether to the
ground.

Before she'd stopped trembling, he slipped another finger into her channel, the walls contracting around the digit. The fullness felt so necessary, so perfect, that she cried out again, his touch dragging out her climax until she was limp. As she recovered, his fingers rested inside her and he kissed her sex softly, his dark head bent between her legs. He seemed in no hurry to move on to other business, and her brain was still floating somewhere up above them.

"Are you ready for more?" His voice was silky and dark, a temptation in itself.

If this was just a prelude to what she could expect tonight, then there was only one answer. "Absolutely."

Chapter Sixteen

$\mathscr{P}$reston stared at this beautiful woman in awe. That she was here, willing to sleep with him knowing it would never lead to marriage, humbled him. And the way she responded to him, with eagerness and boldness, made him unbelievably hard. He was dying to get inside her, to feel her slick walls gripping his cock.

Reaching for the drawer by the bed, he withdrew a tin containing a rubber shield. When he started to unwrap the packet she put a hand on his arm. "Wait," she blurted.

"Having second thoughts? We don't—"

"No, nothing like that. It's just . . ." She bit her lip as her gaze darted to his cock. "I never had the chance to touch you before. You know, at the ball."

A wave of heat spread through his groin as he imagined her hands—or her mouth—on his erection. Christ, he wanted that, but he was too excited at the moment. He'd spend in seconds if she touched him. "Later," he promised. "You may do all the exploring you like after this first time."

With the shield in place, he positioned himself between her thighs. Her sex was flushed and glistened with her arousal. Though he was dying for her, a sense of foreboding went through him, like he was about to make a grave mistake. "Are you sure, Kat?"

She rolled her eyes and reached for him, pulling him down, and the movement caused his tip to slip inside her. Even through the thick rubber he could feel the warmth of her body enveloping him, welcoming him. "Oh, God," he breathed against her mouth, his eyelids slamming shut.

The need to thrust clawed inside him, but he had to go gently with her. He took several deep breaths and tried to regain his control. Normally he was much more disciplined in bed, not so frenzied.

This has to be good for her.

Her small palm cupped his jaw and feather-light kisses rained over his skin. She was giving him tenderness and care instead and, because he was a bastard, he soaked it in, letting it calm him. After a few seconds, his hands stopped shaking and the vise squeezing his balls eased just a fraction. Grateful, he kissed her, his lips sliding over hers while his body remained perfectly still. He tried to soothe her in return, impart how much he appreciated this gift. How thankful he was for her.

After that, it was easier to press in slowly, to widen her inch by agonizing inch. He didn't want to hurt her, though he knew it probably would. Her walls strangled his cock, the tightest and most heavenly place he'd ever imagined. "That's it," he breathed in her ear. "Let me in, mon chaton."

He felt her shiver against him, so he kept talking. "You're going to like having me inside you, your body full of me. I'll be so deep and when I start moving, you'll see. It'll be so perfect and lovely, just like you."

"Please," she whispered.

He rested his forehead against her temple, keeping them connected as he continued to invade her body. He wanted to hear every sigh, every gasp, feel every twitch as he made her his. It was intense, so much more intimate than any time before, like her reactions fed his own, their bodies completely in tune.

Her fingernails dug into his back as she tensed. He waited, a little more than halfway inside her. "Shall I stop or slow down?"

She shook her head. "Please don't. It feels . . . I feel so full."

"I'm almost there. Just relax. Slide your hand down and play with yourself. Think only about your pleasure."

One hand worked between their hips and she used a finger on her clitoris. The reaction was instant. More moisture flooded her pussy, her body relaxing, and he sank in another inch. "Yes," he hissed, sparks radiating along his lower back, his thighs. "More, Kat."

She was panting, her fingers stirring between

them, and after another few seconds their hips finally met. "There," he rasped. "I'm all the way in. How does it feel?"

"Too much but not enough. Oh, God, Preston."

He knew exactly what she meant.

The pounding of his heart resonated in his cock, all the way down his shaft, and he could've sworn he felt her pulse there, too. It was as if she'd reached deep inside him and twisted his organs, rearranging them. He knew he'd never forget this moment.

He withdrew slowly and thrust once, letting her feel every thick inch of him against her sensitive tissues.

Her eyelids fluttered. "Oh!"

"Good or bad?" he asked, though he already suspected the answer. She was clutching him closer, her hips arching up as if seeking more.

"So very good."

Burying his face in her neck, he inhaled her scent, then dragged his teeth over her soft skin. He longed to devour her, to cause her pain and pleasure, highs and lows that went on for days at a time.

So he rolled his hips, dragging out of her tight clasp and shoving back in. They both groaned, the sound muffled between their mouths.

"Again," she begged. "You don't need to be careful with me."

He shook his head even as his body began moving, rocking, driving into her, and soon his force and pace picked up. The little noises she made, like surprised delight, grew louder as he fucked her, and sweat collected on their bodies.

Her wet heat bathed his cock, and every moan, every press of her fingernails into his skin, felt like the sweetest victory. He wanted to bring her nothing but pleasure, worship her as she deserved. To service her and give her everything she needed.

When she wrapped her legs around his hips, trying to get closer, he pressed up on his arms to stare at her. Lord almighty, she was gorgeous. With her flushed face and lips swollen from his mouth, he'd never seen a more beautiful woman.

"Please, my king," she whispered.

"Oh, Christ," he gritted out, his cock jerking inside of her as he thrust. "I'll spend if you call me that."

Her hand slid down the center of his chest to between their bodies, where she used a finger to stroke herself again. "Would you like to see your mistress come, my king?"

"No, no, no, stop." He closed his eyes, but this made it worse because now he could feel her hand working between them, rolling her clitoris to heighten her pleasure as he rode her.

The tips of her fingers brushed his cock.

It was too much. He felt as if he was going to splinter apart. "I can't . . . oh, fuck. Kat, I . . ."

She widened her legs to give him room, opening herself up for him, and he became like a man possessed. It wasn't supposed to go like this. He was supposed to take care of her, go carefully, remain in control. And yet his hips pounded into hers, his erection so deep, and the orgasm started in the base of his spine, then wrapped around his groin and into his balls. He began filling the rubber, jets of liquid heat erupting from the head of his cock, and he shuddered as it went on and on, his body emptying everything he had into hers.

The room quieted and he stayed there, unable to move. His chest heaved with the effort to breathe, and he couldn't yet force himself to leave the comforting clasp of her sex. He felt . . . wrecked.

And embarrassed.

"God, I'm sorry."

"Why? That was amazing." She ran her hands along his damp shoulders and arms, over his chest. "I like you sweaty."

"I'm glad, but I wish I hadn't climaxed so quickly."

"That was quick?"

For him, yes. "I wanted you to come."

Slowly, he withdrew, holding on to the base of the shield. Then he went to the washroom to clean up, where he found a clean linen and wet it with warm water. Katherine was still stretched out on the bed, watching his approach. He liked that she so openly appreciated his body. "Let me tend to you."

He knelt between her legs and pressed the cloth to the swollen, red flesh. "Are you all right? I was rougher than I'd planned."

"It was perfect, Preston. Honestly. How was it for you?"

How to answer that? It had been the best orgasm of his life, but she'd never believe him. "Perfect. I'll last longer next time."

"Next time?"

He tossed the cloth in the direction of the washroom. "You didn't think this was it, did you? I have an entire year to make up for."

She bit her lip and smiled. "Good point."

PRESTON STRETCHED OUT next to her, relaxed into her soft curves and buried his nose in her hair. Mmm, absolute heaven. Why did she always smell so good? "Will you tell me why you rushed here in such a hurry tonight?"

"Do you really want to hear about it?"

"If you want to talk about it, then yes."

Sighing, she snuggled into his body, her backside digging into his groin. "My father is seeing someone. My mother's best friend. I think he loves her."

Preston struggled not to react. Christ, the last thing he wished to hear about was Lloyd, let alone Lloyd's intimate life. He wanted Delafield miserable and alone, like Ebenezer Scrooge before the ghosts arrived. But his feelings for Lloyd had to be set apart from his dealings with Katherine.

Keeping his voice even, he asked, "And?"

"And I hate it. My mother's gone only two years and he's already found someone else. And her *best friend*? Mama would be appalled. Does he . . ." Her voice trembled, like she was fighting tears. "Does he not even miss her?"

For fuck's sake, Preston was going to have to come to Delafield's defense, wasn't he? It was either that, or let Katherine suffer—and he'd rather cut off a limb than see her cry. And really, there were a lot of reasons to hate Delafield, but him belly-bumping with some older widow wasn't one of them.

Preston kissed her temple. "You miss your mother. It's understandable. But your father isn't replacing her, sweetheart. No one can replace her. More than likely he's just lonely. You know, there are some men who prefer companionship to being alone, especially as they age. You should be happy for him."

"Happy that he's taking down my mother's paintings and fawning over her best friend in public? God only knows what they're doing in private."

Likely what Preston and Katherine had just done, but he didn't point that out. "I understand your hurt and anger, I do. But the idea of him in a new relationship will get easier over time, I would imagine. Do you like her, at least?"

"That's hardly the point. He's been lying to me, keeping this secret for more than a year. I never would've known if I hadn't caught them in the park when I went driving with Lockwood."

Preston tensed. What the hell? "When was this?"

"Earlier today."

Were things turning serious with the duke? Preston didn't like it, not one bit, but he pushed aside his sudden desire to punch Lockwood. "And what did your father say when you asked him about it?"

"That he isn't trying to replace Mama. He merely doesn't wish to spend the rest of his life alone."

"See? Exactly as I said."

"No one likes a know-it-all, Preston."

He chuckled. "I can't help it if I know everything. Besides, I know a little about losing someone you love."

"Your father. I forgot."

"No. I mean, yes. My father passed away a few years ago, but I was very angry with him when he died." He was still angry, resentful of how badly Henry had managed everything before he passed away, leaving Preston with a mountain of shit to clean up. "I meant my friend Forrest."

"It was this past summer, right?"

"Yes."

"I'm sorry. Do you want to talk about it?"

The pressure on his chest increased, like someone was sitting on top of him. He hadn't talked about Forrest, not really. Kit knew more than anyone, but Preston hadn't told his friend all of it.

When he hesitated, Katherine said, "I didn't mean to pry. You don't have to tell me."

"No, I want to." And he did. For some reason, he trusted Katherine with his secrets, the darkest parts of himself. Perhaps because she'd seen him at his worst, he didn't think he could scare her away. And it would be a relief to tell someone all of it.

"When I met Forrest in college, he'd never had anything more than a watered-down beer. I fancied myself experienced, already smoking and drinking spirits, so I used to drag him out behind the buildings between classes and give him my flask." He exhaled a heavy sigh. "From there, it continued. The four of us often went drinking, and Kit and Forrest especially grew to love a party. We rarely went home, sticking together more often than not."

He noticed that Katherine was holding his hand, her other hand stroking his arm, and he soaked in that small comfort for a second. "Then I learned my father had nearly lost everything. He had this gambling problem—"

Katherine stilled and he sensed her surprise. So Lloyd hadn't told her, after all.

Preston kept going. "The business was in absolute shambles. I left school early because we couldn't afford it anymore and I had to take over Clarke Holdings, had to try to turn it around before it was too late."

"Oh, Preston. I had no idea. You were clearly successful, though."

"Due in large part to Forrest's help."

She rolled onto her other side so they faced each other. "What do you mean?"

"The bank was going to take the house, so I went to Forrest and borrowed money. He gave it to me, no questions asked. Told me to consider it a gift, that I never had to pay it back." The lump in his throat expanded. "And in exchange, I allowed him to drink himself to death."

In a flash, Katherine's hands cupped his face. "No, Preston. That wasn't your fault. How could it be?"

More like, how could it not have been?

He pulled her close and tried to breathe through the weight of the memories, the sadness that clouded his mind each time he thought of his friend. "I was too busy to notice what was happening until he was deep into his habit. He had new friends, people who hung around because he could afford to pay their bar tabs. Harrison was in Paris, so Kit did the best he could to keep Forrest in line."

She didn't speak, just stroked his hair, staying close. He tangled their legs together and enjoyed the feel of her as he told her the rest. "I know the ward boss in the fourteenth from doing business together. He cabled me one night earlier this year, said a friend of mine had been drinking, passed out and couldn't be roused. Told me to come get him or they were calling an ambulance. I said to call the damn ambulance. If he was that bad off, I didn't want them to wait."

"That was certainly the right thing to do."

"Forrest didn't think so. He was awake and livid by the time I got to Bellevue, but he nearly died, according to the doctors. When I saw what he looked like, how he started shaking after just a few hours without a drink, I couldn't leave him alone. I dragged him up to my lodge in the Adirondacks and tried to dry him out."

Jesus, the things Forrest had said during those two days. Hurtful, cruel words Preston would never forget. Which reminded him—he needed to sell the lodge. Being inside those walls again would bring nothing but bad memories, completely undoing any point of a vacation home.

Katherine kissed his throat. "Of course you did, because you're a good person."

He winced. No, he really wasn't.

A good person wouldn't have said hurtful, cruel words back to Forrest.

A good person would have reconciled with his father before he died.

A good person wouldn't have taken Katherine's innocence without marrying her.

"I need a cigarette," he said, starting to get up off the bed. "Give me a minute."

She grabbed his arm. "Stay with me. You can smoke later."

He flopped back down and stared at the ceiling, his leg bouncing in agitation. Why had he dredged all this up? The night had been perfect up until he started talking about Forrest.

Katherine moved on top of him, her legs straddling his hips. "You don't like when things don't go your way, do you?"

Sliding his hands up her thighs, he gave her a half smile. "You're just realizing this?"

"No," she said with a tiny laugh, bracing her palms on his stomach. Her luscious hair cascaded around her shoulders, a silky curtain he longed to drag his hands through. She said, "You haven't made a secret of it, I suppose. But you can't bend the world to your will all the time, Mr. Clarke."

"Why not?" He cupped her breasts, molding and shaping them, enjoying the way she looked sitting atop him. He wanted to fuck her like this, with her lithe body riding his cock.

"Because you can't control everything."

After licking his thumb, he used it between her legs to caress the swollen button atop her sex. Katherine arched and threw her head back. He kept going, stroking, circling, while his erection lengthened beneath her. "Hmm, but I do know at least one thing I can control right now."

A pleasure-drunk smile twisted her lips as she began moving her hips. "I'll allow it."

And for the next few hours, he showed her exactly the sort of control he meant.

Chapter Seventeen

❧

Over the next few days, Katherine was busy, putting the finishing touches on the art show at the Meliora Club. She avoided another conversation with her father, still hurt that he'd hidden his new relationship from her for so long. So she focused on the exhibition during the day and Preston at night.

Any moment now, guests would arrive for the exhibition opening, and she was a nervous wreck. Would everyone like the collection? Or would they think her full of hubris, arranging this event to foolishly show off her mother's prized paintings?

Nearly everyone she knew was invited tonight. If no one came, it would be more humiliating than waiting a year on a fiancé who had no idea she existed.

Walking around, she checked to ensure the right cards were placed next to each of the forty-five paintings. She'd done this several times, but once more wouldn't hurt.

"Glass of champagne, gorgeous?"

Katherine's head snapped up at the voice. "Nellie!" Relief flooded her. At least one person was attending tonight. "I'm so happy you're here."

"I wouldn't miss it." She handed Katherine a glass of champagne. "Here. You look nervous."

Katherine took a grateful sip. "Of course I'm nervous. I'm worried no one is coming."

"Balderdash. Everyone will come to support you. I swear, it's like you have no idea how much people adore you."

Katherine was already shaking her head. "You're being kind, but thank you."

Nellie threaded their arms together and began leading Katherine deeper into the room. "I'm rarely kind, but let's leave that for the moment. The collection looks absolutely stunning, Katie."

It did, actually. Katherine was quite proud of it. "Your Monet was just the thing I needed. Would you like to see it or the Renoir you loaned me?"

"I've seen them both enough," Nellie said with a wave. "I'd rather catch up with you, since I have a feeling you'll be bombarded with guests shortly."

"Here's hoping." Katherine held up her glass and they each toasted. Then she blurted, "I slept with Preston Clarke."

Nellie began sputtering and choking on champagne, her eyes watering. For several seconds, she coughed and wheezed, and Katherine pounded her back twice.

"God, Nellie. I'm sorry," Katherine said. "Are you all right?"

Her friend held up a hand. "I'm fine." She drew

in a deep breath, then wiped a tear from under her bottom eyelashes. "Lord, you really must give me some warning before you drop news like that."

"I know. It was awful of me. I just didn't want to miss the opportunity to tell you before everyone arrived."

"Forgiven. First, good for you. Second, how was it? Because I'll have him thrown into the East River in chains if he mistreated you."

The way Nellie said it did not sound like a jest. "Why do I feel as if you are serious about that?"

Nellie's smile was positively devious. "Let's just say I know people."

"Ah, right. The Hell's Kitchen branch of the family." Nellie's mother had been Irish, and her relatives all lived on the west side of the city. They also ran one of the biggest street gangs on the island. "Anyway, you needn't worry. Preston's taken very good care of me each time."

"Each time? Plural?"

Katherine sipped her champagne and lifted a shoulder. "I'm having fun with him." The Jane Street apartment had been put to good use the past few nights. She'd eschewed her society commitments, using the art show as cover to come and go as she pleased. Now that the show was almost over, she'd need to be a bit more creative in her excuses.

"Good," Nellie said. "Whatever you do, don't develop feelings for him. Being intimate with someone can fool you into thinking there are deeper emotions at play, but men are generally able to separate the two far easier than we can."

"I won't develop feelings, I promise. He's too controlling for me. Too intense."

Nellie's eyes narrowed like she didn't believe that statement. "Many women prefer those types of men."

"Well, not me. Anyway, to draw suspicion away from us, I invited Lockwood tonight."

Nellie's shoulders stiffened slightly. "Needed someone to suck all the joy out of the room, I suppose?"

Katherine couldn't help but laugh. "You're too hard on him. He's a decent man."

"Decent, sure. I suppose this means Preston is coming, as well."

"I did invite him. I have no idea if he's coming or not."

"Oh, he'll be here. He'll want to keep watch over you. Scare off any potential suitors."

"That's absurd," Katherine said. "First, there are no potential suitors, and Preston doesn't feel that way about me."

"We shall see, won't we? Tonight is going to be very interesting, I can already tell." Nellie glanced at something over Katherine's shoulder. "Ah, here come your first guests. Time for me to make myself scarce so my presence doesn't offend the smart set. Good luck, Katie." Nellie squeezed her arm. "It's going to be fantastic."

"You needn't stand against the wall the entire night," Katherine said. "You should mingle. You're my friend and I want you here."

"I know, and I love you for it. But you're my friend and I wouldn't dream of causing gossip. I'll be fine. Don't worry about me."

Nellie drifted away before Katherine could say anything else. Dash it. Katherine hated that society had vilified Nellie. Though her friend pretended not to care, Katherine knew it hurt Nellie deep down.

Then guests began streaming through the entryway, distracting her, and she decided that any worries over her friend would need to wait until later.

HE COULD HEAR her laughter from across the room, and Preston fought the urge to smile.

Somehow, he'd allowed Katherine to talk him into attending her art show at the Meliora Club. It was increasingly apparent that he had a hard time refusing her anything. From meeting her downtown or inviting him to rub elbows with a bunch of snobs over art, she merely had to ask and he went along eagerly.

Sipping champagne, he studied an impressionist painting and contemplated the affair he and Kat were having. Their couplings were frantic and naughty, seeing as how Kat was busy with the art show. But now that the show had opened he anticipated having her more often and taking his time with her.

He could hardly wait.

"I can't quite tell if you're smiling or not," a feminine voice said at his side.

He looked down at Nellie Young. "Does it matter?"

"No, but anything other than a scowl looks odd on your face. Is it this painting?" She paused. "Or perhaps something—or someone—else?"

"It's refreshing to discover you are every bit as forward as the rumors say."

She laughed, apparently not taking offense. "And it's refreshing to learn you're not as cold as the rumors say."

Had Katherine told her friend about the affair? He was curious as to what had been said—not that he'd ever ask. "Are you an art lover, Miss Young?"

"Not at all. I much prefer beauty that I can touch and feel." She smirked before sipping from her coupe. "And yes, I realize how improper that sounded, but I meant plants and flowers."

"You don't strike me as a gardener."

"People are rarely what they seem on the outside. Haven't you learned that by now?"

His gaze flicked to Kat, who was talking excitedly to an older couple. Indeed, the remarkable woman surprised him at every turn. "Yes, that's quite true."

"I do feel the need to warn you that I'm very protective of my friends—especially Katie. I won't have her hurt."

"You needn't worry about that. I won't hurt her."

"You might hurt her unintentionally. She's not Arabella or one of your other mistresses, Preston. She's not a woman used to the kinds of relationships in which you normally engage."

"I'm well aware," he said. Annoyance prickled across his shoulder blades, but he tried to remember that Nellie was merely looking out for her friend's best interest. And an affair with a man she didn't intend to marry was definitely not in Kat's best interest. Still, Preston would never harm her—at least not beyond his refusal to marry her.

"Don't take that grumpy tone with me. You know I'm right."

Preston glared down at Nellie. "You don't like me, do you?"

"I haven't made up my mind, not that it matters. I'm more interested in watching out for Katie. I don't want her getting ideas in her head about the two of you, then ending up heartbroken because you're too stubborn to see what a wonderful woman she is."

"I know she's a wonderful woman."

"No, you don't. Because if you did, you'd marry her despite your obvious issues."

His fingers tightened on the coupe, nearly sloshing champagne onto his cuffs. "You have no idea what my *issues* are, Miss Young—and perhaps Kat should make up her own mind regarding her future."

"Kat?" Her lip curled. "You already have a nickname for her? Dear God, it's worse than I feared."

He couldn't help needling her, if only in retribution for the "issues" comment. "I have many nicknames for her. Would you like me to recount them to you?"

"I might vomit champagne on the floor if you do, so please refrain."

"Do you hate all men, Miss Young, or just me?"

He expected a snappy response but she remained silent. Instead, she seemed distracted. Preston followed her eyes and discovered that the Duke of Lockwood had arrived. A growl rumbled out of his chest. "What the hell is he doing here?"

"Perhaps he's publicly courting her, as any decent man would. Now, if you'll excuse me, I think I've seen enough art for one night."

She slipped into the crowd, but he wasn't watching her. Instead he was transfixed by the sight of Kat greeting the duke and introducing him to the couple standing next to her. Lockwood and Kat made a striking couple, Preston supposed, albeit boring. They were both nice, upstanding people, liked by just about everyone.

Lockwood kissed Kat's hand, and Preston thought his teeth would crack, he was grinding them so hard. He had no right to be jealous, though. He couldn't court or marry Katherine. And a respectable woman like her deserved a husband she could be proud of—not a thug awash in criminality and corruption. No, she needed to keep her rose-colored glasses firmly on her face, remain untainted by Preston's vices and sins.

Perhaps he should encourage the duke to pursue Katherine. It would be the honorable thing to do, considering Preston had no plans to marry her himself.

Except he was far from honorable, and he wasn't ready to end his affair with her any time soon. The duke could damn well choose someone else.

Continuing around the salon, Preston looked at the art. Kat's collection was lovely, with some pieces that even he, a novice, could see hanging in his home. Perhaps she'd make some suggestions about paintings to buy, as she'd subtly done with his office.

He'd just edged around two attendees when a hand grabbed his arm. "Preston Clarke!"

The face took him a moment to place. "Tommy Stone?"

"I knew you'd remember." Tommy turned to his friend. "I was a year younger than Clarke in school, but we played baseball together. You've never seen a better first baseman than Preston Clarke."

True, they'd been on the team during Preston's brief stint at Harvard, but they hadn't been friends. Preston kept his tone polite but cool. "Surprised to see you here, Stone. Hadn't thought you were an art aficionado."

"I'm not. Came here with my friend." Introductions were made, but Preston didn't recognize the name of the other man. Tommy smirked at Preston. "You don't strike me as an art lover, either. More of a woman's thing, if you ask me. I guess that's why the place is crawling with pussy. *Meow.*" He imitated a cat scratching, and his friend laughed.

Now Preston remembered what Tommy had been known for—inappropriate remarks and demeaning jokes. Tommy's mouth had landed him in trouble more than once, and Preston would not have this fool ruining Kat's event. He glowered at the other man. "Watch your mouth. We're in polite company."

Tommy held up his hands, but moved closer.

It appeared he intended to continue his commentary, merely at a lower volume. "Polite, indeed. Did you see? There's a real duke here. I suppose the rumors are true, that he's desperate enough to take any old pair of gams at this point."

Preston remained quiet, but the friend cast a curious glance in Lockwood's direction. "Is that so?"

Tommy nodded. "They say he's going to offer for the Delafield girl that's been sitting on the shelf for a few years." He gave a deep chuckle. "Hope he can find his way to her cunt through all the cobwebs—"

Before he even knew what was happening, Preston's fist connected with Tommy's cheek.

Tommy fell to the ground with a sickening thud and the room went deathly silent.

Anger monopolized Preston's system as he stared down at the other man. He could feel the fury, dark and terrifying, as it rolled through his veins. The need to kick or hit Tommy again was so real, so raw, that he could taste it in his mouth. His limbs trembled as he tried to gain control over himself, but the red mist wouldn't leave his brain.

"What on earth . . . ?" Katherine was suddenly there, her expression horrified and concerned as she studied Tommy. "Sir, are you all right? Have you need of a doctor?"

A red spot bloomed on Tommy's cheek, but he was otherwise fine. His confused glare landed on Preston. "No need, miss. I've taken worse." He started to get up, yet Preston offered no assistance. Instead, his friend helped him to his feet. The other attendees moved away, giving them space, except for a waiter, who arrived with a cloth to clean up the champagne and broken glass on the floor.

"What happened?" Katherine looked between Preston and Tommy.

"Nothing," Preston said crisply.

Tommy touched his cheek tentatively, as if testing the injury. "Yeah, nothing. Just seems some people have lost their sense of humor since college."

Preston had never enjoyed Tommy's sense of humor, but he didn't bother explaining that. "I apologize, Miss Delafield. I'll see myself out."

She put her hand up to stop him. "You are not leaving, Mr. Clarke." Then quieter, "We shall discuss this later."

Then she and Tommy's friend helped Tommy to the exit and the room came alive once more, murmurs swelling with speculation on what had happened. Mind reeling, Preston stood there, unable to move, trying to understand his emotions. Never had he lost his temper like that in public—or even in private—before.

A fresh glass of champagne appeared before his eyes. Looking over, he found the Duke of Lockwood there. "Thank you," he said, accepting the glass.

"Figured you could use it. That was a hell of a right hook you have there, Clarke."

They'd never been properly introduced but clearly they were beyond formalities. Preston took a long swallow, wishing it was something stronger to dull his fury. "I haven't punched any-one in a long time. Not since boxing in college."

"If you're rusty I couldn't tell. What did he say to annoy you?"

"I don't care to repeat it."

"Ah."

Lockwood's tone implied he knew exactly what Tommy had said, which was ludicrous. Preston couldn't resist asking, "What does that mean?"

"There's only one reason a man would lay out another man like that in public. Because of an insult to a particular woman." Lockwood watched Preston's face for a reaction, which Preston perversely withheld. The duke nodded, as if the lack of response had confirmed it. "I see I'm right."

The man's smugness grated on Preston's nerves. Wasting no time, he asked the question he most wanted to know. "Why are you here tonight?"

The duke sipped his champagne. "Miss Delafield asked me to attend. What's your excuse?"

The same, but Preston didn't wish to admit it. An ugly feeling settled in the bottom of his stomach, one that had him longing to strike Lockwood, as well. He drank more champagne and forced those irrational feelings aside.

There was no need for jealousy. Katherine was his—for the time being, anyway.

Still, he couldn't resist asking, "Are you intending to marry her?"

Lockwood's head cocked, his gaze turning shrewd. "Miss Delafield, you mean? Well, some-one should, don't you think? Enjoy your night, Clarke."

Preston stared at the watercolor on the wall.

Surprisingly, the image brought him a tiny bit of serenity.

Perhaps I should buy it.

He might need that serenity when Katherine got him alone and demanded answers about his violent behavior.

Chapter Eighteen

⁕

Indeed, it was a first. Fisticuffs at the Meliora Club.

Katherine hoped her membership wasn't stripped away—or worse, that her art show was considered a failure. She needed to generate excitement for her modern art museum, not gossip and scandal.

What on earth had come over Preston? He wasn't the type to react emotionally, with hot anger and swinging fists. He was cool and logical—almost to a frightening degree. So, this aggression made no sense. Why would he strike another man in a public place?

Circling the room, she kept an eye on him while chatting with the other guests. At present, he was frozen in front of an Alfred Sisley landscape, a painting she happened to love. Hopefully he was using the serene brushstrokes and soft pastel colors to calm down, because she would demand answers from him soon.

First she needed to soothe any ruffled feathers in the room.

"This was certainly exciting," Abby Aldrich said as she passed by. "You must do this again soon, Katherine." Abby and Katherine had debuted together, and Abby was one of the driving forces behind the formation of the Meliora Club. There were rumors she might marry the sole Rockefeller heir, John Davison Jr.

"Oh, Abby. I'm so sorry. That behavior was deplorable."

"Nonsense. If anything, you probably sold more memberships for the club tonight. People will be clamoring to attend more events here."

"I hope you're right, because I'm mortified."

"Please. Two handsome men brawling in evening coats? Every woman in the room nearly swooned."

Katherine gave her friend a rueful smile. "Unfortunately, tonight was supposed to be about the art."

"And it is. The collection is superb. I have my eye on a few of these paintings." She flicked a glance toward where Preston stood. "I've never known Mr. Clarke to be so hotheaded. Any idea what it was all about?"

"None," Katherine said. "But I mean to find out as soon as everyone leaves."

Abby's dark brows shot up. "Is there anything I should know?"

"Oh, Mr. Clarke and I are just friends."

"Then why are you blushing?"

"Am I?" Her hands flew to her cheeks.

Abby laughed. "No, but you've just given yourself away. I suppose the rumors about you and the duke are unfounded."

Dropping her arms, Katherine smirked at the other woman. "Tell me, how are things going with John Junior? I hear you're taking long walks together and that—"

"Fair enough," Abby interrupted, though she was smiling. "Let's have lunch soon. We can swap stories then."

"I'd like that."

After Abby left, Katherine searched for Lockwood, and eventually found him engaged in small talk with some matrons. The older ladies were looking up at the duke with stars in their eyes. "Ladies, might I steal His Grace for a moment?"

They tittered and nodded, while one even had the audacity to wink at Katherine. Lockwood executed a perfect bow before she dragged him away. "Are you having a nice time?"

"Indeed, I am. You've put together a beautiful collection."

"Thank you. I apologize for the earlier drama. I have no idea what came over Mr. Clarke, but I don't believe the altercation will hurt your marriage prospects."

"Quite the opposite, if I had to guess. It'll be all anyone will wish to discuss tomorrow. You've given me social cachet as a witness." He leaned in. "And I've discovered you have an admirer in the room."

Did he mean Preston? How on earth had Lockwood arrived at that conclusion? She shook her head. "You're wrong. I have no idea what caused that scene, but I do intend to find out."

"Have you told him about our drive in the

park? Because he seems to believe I am courting you and I got the sense it bothered him."

"I wouldn't worry about that. He's not interested in marrying me."

"Are you certain?"

"Absolutely positive." She hurried to change the subject. "You know, my aunt was hoping you and I would marry. She's quite fond of you."

The side of Lockwood's mouth hitched, his face confident even with the weight of his family's future on his broad shoulders. "I met her earlier in the far room. She asked me all sorts of questions about Queen Victoria."

That sounded like Aunt Dahlia. "She's obsessed with royalty."

"I told her I'd be happy to introduce her to the queen any time she visits London."

"Oh, goodness. Now she'll never let up about traveling there."

"I hope she comes—and I hope you join her. I've enjoyed getting to know you, Katherine."

He was such a kind and decent man. "And I you, Lockwood. I'm glad we are friends."

"Same, Miss Delafield. Incidentally, I'll bring the paintings for your museum back with me when I return after the holidays. I hope that's acceptable."

"That's perfect. Has my father written you a check?"

"Yes, he did. Much appreciated, that."

Hopefully the money went a tiny way to easing some of the duke's immediate financial woes. Though he still needed to marry, but perhaps this would buy him some time.

The guests started to depart and the crowd thinned. Preston hadn't moved, still absorbed in the Sisley painting. She needed to speak with him privately, but she should see Lockwood off properly first. "Shall I walk Your Grace out?"

"Not necessary," Lockwood said as he lifted her hand and brought it to his mouth. "Congratulations on your exhibit. You certainly have an eye for these things. The museum will undoubtedly be a smashing success."

"I hope so. The Lockwood family collection will be a huge draw when we open. Thank you, Your Grace."

After a nod, the duke spun and quit the room, and Katherine turned her attention to the lone man frozen in front of the Sisley painting. What had come over Preston tonight? He'd punched someone, right here in a room full of guests. Why?

Unable to stay away any longer, she drifted to his ridiculously tall side. Before she could open her mouth, he said, "It's quite nice, isn't it?"

They were talking paintings now? Fine, she could play along. "It is. I adore Sisley's landscapes. The colors are soothing."

"I agree. I don't know anything about this artist or art in general, but I do like this one."

"I'm glad. It's part of the same set that I sent for your office."

"Ah. That must be why I'm drawn to it."

The few remaining guests were club members, so she felt comfortable disappearing for a moment. "May I speak with you privately?"

"Are you going to yell at me?"

"Most likely."

Preston folded his hands behind his back. "I seem to like it when you're cross with me. So, fair warning on being alone together."

She rolled her eyes toward the ceiling, though he didn't notice. "I'll take my chances. Come with me, bruiser."

PRESTON FOLLOWED KATHERINE deeper into the club. His hand hurt like a son of a bitch, but that wasn't what he was thinking about as he watched the sway of her hips as she walked. Instead he remembered holding those hips as he sank into her wetness. And the curve of her bottom as she bent over to remove her shoes. The press of her fingers into his flesh when she found her pleasure.

But she was so much more, he'd discovered. Like how quick she was to smile, and the easy way she laughed. She was real and comfortable with herself, unconcerned if her hair was a bit messy, and she seemed in no hurry to cover up when they lounged in bed naked together.

She usually did most of the talking, but he didn't mind. He liked to smoke in bed while hearing her go on about art and her travels in Spain. There were fascinating layers to her just waiting to be uncovered. Some man would be lucky indeed to marry this clever creature.

They ended up in an empty office, and Katherine shut the door behind them. She flicked the switch to illuminate the room, which meant he could see her frown. "Have you gone mad?"

He slipped his hands into his trouser pockets. "I apologize."

When he didn't elaborate, she snapped, "That's it? You've nothing more to say?"

Pressing his lips together, he debated on how to proceed. He couldn't very well tell her what happened. "There's no excuse for what I did. I can only say that I felt justified in the moment."

"You felt justified in hitting a man during my event, the most important night of my life?"

"When you put it that way, no. But I wasn't thinking straight."

"You, Preston Clarke? Not thinking straight? I don't believe it. What on earth happened to cause such a violent reaction from you?"

"I'm no angel, Kat. I told you I was entirely dishonorable."

"Not good enough. You owe me an answer about tonight."

He sighed, wondering how little he could say to explain himself. "The man I hit is an imbecile. I know him from Harvard, and he likes to tell inappropriate jokes and give disgusting commentary. He said something I didn't care for and I punched him."

"What did he say?"

"I can't tell you."

"Preston, I have heard just about every improper word and phrase. I understand that men can lean toward the crude when alone together. What was it? Something about breasts?"

If only. "It doesn't bear repeating, Kat. Let it go."

"Why? I've never met this man so he couldn't have been talking about me." Preston felt his expression slip—a momentary flash of guilt that escaped before he could stop it—but Kat noticed, because of course she did. "He said something about *me*? What on earth could he have said about me when we're perfect strangers?"

"I won't repeat it, but the comment was in poor taste."

Her astonished expression quickly transformed into a smug sort of happiness, with her eyes sparkling like gems. "You were defending my honor."

His collar was suddenly too tight, the cloth of his coat pulling against his shoulders. "Don't be ridiculous. I was doing nothing of the sort. It was merely my way of showing him I disapprove of that sort of talk."

"Hmm." She stepped closer, her lips twisting in a teasing grin. "And how many men have you pummeled in the name of linguistic disapproval?"

"I couldn't begin to say," he lied, fingers twitching with the need to get his hands on her.

"Liar." Now in front of him, she ran a palm up his chest, pausing directly over his heart. He gripped her hips, hating the layers of cotton and silk that prevented him from feeling her soft skin. As she continued to stare up at him, he couldn't help but drag the pad of his thumb over her throat and jaw, along her cheekbone. She bit her lip. "How did it feel to hit him?"

"Satisfying."

She laughed and shook her head. "What am I going to do with you, Preston Clarke?"

"Reward me? There is a desk over there."

"Oh, no. Not here. Besides I need to wrap up the end of the evening."

Bending, he pressed a hard kiss to her mouth, letting their lips linger as they exchanged breath. "Most everyone has departed and the paintings aren't going anywhere. Come downtown with me."

He trailed his mouth along her jaw, to the sensitive spot behind her ear. She loved it when he dragged his teeth over that one place, which he did now. She gave a full-body shiver. "You know I can't, not yet. I need another half an hour, at least."

"I'll wait for you. Then we can—"

A knock interrupted. "Miss Delafield, are you in there?"

Katherine paused, her palms putting some distance between their bodies as she addressed whoever was on the other side of the door. "George, is that you?"

"It is, miss. Your father is here and asking to see you."

Startled, Preston looked at Kat, who'd gone pale. "Tell him I'll be right there," she said. "I'm just finishing with some tallies in here."

"Very good, miss."

They heard footsteps depart and Preston grinned. "Tallies?"

"I never think quickly on my feet." She started tugging him toward the exit. "Hurry, you have to leave out the back."

"Why?"

"Didn't you hear what George said? My father is here. We can't saunter in together. Everyone will think we've been in here doing something naughty."

"But we haven't been doing anything naughty and I'm a grown man. I won't skulk out a back entrance."

"Then sneak out the front." She opened the door. "We can't let him catch us together."

"Fine, but for the record I don't care if he catches us together."

"Right, because you won't marry me, even if he tries to force you," she whispered as they left. "You get all the advantages of a liaison and none of the repercussions. But there are repercussions for me if we're caught. Now, go."

He paused in the corridor to tell her of his plan. "Walk in and greet your father. While you have him distracted, I'll go out the front."

"Yes, fine. Just don't let him see you."

"I won't." She started to turn, but he clasped her hand to stop her. "Excellent show this evening, reinette. You did something tremendous out there. Congratulations."

Twin spots of color stained her cheeks and her body relaxed. "Thank you, my king. I'll see you in a bit."

Before he could ask exactly when, she pulled away and headed toward the salon. He waited a moment and then followed, silently. Kat should be leading Lloyd into the salon to view the art, but Preston listened to make sure they weren't still near the entrance.

When he couldn't hear voices, he kept walking. As he passed the salon, he couldn't resist peeking inside, just to ensure that Lloyd wasn't facing the door.

Preston stopped in his tracks at the scene.

Lloyd hadn't come alone. He'd brought an older woman with him.

This must be Mrs. Whittier, Lloyd's new love and the deceased Mrs. Delafield's close friend. Preston immediately looked to Kat, who stood stock-still, her arms wrapped around her middle, her face alarmingly pale. In fact, she appeared one second away from vomiting on the floor.

He cast a quick glance at the front door and debated what to do. The smart thing would be to leave and let Kat deal with this on her own. His stomach twisted at the idea. She was in hell, facing her worst nightmare on the most important night of her life. How could Lloyd do something this cruel?

It was unconscionable, and Preston hated seeing Kat so unhappy.

He was strolling into the room before he could think better of it. "Miss Delafield," he called out. "I apologize for my tardiness. Have I missed the exhibition?"

Everyone turned his way, and Kat's mouth fell open.

Delafield extended a hand toward Preston at his approach. "Evening, Clarke. Didn't expect to see you here."

Preston ignored the other man's hand and bowed over Katherine's instead. "Good evening. Thank you for inviting me."

"Hello, Mr. Clarke," she said, her voice trembling.

"Clarke," Delafield said, "do you know Mrs. Whittier?"

The poor woman looked uncomfortable, clearly

walking into a situation for which she hadn't been properly prepared, and Preston decided she needn't suffer for Delafield's thoughtlessness.

He offered a polite bow as he took her hand. "How do you do?"

Her gaze filled with what he suspected might be relief. "Mr. Clarke. I've heard so much about you."

Preston could only imagine. "Don't believe any of it," he said, then faced Kat. Her face had regained a bit of its usual color. "Miss Delafield, I trust you are well."

She licked her lips. "Thank you for coming, Mr. Clarke. You must be eager to learn more about modern art."

"I am, indeed. I normally focus on only the outsides of my buildings, but I've recently learned beauty can be found inside, as well."

"So true," she said, though her voice came out like her throat was filled with gravel. "Shall we look around?"

"Please," Preston said. "Give us the tour."

While he didn't offer Kat his arm, he did stick close to her side as they started through the exhibit. The mood in the room was tense, but she stopped by each painting and explained a little about the work, as well as the artist. Though he knew she was knowledgeable when it came to art, the depth of her understanding and her passion for the subject surprised him. It was like watching a surgeon explain a complicated procedure, or an architect describe their design. He found himself fascinated listening to her, even asking a few questions to keep her talking.

When they reached the Sisley landscape that had been his favorite, she added more insight about the color and lighting choices that made Preston appreciate the piece even more. But when they stopped at a Renoir painting, Kat came alive. It was of a couple near a river, and her love of the impressionist work came through as she detailed the scene and why the style was important to the modern art movement as they entered the twentieth century.

Head swiveling, Lloyd took in the entire space. "The collection is impressive, Katherine. It must've taken quite a bit of work."

"Thank you." Her eyes reflected her conflicted emotions. "What you see is a combination of Mama's paintings and loans from both families I know and members of the Meliora Club."

"Including this one?" Preston tilted his chin toward the Renoir.

"This painting belongs to Mr. Young, Nellie's father."

Ah, that made sense. Cornelius Young had more money than God and he was known as an avid collector of all things.

"I think the entire exhibit is lovely. You should be very proud," Mrs. Whittier said to Kat, who just pressed her lips tight and nodded.

"Katherine," Lloyd chastised in a low disapproving tone.

Preston opened his mouth to intervene—to tell Lloyd to fuck off—but Kat reacted first. She smiled but the warmth did not reach her eyes. "Thank you, ma'am. It's kind of you to say."

Lloyd patted Mrs. Whittier's hand where it

rested on his arm and addressed their small group. "Katherine, would you care to join Rebecca and I for dinner? We could get to know each other better."

She didn't move or blink, seemingly frozen in horror at the suggestion, so Preston spoke up. "What say you, Miss Delafield? Too tired for dinner?"

Kat latched on to the excuse with enthusiasm. "Yes, much too tired. Thank you for offering, Daddy."

"Another time, then," Lloyd said before moving in to kiss Katherine's cheek. "I knew tonight was important to you, sweetheart. I didn't want to miss it. Congratulations."

"Thank you, Daddy," she whispered. "I'm glad you came."

Lloyd returned to Mrs. Whittier's side, taking her arm once more. "We should be off. We have reservations at Sherry's. Are you walking out, Katherine?"

"You go on ahead," Preston said quickly. "I'll see Miss Delafield into a hansom. They're not easy to find in this neighborhood."

"Appreciate it," Lloyd said. "I don't want her on the street alone after dark. It's hardly safe."

They all exchanged goodbyes, and the older couple left. Preston regarded Kat carefully. "Reinette," he said softly when she didn't so much as move. "What can I do?"

Her troubled gaze met his, and more than a little desperation swirled in the golden brown depths. "Take me downtown and make me forget."

Chapter Nineteen

❧

They stumbled into the Jane Street apartment, already tearing at each other's clothes. A trail of discarded garments lay on the floor in their haste to the bedroom. Katherine felt as though she were being smothered, constricted, the fabric an impediment to getting necessary relief. She needed to feel his bare skin, as well.

Each time with Preston was frantic, a mindless animalistic coupling. She loved it, from the way he kissed her like she was the air he needed to breathe, to how he growled her name when he found his peak. And she liked cuddling with him after. They did a lot of talking and she discovered he was even smarter than she'd assumed. He had a way of diving straight to the heart of an issue instead of dancing around it, offering clarity and sound advice.

It was making their association . . . problematic.

She didn't want to develop feelings for him. Yet, she couldn't seem to help herself.

Not after the way he'd saved her tonight.

He could have easily left, walked out the front

door of the Meliora Club and never faced her father. Yet, he hadn't. When she asked him about it afterward, he only said, "I couldn't leave you there alone."

Perhaps he was starting to like her in return. Which made this entirely more complicated.

But those were worries for another night, because he was kissing his way down her body, toward her sex. She squirmed, beyond ready. Her body was trembling with need, unable to withstand any teasing. "Preston, please. I want you now."

"Fuck, I can't wait, either. Put the shield on me."

He liked to have her roll the rubber down his shaft, probably because of the way she usually dragged it out, teasing him, but this time she was in too much of a hurry. Within seconds she had him sheathed, and he pushed up on his arms, spread her thighs with his knees and entered her in one thrust.

She gasped at the fullness, the sense of rightness as they joined. Yes, this. She'd needed this very thing ever since the last time he'd been inside her.

His chest and arms surrounded her, his big frame pressing her down into the bed. He gave her a minute to adjust, as he always did, until she began to move her hips, begging for friction. He sucked in a breath. "You're going to make me come."

"Isn't that the point, my king?"

The words caused his nostrils to flare. Panting, he put his face into her throat as his hips rocked.

"I cannot get enough. It's so good. God, I want you every second of the day."

Thank heavens, because she felt the same.

Sweat rolled off their bodies by the time they finished. Her limbs felt like noodles as they sprawled on the mattress together, the night air trickling in through the open window. Sounds from the street kept them company in the silence, while Preston's foot stroked her calf. He'd already disposed of the shield and she was lying on top of his chest. Neither of them had a stitch of clothing on.

"You're very comfortable with yourself," he said, a deep rumble beneath her ear.

"Is that bad?"

"Of course not. It's just unusual."

She propped her chin on her hands to stare up at him. He was smoking with one hand, the other caressing her bare back. She said, "Why? Because I'm a woman?"

He snorted before putting the cigarette back to his mouth.

Pushing up to one elbow, she snatched the cigarette from his fingers and extinguished it in the crystal dish on the nightstand. He frowned. "I wasn't finished with that yet."

He didn't fool her, not anymore. They'd spent too much time together for that. "You use those as a defense, so you don't have to speak. Smoking gives you a reason to just listen, instead of participating."

"That's ridiculous. I happen to like smoking."

"I don't doubt it, and stop scowling at me. You

may light another when we're finished talking. Now, tell me why you snorted when I asked if it was because I was a woman."

A muscle jumped in his cheek. "Men feel uncomfortable and uncertain sometimes."

"Even you?"

"Even me. I was terrified when I took over Clarke Holdings. I borrowed money from Forrest to keep afloat, but I knew it wouldn't last long. And I had no real skills to build upon."

"Pun intended?"

He pinched her bottom. "You think you're amusing."

"Yes, I do." She moved in closer to his warm body. "What do you mean you had no skills? You were so young. What did you expect?"

"Drinking and fucking don't exactly count as skills when running a business."

"Was that all you knew how to do?"

Preston's hand reached for his cigarette case, then pulled back as if he caught himself. "My father made sure I could shoot, fish and play cards. Made me learn how to hit a curveball." He dragged his free hand across his jaw. "That last one actually came in handy, though, when I played baseball in college."

"I bet you were good."

He gave her a slow grin. "I was very good."

She didn't doubt it. "Perhaps your father wanted you to enjoy being a young man before he burdened you with responsibilities."

"Then he shouldn't have gambled the family fortune away."

"Gamblers rarely realize they have a problem until it's too late."

He waited a few seconds, then said, "Your father knew."

"He did?" Katherine frowned at the wall. Daddy hadn't ever mentioned it. He just talked about the joint business dissolving, but never said why.

"Of course. He and Henry were close in those days, but Lloyd quickly disentangled himself when things got bad. Ignored my father for the rest of his life."

"That can't be right," Katherine said. "Surely my father would've helped yours if things were truly that grim."

Preston didn't speak, his leg rocking on the mattress.

"You're saying my father deliberately withheld assistance." Her mind reeled with this knowledge. "I don't believe it."

"Doesn't matter what you believe. I'm telling you the facts."

"This is why you hate my father. Because you blame him for what happened."

"I don't blame him for my father's mistakes. But Lloyd could've helped. He could've helped Henry instead of dropping him off the side of a cliff."

She didn't know what to make of this new information. Her father never talked about the old days, when he ran a company with Henry Clarke. Had he truly turned his back on Preston's father?

"I'm sorry I brought it up," Preston muttered.

"No, I'm grateful to learn at last why you don't like him."

"Trust me when I tell you there is more. A lot more, in fact. I'm sparing you the details, even though you love details."

That he remembered this about her made her smile, despite all that had happened tonight. "My father isn't a bad man."

"After seeing your pallor earlier this evening, we'll need to disagree on that."

She tried to put her thoughts into words. "I just hadn't expected to encounter the two of them as a couple so soon. It's upsetting to see him with someone else."

"Understandable, but perhaps he's trying to get you used to the idea."

By surprising her? On tonight of all nights? "Then he should have warned me. Would it have been so hard to let me know he was bringing her, so I might have prepared myself?"

"As your father, he might not believe it's necessary to ask for permission."

"He doesn't need to ask for permission, but some consideration would be nice. I don't care for secrecy and deception. I thought he and I were close, especially after my mother died, but it turns out we aren't."

Preston was unnaturally quiet, as if he didn't know what to say, so she tilted her face and kissed his chin. "Thank you for staying when they arrived."

He pressed his lips to her temple. "Of course, reinette."

She stroked his rough skin, loving how different it felt from hers. "You're not a bad man, either."

A scoffing noise escaped this throat. "You have no idea how wrong that is. I've spent years doing whatever it takes to build the business back up. It hasn't been pretty. No one in this city plays fair."

"Still, that doesn't make you a bad man."

"It does if I enjoy it and have no plans to change."

More pieces of the Preston Clarke puzzle fell into place. "Was this why you insisted I would hate being married to you? Why you said you were doing me a favor by refusing to honor the betrothal?"

"Yes. You'd be ashamed of me if you knew half of what I'd done."

"Preston, I could never be ashamed of you. Whatever you did, it was because you felt you had to, that it was the only way to save your family. There's honor in that."

"Rose-colored glasses," he murmured. "This is why you belong with someone idealistic and upstanding, a man like Lockwood. You two can wish on rainbows and rescue puppies together."

Was that what he thought about her? "You make me sound awfully naive."

"Are you hoping to marry the duke?"

She paused, unsure how to answer. Her relationship with Lockwood wasn't any of Preston's concern, so why should she give him the truth? "I don't know," she lied. "Why?"

"The two of you look good together, like you belong. He seems to fancy you. Want me to speak with him? I could lean on him to make a commitment."

A lump, huge and unrelenting, wedged in her throat, making it hard to speak. Was Preston so eager for this to end, then? "No, that's unnecessary."

Preston wasn't finished, apparently. "Are you sure? If you want to marry him, then I'll help move it along."

Why wouldn't he drop it? "I don't need your assistance with finding a husband, Preston."

Her tone came out sharper than intended. Sounds from the street filled the room—drunken laughter and wheels clattering over cobblestones—while she tried to make sense of her reaction. Preston was attempting to take care of her, as he did with most everything and everyone else. So, why had it hurt her feelings?

He hadn't led her on or lied to her. His position on marriage had been clear from the meeting in his office, and he'd never wavered. Had she expected him to change his mind?

The truth hit her like a physical blow.

Oh, no. No, please. She hadn't developed serious feelings for him, had she?

Because nothing would be more foolish. This man didn't want to marry—and even if he did, it wouldn't be to *her*, the daughter of a man he hated. A man who'd turned his back on Preston's family when it was most needed.

But what else explained the burning sensation behind her sternum at the moment? The fierce need to cry that prickled behind her eyelids?

I fell in love with him.

Sweet heavens, how stupid was she? This man ignored her for a year, refused to marry her, yet she gave him her innocence *and* her heart.

He doesn't want my heart.

Good, because Katherine was about to do all she could to reel the wayward organ back in. Starting tomorrow. She would remember her purpose, which was to take control of her life. To open a museum and forget about marriage and Preston Clarke.

The devil dragged a hand over her hip. "It's all right if you wish to marry someone else."

"I'm aware."

They were silent for a few minutes until he asked, "May I smoke now?"

"Yes," she said instantly, more than eager to put an end to this conversation.

PRESTON EXITED THE carriage and put on his hat, then waited for Kit to do the same. His friend frowned as he stepped down to the walk. "Tell me again. Why are we all the way up here?"

"We're seeing a piece of land." Preston began walking along One Hundred and Fifty-Ninth Street and Broadway. John James Audubon's estate was just slightly south and to the west, with twenty acres right on the river.

"Does this land we're seeing happen to be lined with gold?" Kit asked. "Because enduring a carriage ride all this way north cannot be worth it otherwise."

"You didn't have to come."

"Then why wouldn't you pull over at Eighty-Second Street when I begged to be let out?"

"Stop being so dramatic." To be fair, Preston had basically kidnapped Kit to come on this journey. He wanted a second opinion on the land he was thinking about buying.

I don't need anyone else's opinion. I've never been wrong before.

True, but this was different. This wasn't land for him; this was for *her*. He'd never picked a piece of property for someone else. Would she like it?

His forger was nearly finished with the Twenty-Third Street deed of transfer, and soon a judge would rule in Preston's favor. He'd made certain of it. This meant Katherine was out of a spot for her museum.

However, there were plenty of other viable plots of land on the island for a museum—and while it might seem far now, this area was home to many large mansions, the wealthy residents who wanted out of the hustle and bustle of Fifth Avenue. Exactly the type who would both fund and attend a modern art museum.

One day the whole island would be packed with people and buildings, crisscrossed with subway trains, electricity and streetcar lines. Soon no one would think twice about coming this far north, and Kat's museum would attract every New Yorker, regardless of socioeconomic status. The problem was most developers didn't care to think about the future, only the city as it stood now. Preston wasn't so shortsighted.

"Other than some fancy homes, there's nothing up here, Pres." Kit stepped around some dog leavings on the walk. "Why would you waste your time and money developing this far north?"

"You have to have vision. Think about the future. It's not about what's here now, but what could be here in one or two generations."

"I'll stick to the here and now, thank you. Some of us like our lives the way they are."

I like my life, Preston wanted to say.

But did he?

For years he'd buried himself in work and women, and it had satisfied him.

Until Katherine.

She wormed her way under his skin with her smiles and kindness. She was easy to talk to, understanding. A sensible head on her shoulders, not to mention incredibly beautiful. He'd never had such a compatible lover, a woman he longed for even when they were apart. If he were the romantic sort, he might even say he pined for her.

But that was ridiculous.

Even if he didn't care about her father, Katherine didn't want to marry him—and he couldn't blame her. Too much had been said and done at this point. He'd been a bastard not to put an end to that betrothal agreement the instant he learned of it.

If he could go back in time and undo everything, he would. But that wasn't how time worked, and she was better off with someone else. A man worthy of her, who was capable of softness and tenderness and all the things women needed to feel happy and secure in a relationship. All of that had been wrung out of him ages ago.

They turned the corner and the lot came into view on the east side of the street. A house recently burned down here, and the owners had decided not to rebuild. The subway was close, and there was enough space to properly build a good-sized structure. The surrounding properties were modest, nothing to obscure her footprint. It could work.

"Odd place for an office tower," Kit said, glancing around. "What businesses would rent space this far north?"

"It's not for an office tower. It's for an art museum."

Kit chuckled until he realized Preston wasn't kidding. "Wait, an art museum? That's a bit highbrow for you, isn't it?"

"It won't be mine. I'm gifting the land to Miss Delafield."

His friend's jaw fell open. "You are purchasing land for Katherine Delafield. The woman you refuse to marry but are having an affair with? Do I have that right?"

"Final judgment on the Twenty-Third Street property should come in any day now. She'll lose that block, as it's rightfully mine. I thought to lessen the sting by buying her land somewhere else."

"Lessen the sting? In a business dealing?" Kit flopped his hands helplessly as if completely baffled. "Who even are you?"

"Fuck off. It's the right thing to do."

"No, the right thing to do would be to let her have the original property, seeing as how you were supposed to marry her a year ago. Let the woman at least have one victory. Now you're denying her the dream she's been working toward, and giving her something less desirable in exchange." He shook his head. "This is a bad idea, Pres."

"You're wrong. Katherine is very levelheaded and reasonable." The most reasonable he'd ever encountered, in fact. "She understands the Twenty-Third Street property was mine to begin with. Her father had no right to gift it to her. Even more, I'm giving her something better. This is twice the size of the plot downtown."

"Not sure she'll see it that way, my friend."

Preston frowned and shoved his hands into his trouser pockets. The land was huge. The museum could have a large footprint that would help develop the neighborhood. While it might not be downtown, this spot was the best available on the island. And it wasn't cheap. He wanted to do this for her. "Come on, let's go look at it."

They crossed the empty street. Preston liked to walk the perimeter of every piece of land he bought. That way, he could see the views, the angles. The possibilities. It gave him a sense of what the building might look like in the end. Then he'd go home and sketch out a rough design. His architects would use that sketch to draft the initial plans.

Perhaps he could draw a few ideas for Katherine. Then he could give them to her along with the deed. He liked the thought of doing this together, the two of them looking over plans and making decisions on ornaments and fixtures, materials and costs.

The fire had scorched the earth, leaving black rubble and ash behind. Preston stepped in and kicked a burnt piece of wood, while Kit hovered on the walk, his arms crossed over his chest. "I'm not ruining my shoes to follow you around. I'll wait here."

"Jesus, you're becoming cranky in your old age," Preston said.

"Go to hell. I'm the same age as you—and hurry up. Some of us have wives waiting."

Preston shook his head and began walking, not caring if he ruined his shoes. Before he wrote the check, he wanted to make sure this plot was perfect for Katherine. This was the part about developing real estate that he loved. The thrill of possibility and new beginnings. Crafting beauty out of destruction, and reimagining the city for centuries to come.

As he walked, he felt it deep in his bones. This was a good spot for a large building, one with soaring Roman columns and wide marble stairs. He would buy the land and gift it to Katherine when he broke the news about the ruling. A shame her original idea for the Twenty-Third Street location hadn't worked out, but that plot had never been hers to begin with.

She would understand.

He met back up with Kit. As they strolled toward the carriage, Kit unwrapped a piece of candy and popped it into his mouth. "So, are you in love with her, or . . . ?"

"Don't be ridiculous," Preston snapped.

"I see. You *are* in love with her."

"Didn't I just say I definitely was not in love with her?"

"No, you bit my head off for suggesting it. You know what Shakespeare said about protesting too much, my friend."

Preston sighed dramatically. "I'm beginning to regret bringing you along today."

"Well, genius, I tried to escape seventy blocks ago. You've no one to blame but yourself."

"How is your wife?"

"Wonderful, but don't change the subject. I want to know about Miss Delafield and what you are planning to do about the betrothal. If you're asking my opinion—"

"Which I'm not."

"—I think you should marry her."

A grimace tugged at Preston's mouth. "I cannot think of a greater humiliation than going to Lloyd Delafield and telling him I want to marry Katherine. Can you imagine his glee? I'd rather swallow arsenic."

"Are you willing to lose her over your pride? Come on, Preston. You aren't getting any younger, and Katherine certainly won't wait forever."

Kit was wrong—she didn't want to marry Preston. That had been made perfectly clear.

Then there was the matter of everything else. His company came first, long before any personal relationship. More than fifty employees relied on him, not to mention the shareholders he answered to, so he couldn't let them down. "It's more than pride and Lloyd. The company isn't exactly a sparkling clean, noble venture. It's . . ."

"I get it. Bribes, grift and blackmail." Kit opened the carriage door. "Isn't it fairly well accepted that any successful business of your kind deals in these gray areas? But if you think anyone will judge you for it, surely you've come far enough that you don't need those things any longer. Saving the business after your father? Fine. But not now."

"It is a necessary part of the game, and everyone knows that." If Preston wasn't willing to play by the rules—dishonest as they were—he might as well close up shop.

"But her father does the exact same thing. She's likely more familiar with your world than you suspect."

Sweet and idealistic Katherine, aware of the crooked and illicit nature of developing the city? No, Lloyd would've sheltered her from it at all costs. "Leave it alone, Kit. I know what I'm doing."

"All right, but I think you're making a mistake."

"Duly noted, and let's not discuss it again."

Kit sighed as he stared out the window. "Fine, but I look forward to telling you 'I told you so' one of these days."

Chapter Twenty

❦

Standing on the corner of Twenty-Third Street, Katherine nearly bounced in excitement. The Duke of Lockwood slid her a glance from under the brim of his derby. "You remind me of a rabbit, about to hop away at any moment."

"I can't help it. I'm both nervous and excited. Do you think she'll take on the project?"

As promised, Lockwood had reached out to Mrs. Phillip Mansfield, New York's only female architect, to meet with Katherine. He'd come along to make the introduction, for which Katherine was grateful. "I have no idea," he said. "I'd say it depends on her schedule at the moment. She's just had another child this spring."

"Well, I hope she makes time for me. I'd hate to deal with another male architect any time soon."

"Understandable. Ah, there she is." Lockwood started toward an auburn-haired woman in a smart green jacket and skirt. The duke bent to kiss her cheek. "Lady Eva."

"Hello, Lockwood. And it's Mrs. Mansfield these days."

"I still cannot get used to it."

"Neither can I, and it's been years." She struck out her hand. "You must be Miss Delafield. How do you do?"

They shook hands and Katherine said, "Thank you for coming. It's an honor to meet you." It was true. Katherine had been researching Mrs. Mansfield ever since Lockwood mentioned her. The architect had stayed busy since coming to America five years ago, from Philadelphia department stores and Newport cottages, to New York City hotels and office buildings. She was making her distinct style known all across the country.

"The duke has told me a bit about your project, but I'd like to hear about it from you."

Katherine launched into her vision for the museum, which would feature classics as well as unknown artists looking for a break. The museum would work on donations and contributions, allowing it to remain free to visitors.

"And you wish to put it here?" Mrs. Mansfield asked as she studied the buildings behind them. "On this block?"

"Yes. My father owns the land and we'll be taking down everything you see here."

"It's an outstanding location," the architect said, walking a bit back and forth. "A bit small, but with the convergence of streets and access to the park, you would have plenty of foot traffic."

Was it too small? Katherine had no idea if the museum would be popular enough to warrant more space.

Still, it was much better than Preston's idea of

the world's tallest office tower, which could literally go anywhere in the city. Katherine's museum needed people and restaurants and the subway trains—basically everything happening right here at Twenty-Third Street.

"Have you thought about the style of the building? Lockwood mentioned you had another architect before, but didn't agree on a vision."

"My father's architect, Mr. Jennis."

"I'm afraid I don't know him," Mrs. Mansfield said.

"He was very . . ."

"Rude?" the other woman finished.

"That's a nice way of putting it. I prefer your style, something more modern, like the Mansfield Hotel. But Mr. Jennis only designs in the classic Empire style."

"And he probably treated you as if you had no idea of what you were talking about."

Katherine nodded, impressed that Mrs. Mansfield had guessed correctly. "That's exactly what happened. He told me to leave it to the men who do this for a living."

Mrs. Mansfield's mouth curled derisively. "Men are very dismissive of women, especially when it comes to architecture and construction. If I had a dollar for every man who tried to prevent me from accomplishing my vision, I'd be one of the wealthiest women in the city."

Lockwood made an amused sound in his throat. "You are one of the wealthiest women in the city."

"See," Mrs. Mansfield said to Katherine, holding up her hand. "Take it from me, you'll have to fight tooth and nail to get what you want, Miss Delafield."

"I'm prepared to do whatever it takes. I just want for someone to love this project as much as I do. A partner who will make it as beautiful and modern on the outside as the art on the inside."

The architect sighed heavily and stared at the street traffic. "I fully intended to come today and say no. I'm incredibly busy with several upcoming jobs, not to mention my children and husband, and I hate to disappoint anyone."

Katherine's heart paused, unsure of what was coming next. "But you've changed your mind because I'm so adorable and charming?"

Mrs. Mansfield laughed. "Now I can see why the duke is so fond of you. No, I like your vision. I think these egalitarian buildings and spaces are what the city needs more of, not office buildings and towers."

"Precisely!" Katherine put her hands together, pleading. "Please, Mrs. Mansfield. I think we would make a wonderful team and money is no object. Whatever you want. Let's put up a building that everyone will be talking about for the next hundred years."

The other woman looked at the duke. "How on earth am I supposed to resist her?"

Lockwood shrugged, his handsome face breaking out into a grin. "Come now, my lady. You don't really want to sit home and play housewife. This will be a monument to modern art, a building for the ages. Are you planning to let Stanford White overshadow you?"

At the mention of the famous architect, Mrs.

Mansfield's mouth pinched. "He's such a cad," she murmured. "Just absolute rubbish. I wish he weren't so bloody talented." Turning back to Katherine, she said, "All right, I'll do it."

Katherine clapped her hands and let out a tiny squeak. "Oh, that's marvelous news. Thank you, Mrs. Mansfield."

"You might as well call me Eva. We're going to be spending a lot of time together."

"And please, call me Katherine. I'll have my father's team send over the site survey."

"No need," Eva said. "I'll have my own people do one. They know what I want. I apologize for intruding, but I have to ask. Is there a special man in your life?"

"No," Katherine said almost too quickly.

"Good. The last thing we need is a fiancé or husband interjecting himself in our partnership."

"What about Mr. Clarke?" Lockwood said from over Katherine's shoulder. "Something tells me he might interject himself."

"Why do you say that?" Katherine asked, spinning to face him. Hadn't she discouraged the duke's suspicions over a future between her and Preston the other night? Or did Lockwood still not believe her?

Lockwood gestured toward the office building behind them. "Doesn't he own half this building?"

"Not any longer, no." Katherine turned back to Eva. "My father bought the rights years ago. You needn't worry about Mr. Clarke."

Eva visibly relaxed at this. "That is a relief. Mr. Clarke's reputation precedes him. I prefer to keep my projects on the right side of the law."

You'd be ashamed of me if you knew half of what I'd done.

Preston readily admitted it, though Katherine refused to believe he would ever do anything *illegal*. He wasn't a criminal. Complicated and talented with his tongue, yes, but not a criminal. He'd saved his family's business from collapse and looked after his friends. Had even defended her honor at the art show, then stayed when her father arrived after.

She knew Preston, probably better than anyone, and deep down he was a good man—even if he wouldn't admit it. He was deep and fascinating, intense and uncompromising. It would take layers and layers of paint to properly portray that man's personality on canvas.

And she really needed to stop thinking about him.

Eva struck out her hand once more. "We'll be in touch, Katherine. I look forward to working together."

"And I with you. We are going to do great things."

When their trio parted, Katherine decided to visit her father. Though it was late in the day, she much preferred to meet with him in his office. Then she could share the news regarding Mrs. Mansfield and leave, avoiding any personal conversations about his new relationship.

Her father's secretary was just leaving as Katherine arrived. "Good evening, Miss Delafield. I'm afraid your father is in a meeting."

"Oh." Katherine toyed with the buttons on

her glove. "Do you think he'll be long? I just had something quick to tell him."

"I couldn't say. He's with Mr. Clarke."

That was unexpected. What was Preston doing here? She dropped her hands and tried to appear uninterested, though her mind was reeling. "Has Mr. Clarke been here long?"

"No, he's just arrived." The secretary's nose wrinkled. "Did you need me to stay? I have theater tickets but . . ."

It was after five-thirty in the evening, so Katherine said, "No, please go. I'm happy to wait by myself." *So I may find out why Preston is here.*

"Are you sure, miss? I wouldn't want to inconvenience you."

"No inconvenience. Enjoy your show."

The secretary waved and set off toward the lift, which left Katherine all alone . . . with the old speaking tube that connected to Daddy's office. It would allow her to hear every word of Preston's conversation with her father.

BARELY ABLE TO contain his glee, Preston sat across the desk from Lloyd Delafield. The other man was carefully examining the new deed, which was faultless in Preston's opinion. One could almost believe it was real.

He felt not an ounce of guilt over what he'd done. Whatever game Lloyd was playing, Preston would beat him at it. Every time.

Finally, Lloyd lowered the papers. "You cannot think this will hold up in court."

"It already has. A judge signed off on it and the

deed's been filed with the buildings department. You lose."

Lloyd removed the spectacles from his face and tossed them on the desk. "A judge you bribed, along with a fat payment to the buildings department, as well."

Preston shrugged. They both knew how this worked. "I told you that property was mine."

"Except it's not. Your father sold it to me before he died."

"I don't believe it. As I said, I went through everything belonging to the estate. That building came to him when your joint trust dissolved, after you cut ties when he got in financial trouble. It never went to you."

"You love to paint me as the villain." Lloyd leaned back in his chair. "You don't know a dashed thing about your father, do you?"

"I know he was a gambler, who almost cost my mother everything. I know you were also aware of this, which was why you dissolved the joint business and ran as far away from Henry as you could manage." Shoving aside the painful memories, he folded his hands across his middle. "But he didn't sell off everything. For whatever reason, he kept this piece of land." Only Forrest's loan had prevented Preston from needing to sell it.

Lloyd shook his head and rubbed his eyes. "Son—"

"Do *not* call me that."

"Preston," Lloyd corrected. "I know you're jaded, but are you not even willing to entertain the possibility that I'm telling the truth? What you've done is illegal. And wrong."

"I have the original deed, so please spare me your sanctimonious speech. I only righted your attempt to steal it."

"Why would I try and cheat your father or you? What would I possibly gain? I have properties all over the five-state area."

"I couldn't say, but I'm assuming it has to do with the broken betrothal agreement and your daughter." Lloyd certainly hadn't wasted any time in gifting the property to Katherine, which was a deliberate attempt to ruin Preston's agreement with Manhattan Surety.

"Do you honestly believe me so diabolical?"

Fucking hell. This angelic act was not fooling Preston one bit. "You abandoned my father and my family when we needed you most. You bid against me on almost every piece of property I tried to acquire during my first year as president of Clarke Holdings. You let your daughter believe she had a fiancé for an entire goddamn year! So yes, I'm quite aware what kind of a man you are, Lloyd."

Color tinged Lloyd's cheeks. "You think I abandoned Henry, but I did not. I tried to save him for years. I ran our business, making us both a lot of money, while your father went out and gambled it away. At some point, people don't want to be saved. I would think you'd know a thing or two about that, considering the way your friend Forrest died this summer."

Ice flooded Preston's veins, his ears ringing with cold fury. "You dare bring that up to me now?"

"This is ridiculous." Lloyd threw up his hands.

"You forged a deed to steal that Twenty-Third Street property from me. If you think I won't fight this, then you're delusional. I'll tie this up in court for years, so bid farewell to your Manhattan Surety project."

Preston's jaw clenched as his fingers squeezed the wooden armrests, imagining it was Lloyd's neck. "Then your daughter will bid farewell to her museum there, too. Who do you think will be more forgiving? Manhattan Surety isn't likely to hold a grudge."

The office door flew open, surprising them both. Preston turned around to see Katherine storm inside, her movements brisk. He shot to his feet and blinked. What on earth was she doing here?

She marched toward them, not stopping until she stood next to the desk, her gaze snapping with golden fire. "I cannot believe this," she hissed at him. "You forged a deed? You knew I was planning on putting my museum there. How could you steal this property from me?"

She'd been listening? A lump lodged in his throat as he wondered how much she'd heard, but he forced it away. This was business, not personal. His regard for her didn't affect this decision at all. "I'm not stealing it from you. Your father stole it from me. I'm merely setting things to rights."

"He didn't steal it!" Katherine said, her arms flopping at her sides as if he exasperated her. "And you of all people know how much this museum means to me. I can't believe you would do something so underhanded and cruel."

He did know how much the museum meant to her. While at Jane Street, she often talked about her mother and her mother's love of art, how she wanted to see that continue. He hurried to say, "And that's why I've purchased a piece of land for you, one that's bigger. It's uptown at One Hundred and Fifty-Ninth Street—"

"I don't want another piece of land, Preston. This one is perfect for the kind of foot traffic and public transportation a museum requires."

Preston's gaze flicked over to Lloyd, who was watching these proceedings carefully, his brow furrowed in thought. Preston instantly regretted having this discussion in front of her father. "May we continue this conversation later, when I'm finished here?"

"No, we'll discuss it now." She pointed to the deed on the desk. "Did you forge that deed?"

He didn't answer. He couldn't lie to her, nor could he admit the forgery.

Her expression changed, the anger quickly replaced by disappointment and hurt. It tore at Preston's chest, though he felt entirely justified in what he'd done. "That property was always mine," he told her.

"Not from what I overheard." She tilted her head toward the ceiling and let out a joyless laugh. "God, I am such a fool."

Then she started for the door, her boot heels thumping on the carpets. He began to follow her. "Katherine, wait."

"Do not talk to me, Preston. Do not come near me or talk to me ever again."

He exhaled heavily and dragged a hand through

his hair, but she never glanced back. She went straight to the lift and disappeared inside. Turning, he went to collect his hat—but came to a halt when he saw the surprise on Lloyd's face.

"Is there something we need to discuss?" Lloyd asked. "Because that exchange seemed quite familiar."

"There's nothing I need to discuss with you— now or ever. And stay out of my personal life." He snatched his hat off the chair.

"Not to mention your presence at the art exhibit the other night. You didn't arrive late, did you? You were there the whole time. And Mr. Jennis told me you interrupted his meeting with my daughter, encouraging her to fire him."

"If you have something to say, then just say it," Preston snapped. He didn't want Lloyd arriving at the wrong conclusion. Katherine could suffer as a result.

"Have you compromised my daughter?"

"No," he lied.

Lloyd scratched his face. "I don't know what to believe with you. It's clear you'll do anything to get what you want"—he gestured to the deed— "but I should say, if you've hurt her in any way or stained her reputation, you will do right by her."

"Or, what? My invitations will dry up? I don't give a damn about society, Lloyd. You have no leverage over me. And I'd worry about your own relationship with Katherine before you worry about mine."

Turning on his heel, he hurried out of the office. Hopefully he could still catch her before she disappeared.

Chapter Twenty-One

❧

Katherine hurried from her father's office building, ready to put as much distance between herself and Preston Clarke as she could.

He'd forged a deed. Swindled the property right out from under her nose.

I may be a dishonest man, but I promise to always be honest with you.

That liar.

As she flagged down a hansom, she could barely breathe through all the anger clogging her throat. The entire time—while he listened to her talk about her mother and the museum, during their intimacies—he was planning this. That unbelievable scoundrel. The immoral cad. That . . . that . . . *criminal*.

How had she ever believed herself in love with him?

Madness, clearly.

He was undeserving of her heart. That man cared only about himself and this ridiculous feud with her father. About winning and getting his way, keeping control of everything around him.

God, she was such a fool. One year! She'd wasted one year of her life, thinking they were betrothed, then she'd fallen into bed with him, more than eager to give him her body and her trust.

And what had he done in return? Betrayed her.

The hansom rolled away from the curb just as the man himself emerged from the office building, his head swiveling up and down the block. She was not embarrassed to admit that she ducked down in the carriage so Preston wouldn't see her. His apologies and explanations meant nothing.

Tears began forming, pools of hot moisture gathering on her eyelids. She was so tired of men dictating her life. It was exhausting. She wanted to be independent, to have control over her own future.

The city crowded around the carriage, the buildings reminding her of their narrow world and all the restrictions that came with it. She wiped her eyes, brushing away her tears of frustration. Part of her longed to go off and live in the woods somewhere, alone, as Thoreau had done. A pure and simple existence where every day was her own.

It was clear nothing would ever change. For all her bluster and planning, she was no better off than she was a year ago. Actually, things were worse. She'd fallen in love with a thug, a wealthy criminal dressed in a fancy three-piece suit who wasn't above lying and cheating to achieve his goals.

God, she was so stupid.

When she arrived home, she hurried inside—then froze as she passed the front drawing room.

Mrs. Whittier was here. Having tea with Aunt Dahlia.

Katherine's back went ramrod straight, her mind scrambling to keep up. Why was her father's . . . lady friend here, in their home? And why was Aunt Dahlia laughing and smiling?

She must've made a noise because both women turned toward the doorway. "Katherine, hello," Aunt Dahlia called, waving her inside. "Come and sit with us. You remember Mrs. Whittier?"

Katherine tried to force a polite smile as she approached. "Good afternoon. I wish I could stay but—"

"Nonsense," Aunt Dahlia said. "Take a lemon cookie and visit for a moment. We should celebrate the good news together."

Good news? They couldn't mean the news that Mrs. Mansfield had agreed to design the art museum. That would be short-lived, in any case, as Katherine would need to put the project on hold until she found another location.

That's why I've purchased a piece of land for you, one that's bigger.

She didn't want anything from Preston. Ever.

Temporarily shaking off her misery, she asked, "And what are we celebrating?"

Aunt Dahlia's smile vanished, the lines of her face deepening in confusion. "Surely your father told you. He cabled to say you'd just left his office."

"Told me . . . ?"

"About the engagement." She gestured to Mrs. Whittier. "He and Rebecca."

Engagement?

Katherine blinked, the pain so sharp and fierce that she dropped back a step. No, this wasn't happening. Her father had asked Mrs. Whittier to marry him? Without telling Katherine first?

She glanced helplessly at her late mother's best friend, who seemed to be growing alarmed, if the pallor of her face was any indication.

Mrs. Whittier set down her teacup. "Katherine, I . . . I had no idea you didn't know. I am so sorry to be the one to tell you. Lloyd—"

A noise escaped Katherine's mouth at that word, her father's given name on this woman's lips. Katherine could still hear her mother calling his name throughout these walls, or laughing at the dinner table when he said something amusing. She wasn't ready to hear this particular woman use it, too.

"No," she said aloud. "I don't believe it. Daddy would not do this without telling me. He wouldn't." She looked to her aunt. "Why is this happening?"

Aunt Dahlia rose, her hands out as if to soothe a wild animal. "Calm down, Katherine. There's no reason to get upset, especially in front of Rebecca. This is happy news."

"Is it?" The terrible pressure in her lungs increased. "If it's happy news then why didn't he tell me? Why didn't he mention this when I saw him?" Not that she'd given him much opportunity during her argument with Preston. Still, he could've asked her to stay or followed her outside. "Why didn't he warn me? Why does no one tell me anything?"

"Katherine," Mrs. Whittier said, "I know this isn't what you want to hear right now, but I love your father. I just—"

"He didn't care how I felt about this," she continued, backing out of the room. "And why would he? I haven't any control over what happens, obviously. All these decisions are made without any thought whatsoever to my consideration."

The betrothal agreement, the gain and loss of the museum property, her father's engagement. Even the land Preston had purchased for her. None of it had been her decision, yet her life was greatly impacted by it.

"Katherine, you're being rude," her aunt admonished. "And I cannot believe you are begrudging your father this happiness."

Katherine shook her head, more tears burning her eyes. It was too much. Today, of all days, it was too much to learn that her father was beginning another life with another woman. She would be forced to see Mrs. Whittier everywhere. At her mother's breakfast table, in her mother's garden.

In her mother's bedchamber.

Katherine bent over, her hand pressed tight to her stomach as she struggled to breathe. She didn't particularly care if anyone thought her rude or childish. This was more than she could handle at the moment, and pretending to be happy about it was impossible.

Without another word, she whirled and ran upstairs.

Tears blurred her eyes as she reached her bedchamber, her limbs shaking with anger and frustration. She considered throwing herself on her bed and having a good cry, but there wasn't any comfort in it. Not in this house, surrounded by the memory of her mother and the specter of her father's new life. Nor did she want to stay in this city, where thoughts of Preston loomed around every corner.

No, she couldn't stay here.

It felt like she was about to crack open, like her bones and flesh couldn't contain all of the emotions inside her. She wanted solace and solitude. Away from everyone she knew, someplace where only she mattered. Somewhere far, like Spain.

Could she board a steamer and sail away?

She grabbed a small traveling case from her closet and threw it on the bed. Just as she gathered an armful of clothing, her bedroom door opened.

Aunt Dahlia appeared, her lips twisted in remorse. "Katherine, I'm terribly sorry. I shouldn't have told you like that. I should've let your father do it, but I . . . well, it doesn't matter now. Are you all right?"

"No," Katherine choked out, wiping away a tear. "I'm definitely not all right."

"Oh, you poor dear." Her aunt came forward and regarded the clothing on the bed. "Wait, what are you doing?"

"Leaving. I need some time alone. Away from New York. Away from this house."

"This is very dramatic, Katherine. You can't just run away from us. You must be chaperoned—"

Katherine gave a harsh bark of laughter. "You're

worried about my virtue at a time like this? You must be joking."

"It has been my primary concern for two years, so yes. I am worried about your virtue."

What would her aunt say if she knew there was no virtue to worry about, thanks to Preston Clarke?

Walking to her wardrobe, Kathcrine gathered more things and tossed them on the bed. "I'm not running away. And I don't care if it's dramatic or not—I cannot stay here."

"Did something else happen? Something other than your father's engagement?"

The knot in Katherine's chest tightened.

Your father stole it from me. I'm merely setting things to rights.

"It doesn't matter," she said as more tears fell.

"It matters to me. Tell me what's happened to upset you."

She couldn't, not without revealing her stupidity in falling in love with Preston. "I don't want to talk about it, not right now. I'm going back to Spain."

Aunt Dahlia put her hands on her hips. "Over my dead body, young lady. You are not going across the ocean, to a foreign country, without a proper escort. It's bad enough you're traveling to the Meliora Club without a chaperone, but I won't allow you to go all the way to Spain by yourself."

Unfortunately, her aunt could prevent Katherine from leaving the house in any number of ways. But there were other properties her family owned where she could be by herself. "Fine, then I'll go to Newport."

"The cottage is closed for the season. Only the lodge in the Adirondacks is open."

"Fine. The Adirondacks, then."

Her aunt's gaze turned skeptical. "You want to sit in the middle of the woods in that musty cabin all by yourself?"

A few days away from the reminders and anyone who wanted to talk to her? That sounded like heaven at the moment.

"Yes," Katherine said, putting her hands together, begging. "That is exactly what I want. Will you help me? I can't stay here." Her voice broke. "I just can't. Please, Aunt Dahlia."

"Oh, you know I can't resist you when you cry. I never had my own children, but you're like a daughter to me." She dabbed at her eyes with her fingers, as if trying to stave off her own tears. "If I let you go, how will you look after yourself up there without a cook or a maid?"

"I'll be fine, I swear. I'll pack some food and extra clothing. And I won't stay long. Just a few days." She didn't know if that was true or not, but figured it would ease her aunt's mind.

Dahlia's nose wrinkled as she asked, "What if I came with you?"

Katherine knew the offer cost her aunt dearly. Dahlia hated the woods and the cabin, saying it was impossible for anyone to happily exist outside of a city. Each sound caused her to jump, convinced a man-eating bear lurked behind every bush.

"That wouldn't be relaxing for either of us,"

she said. "And you know from our travels together that I'm perfectly self-sufficient."

"Your father won't like you on a public train by yourself."

Katherine didn't give a fig about her father's opinion at the moment, but to ease her aunt's mind, she made a quick decision. "I'll ask Nellie if I can borrow her family's private railcar, then."

"Fine." Her aunt huffed, like she knew she'd lost. "But if something happens to you . . ."

"It won't. I'll take the train up and stay in the house the entire time. No one will even know I'm there."

THREE DAYS LATER and Katherine still wouldn't return his notes.

Preston should've followed her right away, but he lost her in the crowd after she left her father's office building. Then when he arrived at her home, he was told she wasn't receiving callers, so he decided to give her space. She was a rational, levelheaded woman. Once she calmed down, she would see he'd done nothing wrong. He'd even warned her not to count on putting her museum there.

When he didn't hear from her the next day, he began sending messages. Two a day, each begging her to let him explain. But it appeared she was planning on ignoring him.

He didn't like it.

At the very least, she should yell at him. Then they could talk it out and everything would go back to the way it was before. He'd take her up to One Hundred and Fifty-Ninth Street and show her the parcel of land he bought for her. Then they would go downtown and fuck like rabbits.

He decided to visit the Delafield home again, hoping she would see him. Lloyd could make of that whatever he wished. Preston owed Katherine an explanation, not her father.

Someone agreed to see him, except it wasn't Katherine. Her aunt patiently informed him that Katherine was not in the city at the moment. While Preston tried to wrap his head around that, Dahlia requested that he leave Katherine alone.

"I'm not telling her father about your visit today, Mr. Clarke," Dahlia had said. "I only ask that you not send her more notes or try to reach out to her in any way. I'm not certain what transpired between the two of you, but I can only assume it was improper. Fair warning: my brother will not take kindly to any disregard of her virtue."

Preston nearly rolled his eyes at the threat of Lloyd, but he let it go. He needed to see Katherine. Had she really left? If so, where was she?

One person would know—except he wasn't sure if she would tell him.

Still, he had to try.

Built in the French Second Empire style, the Young's Fifth Avenue mansion was one of the biggest residential properties in the city. On any other day he would have admired the mansard roof and the ornate window hoods. It was monumental and inspiring, with decorative touches, including iron cresting on the roof and heavily bracketed cornices and quoins.

But Preston couldn't appreciate any of that, not in his current panic.

He rang the bell and presented his card. "Mr. Preston Clarke to see Miss Young."

The butler admitted him and Preston stood in the entry, noting the painting hanging there. It looked like something Kat would love, with soft colors and a dreamy, romantic setting. Similar to the paintings from her art show.

His stomach twisted. He wished she were here so she could tell him about the artist and the inspiration for the scene. Where in the hell had she gone?

The butler reappeared, his footsteps impressively silent on the tile. "Mr. Clarke, Miss Young will see you in the ballroom."

Ballroom?

He left his things on the small side table, then followed the butler up the stairs. As they approached the double set of doors, he could hear the sound of . . . swords?

"Allez! Non, you are much too slow," a man with a heavy French accent was saying. "Quicker, mon petit chou."

Preston walked in to find a fencing lesson in progress, with two men squaring off in white fencing outfits. Who was . . . ?

Oh, wait. One of them was most definitely a woman. Was this Nellie? Good God.

The two continued to spar and Preston couldn't help but be impressed. He didn't know much about fencing but Nellie appeared to be holding her own. What she lacked in strength, she made up for with speed.

"Riposte," the man instructed. "Drive me back!"

She lunged, but it was too late. Her opponent

recovered and scored a touch. They stopped, each breathing hard, and removed their masks. The young man, clearly an instructor, smiled fondly at her. "You are getting better, chérie. We will try again after your meeting, non?"

"Merci, Adrian. I'll be but a moment."

He came forward and kissed her hand, lingering a tad too close. "Take your time."

These two were obviously intimate, not that it was any of Preston's business. He was here to get answers, not to chaperone.

The instructor strode out of the ballroom, while Nellie put down her épée and removed her gloves. "I'm surprised to find you on my doorstep, Preston. What may I do for you?"

He closed the distance between them. "Where is she?"

"I don't know what you mean."

The hairs on the back of his neck stood up as irritation swept over him. "There is only one person she would tell, and that's you. Where has she gone?"

Nellie shoved an errant lock of red hair behind her ear. "Didn't she leave you a note?"

Wasn't it obvious she hadn't? If Katherine had written to him, he wouldn't be standing here. "Nellie, please. I need to see her and explain."

"I'm fairly sure if she wanted to hear your explanations, then she would've told you where she was going."

He crossed his arms and scowled at her. "I need to talk to her."

Nellie lifted her shoulder. "Write her a letter. If I see her, I'll pass it along."

Something told him any letter he handed Nellie would end up in a fireplace somewhere. "Is she here?"

"In my house or in the city?"

"Either," he said through clenched teeth.

"No."

"To which? Your house or the city?"

"She's not staying with me. That's all I'll tell you."

He huffed and let his hands fall to his sides. "I can't believe this. You're keeping her from me."

"No, Preston. You managed that all on your own."

"What the hell does that mean?"

He didn't like the knowing light in her gaze. "It means you screwed this up. You hurt my friend, and if you think for one second that I will help you find her just so you can hurt her again . . . you are dead wrong."

"I don't want to hurt her! I want to explain."

"Maybe she doesn't want to hear it. You're fooling yourself if you think you are good for her."

"What did she tell you?" Clearly Nellie knew more than he'd thought. "Did she tell you what happened?"

"I'm not betraying her trust, Preston. If she did tell me, I won't repeat it to anyone—especially not you."

He turned and began pacing, unable to keep his irritation at bay. "I don't know why you hate me, but I care about her. A lot. She's upset about what I did, but I just need to explain everything to her."

"You obviously believe the world revolves around you, but perhaps something else happened. Something that's nothing to do with you, but has upset her all the same."

"Like, what?"

"Again, her trust means more to me than satisfying your curiosity."

Goddamn it. His hands clenched into fists at his sides. A ball of panic had been sitting on his chest ever since Katherine ran out of her father's office. He didn't like knowing he'd hurt her, even unintentionally. It made it impossible to concentrate on the simplest of tasks, and Mrs. Cohen was threatening to quit if he didn't get his head on straight.

He needed Katherine back in the city, making him laugh and meeting him at Jane Street. And Nellie was standing in the way of that.

"Fine, keep your secrets," he snapped. "I'll just hire a Pinkerton or two. They'll find her in a day." After all, he'd hired the investigators to find Forrest and they hadn't let him down.

"Well, well. Nice to see you aren't made of ice, after all." Nellie leaned a hip against the refreshment table and crossed her arms. "Perhaps there's hope for you yet."

"Does that mean you're going to help me?"

"No."

"Why not? I have her best interests at heart."

"I'm not certain you do, but even still, she's gone and doesn't want to be found. When or if she's ever ready to talk to you, you'll hear from her."

"That isn't good enough."

"I'm sorry, but that's all you're going to get from me." She smiled sweetly, clearly relishing her power over him.

"I see I'm wasting my time here." He spun on his heel and started for the door. He'd cable the Pinkerton office as soon as he left.

"Think about why you're so determined to find her," Nellie called out. "What happens then? She's not one of your mistresses, Preston."

He was aware. But Katherine was alone, stewing in anger and hurt, and he needed to set things to rights between them.

Chapter Twenty-Two

❦

$\mathcal{K}$atherine carried her cup of coffee out onto the porch of the four-bedroom wooden lodge. Though it was early, the morning sun cast a brilliant gold over the still waters of Lake George, with the surrounding trees a glorious panorama of orange, red and yellow. This part of the state was rustic and simple, so different than the hustle and bustle of the city. She could see why so many wealthy families built homes here.

Other than her quick trips to the Hotel Sagamore, she hadn't seen a single person in four days. Since Aunt Dahlia required daily proof that Katherine hadn't been eaten by a bear, she walked to the hotel each afternoon, sent a telegram home, picked up something small for dinner and came back to her lodge. While her decision to come up here was made impulsively, she quickly discovered it was the perfect escape.

And she had no plans to leave any time soon.

Back in New York, she'd still find her father engaged to her late mother's best friend and

Preston out conquering the city, uncaring of who he hurt in the process.

She rubbed her chest, unsure why this ache wouldn't ease. Surely this pain should lessen a little bit every day she was here?

These past few weeks she'd tried so hard to discover herself. She thought being more like Nellie was the answer, having affairs and throwing caution to the wind, but that had certainly backfired, hadn't it? Now she had a broken heart to contend with.

Apparently, she wasn't like Nellie, able to keep her feelings separate from any romantic entanglements. Katherine felt too much for that. Not to mention she'd trusted the wrong man. Preston cared about his company and his buildings in that order. There wasn't room for anything—or anyone—else.

Stupid, stupid Katherine.

So, who was she? At the moment, she was an unmarried woman with no prospects, a lover of lists with a father starting another life. It was depressing.

She wasn't ruined, though. While she might not have a maidenhead any longer, that didn't mean she was unworthy. And someday a man was going to put her first.

Leaves rustled close by and she froze. Was it a bear? No, that was ridiculous. Aunt Dahlia's fears were making Katherine skittish. Still, she took a step closer to the door, ready to dart inside the lodge at the first sign of brown fur or snarling teeth.

An unwelcome visitor stepped out of the brush, and not the one she was expecting.

Preston.

She backed toward the door as if he were really a bear. "What are you doing here?"

He held up his hands. "I've come to see you. Please, don't run from me again, Kat."

"How on earth did you find me? Did my aunt . . . ?" God, she would never forgive Aunt Dahlia.

"No, the Pinkertons found you."

He'd hired the detective agency to find her? She was both flattered and annoyed. Mostly annoyed. "Did it occur to you that I didn't wish to be found?"

"Yes." He lifted a shoulder as if her wishes didn't factor into his decisions. "I needed to talk to you."

"Where are you staying?" Because he was absolutely not staying here with her.

"At my lodge. Over there." He pointed to a huge wooden structure dominating the shore of the lake. "Can we—"

Katherine didn't hear what he said next, because she slipped inside her lodge, closed the door and locked it.

Then she set her coffee down and tried not to scream in frustration. How dare he? Instead of giving her space and respecting her privacy, he'd bounded up here, hell-bent on making her listen to him.

"Kat, please. I need to explain." He stood directly on the other side of the door now, his voice low and deep.

"Go away, Preston. I don't want to see you."

"I understand you're angry, but you know that land was never yours to begin with."

The land, the land. Always back to *the land* with him.

A rush of pain expanded in her chest like a sharp balloon. She closed her eyes and wondered how one smart man could be so perpetually dumb.

"I'm not upset over losing the land," she called. "Yes, the museum would've been perfect there. But I'm upset that you cheated, that you didn't tell me what you were planning."

That you didn't choose me instead.

"I did tell you!"

"No, you didn't." She glared at the door separating them. "You told me the land belonged to you, but you never told me the lengths to which you were willing to go in order to prove it."

"What difference would it have made?"

"You knew it would hurt me, that I was building that museum to honor my mother. You knew I wouldn't forgive you, yet you forged the deed and submitted it regardless. After all that's happened between us, you willingly chose to hurt me."

"Kat." A small thump sounded, like maybe he dropped his forehead onto the wooden door. "I'm sorry. Please believe me. I never intended to hurt you."

"Then why buy another parcel of land in Washington Heights? Admit it, you were trying to lessen the sting. You knew losing Twenty-Third Street would hurt me and you thought another piece of land would make it all better."

"You should have your museum. I bought the land because I wanted to help you."

"And to ease your guilt."

"Goddamn it," he snapped. "Twenty-Third Street had nothing to do with you. It was between your father and me, Katherine."

"Do you honestly believe that?"

He sighed, and she could imagine his brow creased in irritation. He didn't like not getting his way, not being able to control every situation.

Indeed, that was too dashed bad. Katherine was done letting him lead. Whatever happened next in her life would be of her own choosing.

"Please, Kat. Let me in."

Hadn't they said enough? He wasn't going to see her side because Preston was incapable of seeing anyone else's side. He was always convinced he was right. Moreover, it was glaringly clear that he didn't feel the same for her as she did for him. There was lust, perhaps, but no love and certainly no respect.

And indulging in more horizontal time with him was only pulling her in deeper, causing her to fall more in love with him.

She drew in a breath and let it out slowly. She had to come first. *Know your worth.* How had she forgotten?

Though it sounded weak and unsure, she got the single word out: "No."

"Kat, sweetheart. Mon chaton. You're killing me. I . . . I have this boulder sitting on my chest and I can't eat or sleep. I can't even work. I'm terrified that I've ruined things between us, that you'll never speak to me again. Just let me see you."

Lured by the genuine emotion in his voice, she took one step toward the door. Then she caught herself. What was she doing? Running off to make him feel better? He should be making *her* feel better.

Straightening her spine, she focused on the wooden grooves running along the front door. The truth of how deeply he'd hurt her burned her tongue and she swallowed it out of habit. But maybe this was what they needed, a dose of total honesty between them. It would undoubtedly cause him to go running back to the city, back to his carefully ordered life of work and mistresses.

He would finally leave her alone.

"You *have* ruined things between us," she said quietly. "You broke my heart, Preston. That can't be repaired with a few apologies and endearments. I was in love with you, and you broke my heart. It can't be repaired."

The silence coming from the other side of the door was telling.

She'd clearly shocked him. Horrified him. He was probably pulling out a railroad timetable at this very minute to research the next train back to the city.

That was that. At least she didn't have to worry about Preston bothering her any longer.

So, why did that hurt so badly?

It should've come as a relief. But as she heard his footsteps retreating from the porch and going down the steps, away from the lodge, tears began tracking down her face. Relief didn't factor into it at all.

THE GIFTS BEGAN arriving the next day.

They weren't traditional gifts, not the kind usually given in their world. These weren't bracelets from Mr. Tiffany or Cartier diamonds, fancy flower bouquets or expensive Worth gowns.

No, they were simple tokens from a man who clearly had no idea how to fix what he'd broken, but was determined to try all the same.

In the afternoon, Katherine found a bunch of freshly picked apples outside the door. A cinnamon sugar breakfast roll the next morning. For dinner, broiled fish in lemon sauce.

She didn't know what to make of it. Wasn't he horrified by her revelation? Repulsed that one of his lovers—the daughter of a man he hated—had developed feelings for him, just as his last mistress had? She couldn't believe he hadn't gone straight back to the city, to his fancy office and towering projects.

Why was he still here?

She tried not to care or think about him, but it was impossible when he visited every day and kept leaving things outside the door. Against all reason, she found herself eagerly listening for his footsteps on the porch, then running out after he departed to see what was waiting for her.

Her favorite gift so far was the small acorn he'd whittled out of wood. It was far from perfect, but she loved the effort he'd put into the token. She placed it on her bedside table and stared at it in the dark. Could she forgive him?

She wasn't sure.

At least Preston's appearance had distracted her from Daddy's engagement to Mrs. Whittier.

It still hurt to know her father was moving on, but the sting wasn't quite so fresh. And yes, she could admit it wasn't fair to expect her father to remain alone for the rest of his life. She just hadn't thought it would happen so soon or that he would keep it from her.

She always assumed she'd be happily married, building her own family, when her father decided to take another wife. Which sounded selfish. And small. So, perhaps her issues with his remarriage had more to do with the uncertainty in Katherine's life?

Was it true?

There was one person she could ask.

Sighing, she tore off another piece of blueberry muffin, a gift from Preston this morning, and stared out at the water. His lodge sat on the other side of the lake, and she wondered how he was spending his days. Probably working. Mrs. Cohen, the poor woman, was likely going back and forth from the city, carrying mounds of paperwork for Preston.

Would it hurt to walk over and see him for a few minutes?

If she did, perhaps then he'd realize she meant what she said the other day. That he'd broken her heart and it couldn't be mended. Then he'd leave and return to the city.

Yes, that was what she'd do. She'd go to his lodge, ask him about her father, then tell him he was wasting his time and order him back to the city.

Carrying a big stick to ward off bear attacks, she started for Preston's lodge. The walk took longer than expected, but it was pleasant, with the occasional squirrel and chipmunk darting across her path. She even saw a family of beavers.

When she was almost to Preston's lodge, the skies darkened. All at once, the heavens seemed to open up and dump rain on top of her.

With a squeak, she began running as best she could in the direction of his lodge. It was a struggle in wet skirts and sodden shoes, especially when the path turned slick, and she lost her balance twice. Now she was freezing, covered in mud and looking like a bedraggled mess.

This will really scare Preston away.

Finally his large wooden cabin came into view. Gasping for breath, she hurried toward the steps. Lights blazed from inside, smoke curling out of several chimneys. The devil could've been waiting inside and she would willingly sell her soul to stand next to one of those fires.

She practically fell against the door, her body trembling from the cold. When the wood opened, Preston's eyebrows flew up, his gaze layered with concern. "Katherine, Jesus. Get inside." He grabbed her elbow and dragged her into the warm entryway.

Water sluiced off her clothes and onto his wooden floor. She wrapped her arms around herself, but it didn't help with the shivering. "Th-thank you," she got out. "Do you h-have a cloth or—"

Preston scooped her up and began carrying her deeper into the lodge. No doubt she was getting him—and the entire place—wet. "Put m-me down."

"I won't, so save your breath. Your lips are blue, Kat."

She stopped arguing and shamefully pressed her face into the warmth of his throat for body heat. Yes, definitely body heat. And if she inhaled his scent once or twice, that was no one else's concern.

They entered a bathing chamber that was larger than her bedroom in the city. It had a huge clawfoot tub, a rain shower, sink and skylight. He set her down onto the rug. "Let me start a hot bath, all right?"

She was pretty certain she nodded, but her whole body was shaking, so who could tell?

He strode to the tub and turned the taps, adjusting the water to where he liked, then came back to the rug. He was dressed down, in just a plain white shirt, no necktie or collar, and navy-blue trousers. The sleeves of his shirt were rolled up to his elbows, revealing a smattering of dark hair on his arms. She could remember feeling that hair tickle her palms as she stroked his arms in bed.

"I'm going to help you out of these wet clothes and into the tub."

"I c-can do it."

"Can you?" He quirked a brow. "I have my doubts, and I'd rather get you into the hot water quickly. What if I get you down to your chemise? Then you can do the rest."

"All r-right."

Preston worked with impressive speed, removing her wet garments with the dexterity of someone who hadn't been outside in the cold rain. Her chemise offered a small amount of modesty as he untied her drawers and removed them, along with her stockings. Then she was bare, except for the thin undergarment. He helped her step into the tub, then dropped her elbow. After he released her, his eyes raked the length of her body, and everywhere he looked broke out into a fresh round of goose bumps. She'd forgotten the power of that intense stare of his.

Clearing his throat, he turned and went to the rug. "I'll take your things and put them by the fire. They'll be dry in a few hours. In the meantime, I'll bring you something to wear and leave it outside the door."

He paused on the threshold. "Just shout if you need anything. I won't be far." Then he disappeared.

She whipped off her sodden chemise and tossed it to the tile. Then she sank into the tub, groaning as the hot water enveloped her frozen skin. Steam wafted up and filled the room like smoke. She closed her eyes and wiggled her fingers and toes, grateful to have feeling finally returned.

Hmm. Preston's washroom. She looked around, trying to find little touches of him here. Other than some shaving supplies on the sink, there wasn't any hint of him. The decor was fairly impersonal, in his usual function-over-style manner. Some prints would go a long way toward—

Why? Why was she trying to redecorate and bring softness to this man's life? He clearly didn't want it—nor did he deserve it.

After a bit, she added more hot water and continued soaking until her skin wrinkled. There was only so much she could sit with her own thoughts, though. She decided to get out and go talk to him, even if she'd need to do it while severely underdressed.

She used the towel to dry herself off, then peeked around the door to see what clothes were waiting. She found a union suit and one of Preston's shirts. Strange to wear men's clothing, but she liked it. The garments were easy to put on and quite warm. Moreover, the cloth smelled like Preston, which gave her a tiny thrill. It was like having him close by all the time.

When she wandered downstairs, she was surprised to find him in the kitchen, a small towel slung over his shoulder with fish spread out on the marble workbench.

"There you are," he said, his gaze darting to her legs. Did he swallow, or was that her imagination?

"Thank you for the clothes. I had to roll up the bottom cuffs on the union suit a bit."

"I see that. Do you feel better?"

"Yes. I apologize for crashing in here like a soaked sponge."

"I admit I was surprised, but pleasantly surprised. I'm glad you came to visit. Though, didn't you know about the impending storm?"

"No." She sat on one of the stools at the workbench. "How would I have heard?"

"I know you're walking to the hotel every day." He lifted his shoulder but didn't take his eyes off the fish. "I assumed someone there would've told you."

She generally didn't stop to chat in the hotel. Inviting friendship meant explaining she was here by herself, which seemed risky to a city girl. "What are you doing to those fish?"

"Cleaning them for dinner." He dragged a knife through the belly of a fish and peeled it open, then reached in to pull out the insides. "Would you like to help?"

"Absolutely not." Her stomach roiled just watching him do it. "That's disgusting."

"Do you like to eat fish?"

"Yes, of course."

He looked up and gestured to the dead fish as if to say, *Well, here you go.*

"I'll step in if you need help," she offered. "But I think you have it well in hand."

He hummed in his throat and went to rinse the fish at the sink. She was suddenly reminded of what she'd been eating for dinner. "Wait, did you catch and cook the fish you've been leaving me every day?"

"Yes." He glanced over his shoulder. "Who did you think was cooking your dinners?"

"I didn't know." She played with the buttons on his shirt she wore, unsure about this new side of Preston. "I assumed you were buying the meals at the hotel."

"Didn't you like them?"

"I loved them. Really, Pres. Each one was amazing."

"Good," he said and placed the fish onto a clean platter. "I'm not as skilled a cook as Alice, obviously, but I can make a decent fish dinner every now and again."

He was being humble. Katherine had dined in enough fine restaurants to know Preston's fish dinners were delicious, seasoned perfectly with herbs and sauces. "Where did you learn to do this?"

"My father." A shadow passed over his face, like a bad memory had surfaced. "He loved coming up to the Adirondacks."

"I can see why." She glanced around at the huge, well-appointed interior. "This lodge is spectacular."

"Oh, I sold the Clarke lodge ages ago. The van Allens bought it. I built this about three years back. I made sure it was bigger and in a better location than the old one."

She had no doubt. Preston was the most driven, capable man she'd ever encountered.

Which led her to the one question she'd come to ask. "Why are you still here, Preston?"

He paused and lifted his head, his expression full of a promise she didn't understand. "Why else? Because you're here."

Chapter Twenty-Three

❧

$\mathcal{P}$reston noted the confusion on Katherine's face, so he resumed work on the fish, giving her a moment. In truth, he barely understood his motivations himself.

When the Pinkertons informed him of Lloyd's engagement, Preston knew losing the museum property was only part of why Katherine had retreated upstate. So, he'd raced up here, fully expecting her to accept his apology, then allow him to comfort her. Everything would go back to the way it was before.

Only, she'd refused to see him.

I was in love with you and you broke my heart. It can't be repaired.

Was, past tense.

The words ripped through him with a ferocity he hadn't been prepared for. The knowledge twisted and slashed, opened a thousand tiny cuts in his chest, and he knew he had to fix this. He absolutely could not live in a world where Katherine was broken in any manner, especially when he'd played a part in it.

So despite the bad memories lingering in the lodge from his time with Forrest, Preston decided to stay and try to repair the damage he'd inflicted on Katherine in whatever way he could. It wasn't much, but he would keep close until she was ready to talk.

"I don't understand," she said, her fingers absently playing in the folds of the shirt she wore. "There must be a mountain of work waiting for you. Or is Mrs. Cohen here somewhere?" She glanced over both shoulders dramatically.

He did have a mountain of work waiting, and each cable from Mrs. Cohen grew increasingly alarmed. But he couldn't think about that now, not when Katherine was in his kitchen and they were alone.

He set down the knife and flattened his hands on the marble. "I'm not leaving you up here by yourself. You're upset and hurting, and I know I'm partially responsible. For that, I'm terribly sorry, Kat. If I could do it all over again, I would. But I can't change what's happened."

"Why did you do it, then?"

The answer was tricky. How could he explain the burning drive inside him, the relentless ambition combined with incessant fear? He barely understood it himself. "Because it was your father. Because of all that happened with my father. Because I can't stand to lose."

"Even when it hurts someone else?"

Leaning on the workbench, he gave her an honest answer. "I never had to worry about that before, possibly because I never cared about anyone the way I do you. Unfortunately, I didn't realize it until it was too late."

"That certainly is convenient. You get everything you want, then realize how you've hurt me and beg for forgiveness."

"I don't have everything I want." He paused to let that sink in, his eyes holding hers. "Not by a long shot, Katherine."

I was in love with you.

He wanted all of it back. He wanted her smiles and laughter, the way she stroked his skin and made him forget every terrible thing he'd ever done. To hear the way her breath hitched as he first sank inside her, as if she couldn't believe how good it felt.

He needed her to buy him paintings and tease him and recite the lists of everything in her head.

Her nose wrinkled as if she hadn't liked his answer in the least. "Right. You want me. As a lover or mistress, or whatever we were to each other."

"I won't apologize for it. I enjoyed our time together, and I think you did, too. It would be a shame for this to end prematurely because of Twenty-Third Street."

"It's not merely because of Twenty-Third Street."

That surprised him. "Then what else?"

"I suppose I realized how little I know you, not to mention how little I matter to you."

"Wrong." His voice was sharp and loud in the cavernous room, but he didn't care. "You know me better than anyone. I've told you things no one else knows about me. And you matter, Kat. Very much. To me." The words were awkward coming off his tongue, but he meant them.

"I don't think I can forgive it, Preston."

Fuck, this was what scared him, that he truly couldn't repair their relationship.

And really, what more could he say? He'd apologized, said he would do it all differently. Told her how he felt about her. If she was hoping for a declaration of love or a marriage proposal, then this was doomed. Even if he accepted saddling her with his burdens, her father would never agree.

Katherine deserved a husband who could take her on trips and give her enough time and attention. One with decency and honor, who wasn't in the muck with the other vermin every day. Though he'd rebuilt an empire, Preston was hardly quality husband material.

But was he ready to give her up? He knew the answer to that. It was why he'd chased her here. Why he was hanging about, waiting for even a crumb of her affection. He was absolutely besotted with this girl.

He returned his attention to the fish. At least she was here with him. He could feed her dinner and try to convince her to return to the city. Being up here alone wasn't safe, and he couldn't watch over her every second.

"I like your lodge," she said, her head swiveling to take it all in. "How many rooms is it?"

"Eighteen, with five bedrooms. There's a teahouse pagoda out near the lake, if you'd like to see it tomorrow."

"I didn't realize you liked tea."

"I had it put in for my mother." Though she rarely came up anymore. She said she hated being here alone, and Preston was usually too busy to make the trip.

"I think this is the first time I've heard you mention your mother."

"Not because I don't care about her. In fact, I'm overdue for a visit. We don't see each other as often as we should, which is entirely my fault."

"Because you're working."

He could feel the frown tugging at his lips. Yes, he worked hard, but had he any choice? The Clarke empire, the family name, rested on his shoulders alone, and he'd inherited a steaming pile of shit after he left college. "She understands. After all, she suffered the worst of it with my father."

"I'm sorry," Katherine quickly said. "I shouldn't have passed judgment."

"It's all right. And you're not wrong. I should make more time for her, now that I've moved out." He gave a rueful shake of his head. "She likes to remind me I don't have to save the world in a day."

"You know, I haven't the first clue where you live."

She didn't? "A town house on East Seventy-Fourth. It's not very glamorous. I'm hardly ever there." The rooms weren't even fully furnished. He'd considered hiring a designer—he knew of several who did that sort of work—but it seemed like a waste. He slept there, that was all. Most nights he ate out, and he always used hotels and Jane Street for liaisons.

"Let me guess? The walls are completely bare."

He chuckled. "To be honest, I'm not sure. I suppose they are, though I've never noticed."

"That is an absolute travesty." A companionable silence fell until she said, "My father is engaged."

"Yes, I heard."

She recoiled, her skin paling. "Has it been made public, then?"

"No," he rushed to say. "The Pinkertons told me."

"Ah." She traced the marble with her fingertip and worried her lip with her teeth. "It's only a matter of time before everyone finds out. Do you think . . . ?"

When she didn't continue, he forced himself to wait patiently. It went against every instinct not to push her, but he sensed that Katherine needed to ask this in her own way. So, he continued gutting fish.

"It sounds absurd to say it out loud," she finally said, "but do you think I'm only upset about my father and Mrs. Whittier because of my own lack of matrimonial success?"

Guilt stung his insides, but he shoved it aside for the moment. "I don't think it's absurd. I think it's natural to be envious of another person when they have something you want."

"Have you ever felt that way?"

"Of course. While I was struggling to rebuild Clarke Holdings, I hated every developer in the city. They made it look so easy and I was drowning in paperwork and legalese I barely understood."

"Including my father?"

"Especially your father." He put down the last

fish and went over to clean his hands at the sink. "But I had more reason to hate him in particular, considering he deserted my family when we needed him the most."

"So, how did you get over it?"

"Well, with your father I haven't and probably never will. With everyone else, I don't know. It just . . . went away after a time. I got busy and had my own successes, my own properties to focus on. I stopped worrying about what others were doing and concentrated on myself."

She nodded. "That's what I was attempting to do after the betrothal contract dissolved. I thought I'd have a string of affairs up and down the island, build my museum and never think about marriage or husbands ever again."

Though the plan made him smile, he couldn't see her succeeding with it. "Kat, you aren't Nellie. Nor are you Alice or Maddie, who both rushed into marriage. You're you, and that's enough. You have a big heart and an easy, natural charm, with an infectious personality that's impossible to refuse. So, do what makes you happy, not what you *think* you should be doing."

Seconds stretched as they stared at one another, with rain continuing to pelt against the windows. It was intimate, like they were isolated from the rest of the world. A glen in the middle of nowhere. He loved the city, with its towering steel and rough cobblestones, but he wouldn't care to be anywhere else at the moment except for in his lodge with this particular woman.

She licked her lips and the sight of her small pink tongue sent a wave of heat through him.

Christ, this girl. Even the simplest things she did were damn arousing.

When she began walking around the workbench, the bottom of his stomach hollowed out as hope ballooned in his chest. She stopped just out of reach and looked up at him, and a familiar sparkle in her gaze sent his blood rushing south. Her voice was soft. "Want to hear what I would like right now?"

The possibilities nearly made him light-headed. "With every single bone in my body."

"I want you . . . to teach me how to cook those fish."

Air rushed out of his lungs and he shook his head, trying to clear it. "Go and wash your hands, reinette. You can help me make dinner."

THEY ATE THE fish and drank champagne, all the while chatting companionably. It was nice. They hadn't shared a meal before, and Katherine was surprised by how charming and funny Preston was outside of the bedroom. Nearly all of their interactions the past month had been about kissing, rather than actually talking, and she liked this side of him.

You're you, and that's enough.

When she remembered the words, along with everything else he'd said, she felt warm and bubbly inside. Was that truly how he saw her?

It was all so confusing. Three hours ago she was prepared never to forgive or see him again. But then he caught and cooked her fish from the lake and said wonderful things about her, and she felt her resolve weakening. Was she so shallow, then?

It had been fun teasing him earlier. Probably cruel to make him think she was going to demand something naughty, but he deserved a little torture after everything he'd done.

Though honestly, her desire hadn't been a lie. Arousal had thrummed in her blood ever since she emerged from the bath and found him in the kitchen. Preston Clarke, domesticated. Who would've ever believed it? And how utterly fascinating.

"Are you finished?" he asked, gesturing to her plate.

"Yes, thank you."

He carried both their plates to the sink. "I'll clean those later. Would you like coffee?"

"Can you make coffee?"

"Of course. I don't keep day-to-day staff at the lodge. They come once a week to look after the place. So when I'm here, I generally fend for myself."

Strange, but it hadn't occurred to her before now that they were totally alone. She didn't mind, though. And, considering what she was wearing, it was preferable.

The rain hadn't let up and the sky was even darker. In another hour, it would be nighttime. Should she attempt to find her lodge? Not sure that was wise with two glasses of champagne in her stomach.

And what about the bears?

She peeked at Preston through her lashes. Of course, there were dangers here, as well. But this was a danger she well knew.

His mouth hitched as he leaned on the marble

toward her. "You're wearing an odd expression. Care to share?"

She gave him a half-truth. "I was noticing the hour and wondering if it's safe to return."

"It's still pouring, but if you want to go I'll find slickers and galoshes for us. I'll see that you get back to your lodge safely."

"You would do that for me?"

His expression softened, and the warmth she saw in his dark gaze curled her toes. "Haven't you realized by now the lengths I'll go to for you?"

Because he wanted to sleep with her again. It was the only reason he needed her forgiveness, so everything could go back to the way it was before.

Too much had changed, however.

Nothing would ever go back to how it was before, not now. He'd proven how little she meant to him. He would never love her, never care more about her than his company and buildings, and that hurt. She'd wanted to be more than a fleeting affair to him. She wanted to be his everything.

Silly, stupid Katherine.

She'd set out on an adventure, desperate for excitement, and ended up scorched instead. Somewhere along the way, between the games and the attention, she forgot her worth. She'd lost herself. But she wouldn't let him hurt her again. It was time to reclaim her dignity and self-respect.

Though perhaps after one more time together?

They were stuck here tonight, just the two of them, and it seemed fitting to enjoy one last round of meaningless pleasure with him. It was what he was good at, after all. She'd make certain to keep her heart firmly in her chest, locked away for the entire experience. Men did it all the time, so how hard could it be?

I'm rationalizing so I can sleep with him again.

"Katherine?" he asked when she didn't respond. "What's going on in your head?"

If only she knew.

Slipping off the stool, she headed toward him. "Why must I be so attracted to you?"

The lines of his face sharpened, intensified, as he tracked her approach, and ribbons of longing unfurled in her belly, her skin turning hot and itchy. He straightened but otherwise didn't move. "Is this the champagne's influence?"

"I wish." She was now directly in front of him, her neck craned to see him because of his obnoxious height. He was so big and solid, like a giant marble sculpture come to life. "Blaming the alcohol would make things easier."

"I would never force you."

She dragged her fingertips along the opening of his shirt, right at the base of his throat, to feel the warm smooth skin, and his chest rose and fell on a quick breath. "I know," she said, flicking open the buttons along his chest.

"Then, why? If you don't want to—"

"I want to." After sliding his suspenders off his shoulders, she yanked his shirttails out of his trousers and shoved the cotton up over his head. This left his impressive torso clad in a thin sleeveless undergarment, and she was impatient to see the rest of him. Her hands swept his shoulders. "You are annoyingly handsome."

"Annoying, is it?"

"Very."

He kept his arms at his sides while she plucked at the fastenings of his trousers. "Are you determined to do this here? The workbench is a good height for it, but the stone might not be comfortable for you."

The workbench? She looked in horror at the marble. "Where you were gutting the fish?"

Chuckling, he bent and lifted her up, guiding her legs around his waist. "Come along and let's find a proper bed. I want to take my time with you and I don't want you thinking about trout."

She wrapped around him and pressed her corset-less breasts against his chest. "I want to see where you sleep." She'd only yet seen the place he used for liaisons, not somewhere he actually lived. She was curious to see where he let down his guard and relaxed.

"It's not very exciting." He started up the wide staircase. "You'll be disappointed."

"Doubtful." She noticed the walls were bare here, too. "What do you have against works of art decorating the walls? That Sisley you were admiring at the exhibition would be perfect. Or perhaps a Turner or Cole painting."

"Make a list and I'll have them purchased and hung."

While she was flattered, she knew she wouldn't be around to see a list through. After tonight, she'd return to the city and move on from Preston Clarke. In time her broken heart would mend. She would eventually recover. Little by little, day by day, she'd find herself again.

They finally entered a large bedchamber that was both impersonal and yet utterly Preston at the same time. The bed, a huge wooden affair, was perfectly made, as if it hadn't been slept in. Plain walls—because this was Preston—and rustic wooden furniture that fit the style of the lodge. The curtains and bedclothes were dark blue, and there was a stack of papers on the nightstand with a pair of eyeglasses.

Instead of dropping her on the bed, he laid her down and followed, his big body covering hers. With so few layers separating them, she could feel every bit of his large frame, the weight of him overwhelming her senses. She couldn't resist running her foot along the back of his leg.

He propped on an elbow and used his free hand to caress her cheek. The tenderness in his gaze nearly did her in. "Tell me what you need, sweetheart," he whispered.

"You. This. Tonight."

A crease formed between his brows. "You aren't going to disappear on me again, are you?"

"No," she lied. "Though we can't stay here forever."

Warm lips began coasting over her throat, sending shivers of pleasure all along her skin. "Maybe we can," he whispered. "Maybe I'll keep you here and never let you go."

"Who will conquer New York City, then?"

"I'm only interested in conquering you."

They both knew that wasn't true—and she

didn't want more of his lies. Despite his promise to always tell her the truth, he'd schemed behind her back to get his hands on the Twenty-Third Street property. So she needed to keep this light and easy, nothing more than this bed and their pleasure. "Stop talking and get busy, Preston."

"I'm enjoying this take-charge side of you." Coming up onto his knees, he removed his shirt from her body. Then he worked to unbutton the union suit she wore, his fingers working too slowly for her liking.

She reached and unfastened his trousers. Then they worked together to rid themselves of their remaining clothes until they were both bare. Preston was a slab of sinewy muscle, with fascinating ridges and angles, and she just had tonight to explore him.

Pushing on his shoulder, she got him flat on his back and stretched out on the mattress, his hard cock resting on his belly. She'd taken him in her mouth only a handful of times, but she loved the way he'd responded to it, with a combination of surprise and savagery. Like he couldn't believe she was sucking him and he'd die if she stopped.

She untwisted the simple knot holding her long hair up, letting the strands fall around her shoulders, and leaned down to press kisses along his sternum. His hands threaded her hair as he moaned. "Christ, Kat," he whispered. "You're so beautiful."

His skin was warm and rough, the light coating of dark hair along his stomach tickling her nose. Then she reached his erection, the head swollen and smooth, with a glistening drop of moisture waiting at the tip. With a flick of her tongue she captured it, and he gasped. "Fuck. Do that again."

She licked him again, pressing harder this time, and he jerked, nearly levitating off the bed. "All of it, reinette," he growled. "Take all of it in your mouth."

He was demanding in bed, but she liked that about him. There was no fumbling or guesswork, and she loved driving him wild. So she opened her lips and engulfed the head, letting him feel the tight heat of her mouth. His hips rocked slightly, like he couldn't help himself, and she swallowed more of him.

"Oh, God. That's so good. Keep going."

The urge to tease him resurfaced and she pulled off, letting go of him with a pop. He huffed in frustration, so she clasped the base of his erection and gave him a long lick. "Patience, my king."

He chuckled softly. "You're killing me."

She took her time, using her mouth on every steely inch of him, going over him with her tongue, memorizing him. If this was their last encounter, she would use it to her advantage, build memories for years to come. She explored and mapped, even licking the heavy sac between his legs. By the time she took his cock in her mouth again, his thighs were shaking.

His fingers clasped the sides of her head, guiding her to move faster, then he jerked out of her mouth without warning. Confused, she looked up at him. His eyes were nearly opaque, glittering and dark with lust. "Get on your back. I need you. Right now."

Chapter Twenty-Four

❧

Something had changed between them tonight.

Preston could sense a restless desperation, one much different from the fervor of previous encounters, and Katherine hadn't smiled once. She was normally so playful, so responsive in bed, but she seemed serious this time. Dedicated to her task like she was being graded on it.

As she moved to lie on her back, he forced himself to drag in a deep breath and calm down. With her mouth on his cock, he'd been perilously close to coming—and he didn't want to rush this. Instead, he needed to take his time and shower her with attention, slow down to capture her every sigh and moan. He wanted to spend hours worshiping her, a penance they would both enjoy.

Exhaling, he leaned over and brushed his knuckles along the side of her breast. "Does this mean you've forgiven me?"

Instead of answering, her hand slid down his stomach to grasp his cock in a rough stroke. "I need you, Preston."

Pleasure punched along his shaft, through his

balls and wrapped around his thighs. "Damn it, Kat. You're going to make me come too soon."

Bending, he began lavishing attention on her breasts, sucking on her nipples until they were swollen and she was writhing beneath him. Then he kissed his way up her chest, along the side of her neck, her jaw. She continued rubbing his erection with a distracted hand, which was both a relief and incredibly frustrating.

"Part your thighs," he whispered against her mouth. "Let me feel you."

Her legs widened and his fingers skimmed her folds. The skin was slick, her arousal scenting the air between them, and desire tightened like a fist in his lower back. "Ah, yes. Feel how wet you are. Christ, sweetheart."

She rose up and sealed her mouth to his, her lips soft as they moved, drugging him with her sweetness, and he couldn't get enough. Circling her clit with two fingers, he slanted his lips over hers again and again, their breath mingling while their tongues tangled.

Her fingernails dug into his arms and her hips chased his touch. She broke off from his mouth on a long moan. "Please. God, please now."

He couldn't take it any longer.

Shifting between her legs, he angled his erection toward her entrance and began guiding himself in, staring at her the entire time. Katherine had never been more gorgeous, with her swollen lips and flushed skin. He loved this first part, when he slid into her wet heat and her eyes fluttered like she was overcome by the sheer bliss.

Suddenly, he froze. "Kat, I don't have a shield. I never keep them here and—"

"It's fine." She dragged him closer. "Just pull out before you finish. Don't stop."

Jesus, this was stupid. He never had intercourse without a shield. But this was what Katherine did to him. She unraveled him, altered his plans and obliterated all his good sense.

He needed to savor this, to enter her slowly, but her channel burned his skin while bathing his cock in slick warmth, and sweat gathered on his skin. It was the best kind of torture. His body screamed for him to thrust, to take, but he fought it, his teeth clenched in blissful agony.

She shifted to raise her knees up by his sides, widening herself, and he sank in the rest of the way. The breath left his lungs in a rush. "Fuck," he exhaled. "You're driving me out of my mind."

"Good. Stop being so careful. You can't control everything."

"Oh, I can't?" He gave a rough grind of his hips, making sure to drag his pelvis over her clit. "Are you certain about that?"

She threw her head back on a moan, the slim column of her throat stretched tight. Pressing his face there, he licked and bit the sensitive skin, and her walls contracted around his shaft. "Do that again," he whispered.

Her muscles squeezed him, sucking him even deeper, and his balls drew up tight, the ache nearly painful. He was lost. This sweet and playful girl was his undoing in every way. He growled into her ear. "Hold your knees up. Then I may show you how not careful I can be."

She placed her hands behind her knees, holding her legs high and wide, and he thrust so hard the bed jolted into the wall. For half a second he worried it was too rough, but then he felt her teeth sink into the meat of his shoulder, her groan echoing against his skin. Instinct took over. He braced his knees on the mattress and drove into her again and again, their bodies slapping together, while rough exhales filled the room.

He didn't stop, even when her moans turned to whines, her back arching. She whispered, "It feels so good. Keep going."

Slamming his lids shut, he churned his hips and used his body to give her as much pleasure as possible. Except the angle and the way she gripped him meant he wasn't going to last. The friction on the underside of his shaft was too delicious to be believed. "Use your fingers," he rasped. "Please, hurry."

When her hand moved between them, he could feel her fingers circling, rubbing, and he prayed she would peak soon. "Come on, darling. I want to feel you."

"Oh, God," she whispered as her body tensed.

He pushed up on his hands and continued moving. With her lips parted and her hair spread all around her, she was the most gorgeous thing he'd ever seen. Then she froze, and he was able to witness the exact second when the pleasure dawned over her. He noted every change, every twitch, as she came, and it was more satisfying than any project, any business deal he'd ever made. In this moment, he did feel like a goddamn king.

When her walls milked him rhythmically, he was forced to grit his teeth. That tight, warm clasp . . . it was too much.

Before she'd even stopped convulsing, he yanked out of her body, spend already gathering at the base of his cock. Thick ropes of white fluid shot across her thighs and mound as he trembled, a shout ripped from the depths of his soul. His vision temporarily wavered, and he struggled not to collapse on top of her as the orgasm went on and on. "So good," he groaned. "God. It gets better every single time."

When he finally returned to himself, he felt drained and totally content. Like everything had righted itself. Katherine wasn't angry with him anymore, and he had her back in his bed where she belonged.

Dropping onto the mattress beside her, he cupped her head and kissed her temple. "You've wrecked me."

She gestured to her lower half, where his fluids were currently drying on her skin. "I'd say I'm equally wrecked, then."

He chuckled and yawned. Satisfaction cloaked him like a soft blanket. "Give me a moment to catch my bearings, then I'll clean you up. Though I rather like seeing the mess we've made."

"Why am I not surprised?"

Pulling her close, he wrapped his arms around her. "Because you know me so well."

She hummed in her throat. "Right, which is how I know you'll start smoking at any moment."

Actually, it hadn't even occurred to him. He hadn't smoked in days, the itch completely absent while upstate. "Huh."

"What does that mean?"

"I just realized I haven't touched my cigarette case since I've been here."

"That's good. You should quit—either that or move up to the Adirondacks. It's clear you're a more relaxed and less intense version of yourself here."

"Less intense version? Am I so intolerable, then?"

"Well, I was attempting to be polite," she deadpanned.

He slid a hand to her ribs and dug in with his fingers, tickling her. It caused her to squirm and give the most delightful-sounding laugh. It also caused his spend to drip onto the bedclothes.

Fighting the urge to fall asleep, he grabbed her hand. "Let's clean up in the bath."

"I already took a bath." She pushed off the bed, slipping out of his grasp. "I'll just wipe off and return in a moment."

He enjoyed the sight of her luscious backside as she headed across the room toward the bathing chamber. "Should I help?"

"You've done enough, Preston."

He had, hadn't he? And he couldn't wait to do it again as soon as his body recovered.

The door closed behind her and he shut his eyes, allowing himself just a brief moment of rest before she returned.

Except when he awoke it was morning.

And she was gone.

As KATHERINE STEPPED onto the platform at Grand Central Depot, she was surprised to find Nellie there waiting for her. "I can't believe it. You're here."

Nellie reached to take Katherine's satchel. "Of course. You sounded upset on the telephone this morning. I wasn't about to let you struggle alone."

Gratitude filled Katherine's chest like a balloon. Using the hotel's telephone just after dawn, she rang Nellie and asked for help getting out of the Adirondacks as quickly as possible. Her friend had moved heaven and earth to have a private railcar waiting at the connection in Saratoga Springs. "Still, you didn't need to come," she said as they started walking. "The use of your father's private coach was more than enough."

"It was no problem. I had it rerouted from Albany. What's the benefit of having a father who owns most of the railroads on the East Coast if I can't rescue a friend in need?" Nellie studied Katherine's face. "You look exhausted."

Indeed, she was. She'd lain awake most of the night, thinking, wrestling with her feelings, and departed just as soon as the sun peeked out over the lake. Preston hadn't even twitched when she dressed and left.

Nellie held open the door at the top of the stairs. "Are you going to tell me what happened?"

"Preston happened."

"What? How?"

"He's been up there all week. Leaving me breakfast, cooking me fish for dinner. Mind you, this was after I told him to go away."

"That's . . . odd."

"Very. But last night, we had dinner together and . . ." She didn't need to say it, did she?

"And more." Nellie edged around a family stopped to study a departure board. "Were you ready for more?"

"I asked for it, actually. I wanted one last time with him."

"I'm sure he didn't argue about that."

"He didn't know. He thinks it means I've forgiven him."

Nellie wrinkled her nose. "I'm not one to take Preston's side, but that seems a bit harsh, Katie. Why didn't you talk to him?"

Katherine ignored the small sliver of guilt that tried to wrap around her heart as the two women continued through the busy station. The chaos made it impossible to carry on a private conversation, which suited Katherine just fine. Nellie went directly to a side door and stepped through, and soon they were outside, where a closed carriage waited at the curb.

"This is us," Nellie said, tilting her head toward the conveyance.

When they settled inside, Katherine exhaled. "You are the very best friend a girl could ask for."

"I know. But don't think I won't return to our earlier conversation. I don't understand why you didn't talk to Preston about how you were feeling."

"What good would it have done? He's already apologized and I told him I can't forgive him."

"Can't?" Nellie cocked her head, her expression almost disappointed. "You have the biggest heart of anyone I know. Can you really not get past this?"

"He stole that property away from me!"

"And are you surprised?" Nellie huffed a laugh. "This is Preston we're talking about. You know his reputation. He didn't hide his feelings about your father. And he repeatedly warned you the property was his and not to get attached to it. You want to know what I think?"

Katherine picked at a loose thread on the quilt, not meeting her friend's eyes. "No, not anymore," she grumbled.

"Ha! You just want me to take your side. Well, I will always tell it to you straight, Miss Let's-go-cavorting. I think you've fallen in love with the man."

"Don't be ridiculous," Katherine lied instantly. "That would be incredibly stupid of me."

"Not if he shared your feelings. And, considering he trailed you up to Lake George and played private chef for five days, I'd say that he does."

Haven't you realized by now the lengths I'll go to for you?

Still, it was impossible. Preston, in love with her? She nearly snorted. He merely wished to bed her again, to begin their trysts once more. To distract her from the fight over Twenty-Third Street.

And even if all that weren't true, she was a Delafield. He could never love her, not after what happened between their fathers.

"You're wrong," she told Nellie. "He doesn't feel anything for me."

"I disagree. You should've seen him at my

house, Katie. He was like a rabid dog, wanting to know where you were."

"What? Preston came to see you?" She angled toward her friend. "When?"

"A few days after you left. He begged me to tell him where you were. *Begged*, Katie. And he was livid when I wouldn't." Nellie bumped Katherine's knee with her own. "Told me he cared about you. A lot."

"He did? Those were his words?"

"Yes. I almost felt sorry for him—but then I remembered how he hurt you and I was cured of any sympathy."

Katherine couldn't believe it. Preston had begged Nellie for information? "He must've hated that you wouldn't help him. He's used to getting his way."

"Like I said, he was quite angry when I refused. All in all, I think this is very good for Preston. You're humbling him. Showing him that he can't have everything he wants by sheer force of will alone."

"I'm not doing it intentionally. He hurt me."

"I know." Nellie rubbed Katherine's shoulder. "How are you feeling about your father and his engagement?"

"Better." Katherine exhaled slowly. "I think if I were married and settled it wouldn't have bothered me as much. But I felt like he was creating a new life for himself, while I still have no one."

"Your father is still your father, no matter who he's married to or sleeping with—"

"Ew, Nellie. Please." Katherine did not want to picture Daddy and Mrs. Whittier in bed. Ever.

"I hate to break it to you," Nellie said dryly, "but they are screwing, Katie."

"I know, but that doesn't mean I want to think about it."

"Fine, but you're not losing him. Or the memories of your mother. He's lonely. That's all."

"Would you mind if your father married Mrs. Paulson?" Mrs. Paulson was Cornelius Young's longtime lady friend, a woman with whom Nellie was quite friendly.

"I wouldn't mind at all. I want him to be happy, and if Mrs. Paulson makes him happy, then so be it. He still loves my mother. Nothing will ever change that." Nellie sighed. "Death doesn't mean we forget. The pain becomes easier to manage, but we have to keep moving forward. All of us have to continue living the best way we know how."

"You're so wise. I wish I were as well adjusted as you are."

Nellie snorted and rested her head on Katherine's shoulder. "I'm not well adjusted. I'm a mess, just like every other human on the planet. But I have experience with grief and loss."

"It will be so strange to see her in our house, in my mother's chairs."

"At first, but you'll grow accustomed to it. Would your mother want him to be alone and sad for the rest of his life?"

Katherine swallowed hard. No, Mama wouldn't have wanted that. She'd loved him fiercely. Before she died, Mama asked Katherine to take good care of him.

Shame crawled over her skin like a swarm of

insects. She truly had acted selfishly, like a spoiled child. God, would Daddy ever forgive her? What about Mrs. Whittier? Instead of congratulating both of them, Katherine had run off to the woods to hide.

"I owe both of them an apology," she said quietly. "Running away wasn't like me at all."

"You were taken by surprise. Your father should have told you ahead of time, made sure you were comfortable with the idea of it. But I think your escape upstate had more to do with Preston than you're letting on."

Probably. Katherine hadn't expected him to betray her, even though he'd told her he was dishonorable. Why hadn't she listened?

Because she'd wanted to believe that he cared for her more than everything else.

Which meant she was a fool. Perhaps someday he might feel that way about someone, but Katherine wasn't waiting around for it. She would find another property for her mother's museum and put Preston Clarke firmly out of her mind.

She yawned and rested her head atop Nellie's. "Thank you, Nels," she murmured. "I don't know what I would do without you."

"Obviously you'd have a lot less fun."

Katherine chuckled. "True. Promise me you won't ever leave New York. We'll remain friends forever and throw fabulous parties, like Mrs. Fish and Mrs. Vanderbilt."

"I promise, but only if we choose more broadminded role models."

"I'll leave the planning to you," Katherine muttered and closed her eyes.

"So, are you coming home with me or am I dropping you off at home?"

As much as Katherine dreaded the conversation ahead, she had to clear the air with her father. "My home. I can't hide out any longer. I need to apologize."

"And what about Preston?"

"Who?"

A sound of surprised amusement left Nellie's lips. "I see. Good luck with that. Something tells me Preston won't like being ignored, so you'd best prepare yourself."

Chapter Twenty-Five

❧

$\mathcal{H}$e went straight to the Delafield mansion.

After frantically checking for Katherine everywhere within a five-mile radius of the lodge, Preston finally learned she'd left for the city on the morning train. The relief at discovering she hadn't been mauled by a bear or lost in the woods nearly sent him to his knees. Thank God she wasn't hurt.

Anger quickly followed, however. She couldn't have jotted a quick note to tell him not to worry, that she was going back home?

So he raced from the Adirondacks to Manhattan, fueled by the desperation to see her and the need for an explanation. Still, it took most of the day. By the time he arrived on her doorstep, it was almost four o'clock in the afternoon.

After pounding on the door with the knocker, he smoothed his wrinkled suit. He hadn't even bothered to shave this morning and had thrown on whatever he could find. His boots were still caked with mud from tromping around the lodge, yelling her name.

The door swung open and the butler's brows rose dramatically. No doubt Preston looked a disheveled mess. "Miss Delafield, please."

Despite the height difference, the butler looked down his nose at Preston. "Do you have a card, sir?"

"I'm fresh out at the moment. Tell her it's Mr. Clarke. She'll see me."

"Come in and I will inquire as to whether she is available."

When Preston tried to step in, the butler held out an arm, stopping him. "Your feet, sir."

He glanced down. Right, the mud. Bending, he ripped off his boots, left them on the stoop and walked in. The butler appeared scandalized, but Preston didn't care. He didn't have time to waste.

"If you'll wait over there, sir," the man said with a sniff and waved Preston toward the drawing room.

Once inside, Preston paced and awaited Katherine's arrival. She owed him answers. After last night, after everything they'd shared, she'd snuck out of his lodge and disappeared this morning. Hadn't she realized the danger? Hadn't she cared that he would be worried sick about her when he woke up?

When had his reinette become so reckless? So inconsiderate? This wasn't like her at all.

"Well, this is a surprise."

Preston turned at the deep voice and found Lloyd in the doorway. Katherine's father was staring at Preston oddly—and not because of his bootless feet.

"Lloyd," Preston said by way of greeting. "I am calling for Katherine."

"Yes, that's what my butler said. What I don't understand is why."

Preston gnashed his teeth together. He didn't owe this man an explanation. Furthermore, it was still working hours. Why was Lloyd even here? "To check on her well-being."

"I see." Lloyd strolled deeper into the room, closing the distance between them. "I heard you were out of town this week. You weren't up at Lake George by any chance, were you?"

"I don't see what business it is of yours."

"It's my business when you have clearly ruined my daughter, Preston. Do you plan to do the honorable thing?"

Honorable. He nearly snorted. "Don't lecture me about honor as if you're familiar with the concept."

"Whatever my transgressions, I never ruined an innocent girl. Do you really think this will stay quiet? That no one will find out about you following her up there?"

"This is between Katherine and me, no one else."

"Wrong. None of us exist alone, Preston. Not even you. Do you think the Manhattan Sureties of the world will do business with you if it gets around? These companies value family and respectability. Trustworthiness. Do you honestly think you'll convince any of them to work with you if I let it be known what you've done?"

"Is this . . . ?" Preston pinched the bridge of his

nose between his thumb and forefinger. "Are you *blackmailing* me?"

"No, I'm stating facts."

"Jesus Christ This is low, even for you. Do you think she'd forgive you for forcing us together like that? You've already caused her enough grief by springing your engagement on her. Did you ever once consider how such news would affect your daughter, you selfish piece of shit?"

Lloyd's face turned red. "Selfish, right. I'm the selfish one for committing to the woman I care about. Just so we're clear, Clarke, I planned on telling Katherine myself but my sister got overly excited and shared the news before I could. I love Katherine. I would never purposely hurt her. Can you say the same?"

"I don't want to hurt her, either."

"And yet you have. You let your greed and ambition get in the way of her happiness, not to mention your bitterness. If not for your misguided opinions of me, you would marry her."

"They're hardly misguided." Preston snarled. "I know exactly what kind of man you are, about your greed and ambition."

Lloyd's nostrils flared, his gaze turning hard. "Yes, I was so awful that I carried your father, ignoring his gambling problem and covering his losses, for eleven years. Eleven *years*, Preston. However, I did it because I cared about him and I knew he would lose everything once I stopped. At the time, you were still young and incapable of taking over, so I had to wait until you got older. When I was sure you were competent, that's when

I dissolved the joint business and distanced myself from Henry."

"You make it all sound so benevolent. Why not try to help him instead?"

"Do you think I didn't try? Your father wouldn't listen. I went to the usual haunts and told them not to lend him any more money. He just found others who would. It was like trying to stop water running through a sieve. I did the best I could until you were older."

"You couldn't wait two more years until I graduated? I was in my sophomore year at Harvard, for God's sake."

"There wasn't time. Your father knew he was sick, and began gambling even more. He wanted to win it all back before he died, except he had terrible luck. Another few months and it all would've disappeared."

"Fine, that explains why I had to quit school. But why bid against me on every parcel I tried to buy? If not for Forrest's loan, I would've lost the house."

"I thought it was best if you learned to handle things on your own."

Preston dragged a hand down his face. "Thank you for that. You abandoned Henry and me, then tried to sabotage me at every turn."

"I never sabotaged you. I wanted to force you to learn what it takes to survive in such a cutthroat and dangerous business. Sometimes the only way a man can make his way in this world is by making it."

"Insightful. Read that in an advert for union suits, did you?"

Lloyd's arms dropped against his sides as if he were exasperated. "What I'm saying is that you would never have gone so far in such a short amount of time if I helped you. You didn't need it, and look at how successful you are now."

This was more than Preston could handle at the moment. He didn't want to acknowledge that there might be a grain of truth to what Lloyd had said. He didn't want to feel anything besides hatred for this man. "Where is Katherine? I want to see her."

"She doesn't want to see you."

"I don't believe you." Though a sickening feeling settled in Preston's stomach, the fear that Lloyd may be right. She left without a word, after all.

"I was with her when you were announced," Lloyd said. "She's not coming."

"You're lying." Preston strode out of the drawing room and headed for the stairs. A hand landed on his arm, stopping him.

"Have you lost your mind?" Lloyd's mouth was flat and unhappy. "You are not going to bumble around my home, looking for her."

Fine. If that was how they were going to play this, then he'd find another way. Preston threw his head back and bellowed, "Katherine! Come out here right now."

"Get out of my house." Lloyd began shoving him toward the front door, but Preston kept watch on the steps.

"I want to speak with her."

"Marry her and you can speak with her all you like."

Marry her.

The words whispered across Preston's skin and sank into whatever was left of his soul, the idea both tantalizing and fantastical at the same time. He hated that it was Lloyd who teased him with it, dangling his own daughter out like a piece of fruit to a starving man. Anger caused him to snap, "You'd like that, wouldn't you, if I honored that ridiculous betrothal agreement?"

"Actually, no. I want her to marry someone who loves and respects her. I'm not convinced you are—"

"Daddy, stop."

Both men spun toward the stairs and there she was, looking tired but incredibly beautiful. Preston's heart thumped hard in his chest, as if the organ beat just for her. "Katherine."

Her gaze held no warmth, no hint that they'd exchanged bone-rattling orgasms last night. "Mr. Clarke, I'll see you in the drawing room."

RIPPING HIS ARM from Lloyd's grip, Preston returned to the drawing room, where he paced like a caged tiger. He heard Katherine having a quiet word with her father in the corridor, but he was too far away to make out what they were saying. Then she entered and he had to suppress the impulse to take her into his arms. He wanted to hold her close, to feel her skin and smell her hair.

He never wanted to let her go.

She slid the pocket door closed, giving them some privacy. When she turned, she crossed her arms and glared at him. "Have you lost all your good sense? I spent most of the day trying to convince my father nothing happened between you and I, and you've ruined that effort in just a few seconds."

"I woke up and you were gone, Kat. I have been worried sick."

"I wrote you a note."

"Where? I didn't find any note."

"On the workbench in your kitchen."

He hadn't done more than poke his head into the kitchen while searching for her. "Rather an odd place to leave such an important piece of paper, wouldn't you say?"

"I thought you'd see it first thing, while you were making coffee."

"Why on earth would I be making coffee when you are missing?"

"I wasn't missing, Preston. I left."

"I thought you were lost in the woods or had been eaten by a bear."

"I apologize. I didn't think you'd be so worried."

A frustrated noise escaped his throat. "You didn't think I would worry? My God, Katherine. I think today took ten years off my life."

"I'm sorry. Truly."

He stepped closer, needing to erase the distance between them. "Didn't you believe me when I said I care about you?"

"Yes. I think, in your own way, you care about me. But it's not enough, Preston."

"In my own way? What does that mean?"

She was calm and poised, as if the answer was obvious. "It means you care about your projects and your company more than anything else. Your priorities are clear."

It was an accusation he'd heard before from countless people in his life, but this was the first time it felt unwarranted. "Is that why I chased you to the Adirondacks for the better part of a week? I've ignored everything for days in order to look after you."

"Out of guilt! You stole that property from my father, from me, and because you'd like me"—she dropped her voice to barely above a whisper— "back in your bed, you rushed upstate to calm my ruffled feathers."

He opened his mouth to deny it . . . and promptly shut it. She wasn't wrong, though he didn't like how it was phrased. "First of all, I didn't steal that property. Your father stole it from me, and I rightfully took it back. Next, I can't deny that I'd like to carry on with our relationship."

"Of course you would," she murmured dryly. "And you get everything you want, don't you?"

"You know that's not true."

She pressed her lips together and gave him her profile, her gaze on the painting above the mantel. He forced himself to be patient, though he longed to hear what was going on in her head. "Preston," she finally said, her voice tight and low. "I lose at every turn with you. The betrothal agreement, the property. Even my heart. I keep losing and losing. Eventually I need to—" She broke off and dragged in a deep breath. "I need to put myself first or else I fear there'll be nothing left."

A wound opened up in his chest, like his skin was being torn apart. Was that how she saw him? Their interactions? "I never meant to hurt you.

With any of it. God, Kat. I'd rather die than cause you any pain."

When she faced him again, her eyes were glistening. "But you did, intentional or not. I'm sorry, but I can't do this any longer."

I was in love with you, and you broke my heart. It can't be repaired.

Those had been her words upon his arrival upstate and, even after the last five days, nothing had changed. She couldn't forgive him.

Yes, but do I deserve her forgiveness?

Perhaps not, but he knew in this moment that he was not ready to give up on her, on *them*. He couldn't see his life without her in it. There'd never been a woman who owned him body and soul like this, and the idea that he might lose her made him want to drop to his knees and beg her to stay.

He hadn't ever said the words to a woman before, but he knew what this bone-deep fear meant. This obsession with everything about her, the need to constantly be at her side.

He had to tell her. Now, before it was too late.

Closing the distance between them, he cradled her jaw in his hands. "Katherine, I love you. I'm in love with you. Please, say you will love me back."

A single tear escaped her lashes and slid along the slope of her cheek. She eased away from him and his arms fell uselessly to his sides. "I can't. It's not fair to myself. I cannot be a pawn for you to dismiss and manipulate. I must stand on my own."

"I will help you to do that," he rushed to say.

"Take the property in Washington Heights. Let's build your museum there."

"How is that standing on my own, exactly?"

"Katherine, I know how to oversee these sorts of projects and get them done quickly. It'll make it easier for you."

She clasped her hands together and placed them under her chin, gazing heavenward as if looking for patience. "You are not listening to me, which only proves my point. It proves how ill-suited we are."

Panic began to fill his chest, like water rising in a flood. He struggled to breathe, the air in the room in shorter and shorter supply. "No, you're wrong. We're perfectly suited, and we share the same interests. In fact, I think you should marry me."

While he'd blurted the words, he didn't consider taking them back. He wanted to marry her.

She didn't appear thrilled by his declaration. Quite the opposite, as more tears tracked down her cheeks. "That was the most astonishingly terrible proposal of marriage I've ever heard, and that is saying a lot considering *Pride and Prejudice* is my favorite novel."

This was rapidly turning into a disaster. "I didn't have time to plan out a proper proposal, but I will. I'll give you all the romance and heartfelt emotion you can stand."

"I don't want it. Furthermore, I'm not certain I'd believe it."

Ouch. The words stung. "I've never lied to you, Kat."

"Not directly to me, no. Yet you forged a deed

to get it out of my hands. You told me you were dishonest, but I didn't listen, did I?"

"I will repeat this until you believe me: that land always belonged to me, never your father."

She edged toward the hallway. "We're done here. I have things to do and no doubt you have a mountain of work awaiting you."

His hands curled into fists at his sides. This wasn't it. "We aren't done discussing this. If you think I won't fight for you, that I won't tear this city apart with my bare fucking hands to make you mine, then you are dead wrong."

A clock chimed somewhere nearby but he didn't take his eyes off her as they studied one another. He didn't know what else he could say.

Her expression never changed as she said, "Goodbye, Preston."

She started for the door and alarm filled him, so he darted to block her path. Swallowing, he blurted, "Please, Katherine. Don't hate me. I need you so much."

Her palm stretched to rest on his jaw, her thumb brushing his cheek. "I don't hate you, you complicated man, but I need more than what you're willing to give me. You're like those towers you build—solid and impenetrable. As unshakable as bedrock. Go, conquer the world." Her voice cracked slightly. "You'll be fine without me."

"No, please. Don't do this. Give me a chance to make it right."

She let her hand fall slowly. "There's no point. We don't need more chances to see what we both know is impossible." Edging around him, she slid open the door and disappeared.

Chapter Twenty-Six

❧

His hands were sweating.

Preston sat in the anteroom, leg bouncing, as nerves assaulted his insides. This had to work. He'd mapped out the entire plan in his head and it all hinged on this meeting right here.

He hadn't been this worried since he returned from Harvard and learned his family was on the precipice of losing everything.

The office door opened. "Mr. Delafield will see you now, Mr. Clarke," the secretary said, moving aside.

Preston rose and walked in. Lloyd was behind his desk, surrounded by papers. He didn't bother to stand. "You have a lot of nerve coming here, Clarke. Almost as much nerve as when you shouted down my house the other day."

"I apologize for that." He lowered himself into one of the armchairs. "However, I'm not here to discuss your daughter."

"I'm not sure what else we have to discuss."

Preston folded his hands, took in a deep breath

and let it out slowly. "I want to merge our companies again."

Lloyd's mouth fell open and stunned silence filled the room. "You . . . what?"

"Clarke Holdings and Delafield & Associates. I want to merge them together, as they were before."

Lloyd stared across the desk, his fingers drumming on the wood. "Why?"

"Because I found someone I want to marry. A beautiful and smart girl I can't live without—and I want to spend time with her, take her traveling. Raise children together. I want to build a life with her, not a fraction of a life, which is all I could give her if I continue running Clarke Holdings by myself."

"This is about my daughter."

"Yes. I'd like your permission to marry her." The words weren't hard to say. He no longer cared what Lloyd thought or anything about their history. The only person who mattered was Katherine.

Lloyd stroked his jaw. "Something tells me if I say no that you'll pursue her, anyway."

"Correct, but I know she'd prefer to have your blessing."

"Have you ruined her?"

Preston shook his head. "She has ruined me. I love her more than anything else on earth. More than reason, certainly. And more than any grudges I've been holding."

"I actually believe you."

Preston reached into the satchel he'd brought,

withdrew a brown folder and tossed it onto the desk. "A gesture of good faith."

Lloyd lifted the cover of the folder, then his eyebrows climbed toward his hairline. "This is the deed to Twenty-Third Street."

"I want you and Katherine to have it."

"What about Manhattan Surety? The tallest building in the world?"

"I told Manhattan Surety I no longer own the land. Whatever they decide to do now is up to them. If it falls through, there'll be other buildings and other projects."

Katherine's father gestured to the deed. "Are you trying to bribe her? Because I'm not certain it will work. She's put in an offer on a piece of land in Brooklyn."

That was fast, but he'd expect nothing less from Katherine. When she set her mind on a task, it was accomplished. No doubt she'd already comprised lists of things that needed to be done.

"Not a bribe," Preston said. "If you say Henry sold it to you, then I choose to believe you. Therefore, I never had any legal claim to the property."

"Until we merge the two companies together, of course."

Preston held up his palms. "If you want to exclude existing assets from the merger, I would agree to that stipulation."

"You're serious."

"Absolutely."

"I don't know what to say to all of this." Lloyd leaned back in his chair. "What happens if Katherine refuses the marriage proposal? Will you renege on the offer to join companies?"

"She won't refuse." He tried to sound confident, though doubt plagued him. There was every chance this wouldn't work, that he was handing over his entire family business to Lloyd Delafield for nothing. "But I'll honor our deal, no matter what happens with your daughter."

Lloyd still didn't look convinced, the skepticism plain in the creases on his brow. "What makes you think I wish to hand over half of my company to you?"

"Three reasons. First, because I'm turning over half of mine to you in exchange. Second, you'll want more time to spend with your new bride."

"And the third?"

"I'm about to become your son-in-law."

A small smile tugged at the other man's mouth. "You certainly have confidence, I'll give you that. Fine, I accept on one condition. If Katherine agrees to marry you, we'll merge the two businesses."

The knot between Preston's shoulder blades eased ever so slightly. That was one mountain scaled. "Excellent. I'll have our lawyers get in touch." He stood and reached out to offer his hand. "I look forward to working together."

Lloyd smirked and rose out of his chair, then shook Preston's hand. "Don't get ahead of yourself, son. Whatever happened between you two has hurt her. I haven't seen her this sad since her mother died."

That news tore through Preston's gut like a dull blade, causing him to wince. "I have a lot to atone for, but no one is more determined when they set their mind to a task."

"I believe it. Good luck."

It was said with complete sincerity, which Preston didn't expect. "I'm surprised you're being so supportive."

"Do you know why your father and I betrothed our only children?"

"A temporary fit of insanity?"

Lloyd buttoned his coat and shook his head. "No, not quite. We never intended to force either of you to marry. The goal was to put you in each other's path, hoping if you met there might be an attraction."

"Was that why you encouraged her to come see me about the wedding details?" The sparkle in Lloyd's gaze gave Preston all the answer he needed. Which made him realize something else. "So, the Twenty-Third Street deed? You did this to bring Katherine and I into contact again?"

Lloyd shoved his hands into his trouser pockets, looking quite pleased with himself. "Remind me to give you the name of my forger. He's a lot better than yours."

"Jesus Christ," Preston breathed, dragging a hand across his jaw. "You are one devious son of a bitch."

"As are you, son, which is why I trust Katherine with you. You'll do whatever it takes to look after her."

"Yes, I definitely will."

Lloyd gestured to the door. "Go get her, then."

"THANK YOU FOR coming with me this afternoon, Katherine," Alice said as the carriage bounced along East Seventy-Fourth Street. "Kit is busy at the supper club and I need a second opinion on a town house we're thinking of buying."

Alice rang this morning to ask Katherine to tea and to accompany her uptown for an errand. As Katherine was still waiting to hear about the offer on the Brooklyn property, she wasn't terribly busy these days. Also, she hoped an outing with her friend would provide respite from her heartache.

God, Kat. I'd rather die than cause you any pain.

Yet he had, again and again. She was so tired of thinking and remembering, allowing Preston to take up space in her heart and mind. When would this end?

Katherine peered out of the carriage window as they began to slow. "Alice, are you certain this is the house you and Kit are thinking of buying? It doesn't look for sale." The town house had no plants on the stoop, no flower boxes. The curtains were closed. It looked about as welcoming as a graveyard.

"I love the neighborhood," Alice said, in a voice that sounded distracted.

East Seventy-Fourth . . . Didn't Preston live on this street somewhere? No wonder Kit wanted to move here. The two friends would ride downtown together and attend dinner parties at each other's home. An ache sharpened in Katherine's chest, like a clamp was squeezing her ribs.

When they stopped, Alice got out first. "Shall we go poke around inside?"

Katherine started to examine the surrounding town houses, wondering, but quickly caught herself. He wasn't here—not at this time of day, anyway—and she didn't care. Lifting her chin, she tried to smile at Alice. "Lead the way."

At the top of the steps, Alice withdrew a key from her bag, which seemed odd. Before Katherine could ask about it, though, Alice had thrown open the front door and started waving Katherine in. "After you," her friend said.

Katherine stepped inside the foyer—and drew to a halt. The walls . . .

Paintings covered the walls, many of the frames so close they touched, as if the owner needed to adorn every bit of plaster with artwork. She recognized some of the works, but many were unfamiliar landscapes and cityscapes. Flowers and fruit. People and animals. The images surrounded the foyer and swept up the main stairs.

The door snapped shut behind her. Katherine turned to make a comment to her friend . . . but the space was empty. "Alice?"

"Katherine, I'm sorry! I hope you forgive me."

Forgive her? Whatever for?

Then it hit her. East Seventy-Fourth Street. The paintings. Alice disappearing.

Preston.

Dash it. Katherine closed her eyes and drew in several deep breaths. "Alice Ward, you come back here right now."

There was no answer. Unbelievable.

He wanted to see her? Fine. She'd tell him it didn't matter how many paintings he hung, she wasn't interested. Her mind had been made up in the Adirondacks. Preston would always love his company more than any woman. Certainly more than *her*.

She turned and looked at the interior of the house. There was no sound, the place as quiet as a tomb. Was he planning on ignoring her? And where were his servants?

A flash of green and white on the ground caught her eye. Orange blossoms. Not just one, either. A string of the flowers trailed up the steps, their delicate citrus scent hanging in the air. She couldn't help but drag in a lungful of the heady aroma. What was she supposed to do? Did he want her to follow the flowers?

This was a silly game. Still, she had to admit, she was curious. Yes, this fluttering excitement in her chest was only curiosity.

Climbing the stairs, she called out, "Preston, this is a waste of your time."

The flowers continued toward a set of double doors. In most homes the ballroom was situated here. She couldn't imagine Preston actually had a ballroom, though.

She pushed open the door slowly, unsure of what she'd find.

There was no missing him. Preston stood in the middle of the huge room, wearing a formal gray morning suit complete with top hat. Rows of lit candles flickered to give a soft, romantic atmosphere, while a single harpist sat in the corner. Goodness, was that Louis Sherry himself? He and four waiters surrounded a round dining table.

All the breath left her lungs in a rush. "What is happening?"

Preston advanced, closing the distance between them. "Hello." The dying afternoon light cast a soft glow on his features, and he offered her a small smile. Was there insecurity lurking in his dark eyes?

"What is this?"

"You said you needed more than I was prepared to give. But, Kat, I'm willing to give you everything you want, everything I have. Anything to get you to stay with me forever."

Forever? Her gaze darted around the room. "I don't understand."

Then the pieces began to slide into place. The orange blossoms, the harpist. The way he was dressed.

It was everything she'd once imagined for their wedding.

She sucked in a breath and blinked up at him. "My journal."

Preston reached into his pocket and withdrew the book where she'd written all of her wedding ideas. His voice was low, but laced with intensity. "If you marry me, reinette, I will always put you first. I'll dedicate my life to making you happy each day."

It was almost everything she'd hoped for, but didn't he realize that nothing had changed? "Preston, you won't feel that way in a year or two. You'll be back to your projects and long hours. Your need to win at all costs."

"I promise, I won't. Your father and I are merging our companies again."

The room seemed to pause, the air growing

thinner as her brain slowly caught up. "You and Daddy are . . . ?" She shook her head. That made no sense. "You must be joking."

"I told you, nothing matters more to me than you. Your father may not be my favorite person, but he knows our business well. We can form one large company and share the responsibilities."

She pressed her fingers to her lips. "You and my father, co-owning Clarke Holdings?"

"Clarke-Delafield Holdings, but yes." He moved closer, until she could smell the sandalwood and leather, the heat from his body causing bumps to race over her skin. "I don't want to work this hard. I want to travel with you, spend time with you. Play games and raise a family. I want to love you and be loved in return. There is more to life than office towers and apartment buildings, but only if you're by my side."

Slowly, he lowered to one knee, almost as if giving her a chance to stop him. Then he held out a blue box she recognized from Mr. Tiffany's store and opened it. A huge diamond—emerald cut, just as she'd drawn in her journal—winked up at her. "Katherine, will you do me the great honor—"

Bending slightly, she cut him off with a kiss. She didn't care if there were people in the room or that it wasn't proper. They'd ignored propriety from the beginning, so why start now?

His lips were warm and soft, and every bit as demanding as she remembered. God, she'd missed kissing him. This was like air and food and water all rolled into one, and she would never get enough of this man. Not breaking off from her mouth, he rose and held her face in his big palms, his tongue stroking over hers again and again. The faint strains of a harp filled her ears as Preston overwhelmed her other senses, his mouth her only anchor.

When they parted, he pressed his forehead to hers. "Does this mean yes?"

"Yes," she breathed. "But I may want a smaller, not-so-lavish wedding. One we can plan faster."

"I won't argue about that."

She patted his lapel, then stepped away. There was something else she wanted right now, and they didn't need an audience for it.

Within a few minutes, she'd thanked everyone and sent them away, leaving just her and Preston surrounded by flickering candles and orange blossoms. She picked up one of the flowers and held it to her nose. "You are very resourceful, Mr. Clarke. I never would've taken you for a romantic at heart."

"Only when it comes to you, apparently. I love you madly, Kat."

"I love you, too." She gave him a small teasing smile and dragged the blossom along his jaw. "My king."

Heat flared in his eyes at her words and a large hand settled on her hip to bring her closer. "Is my reinette in need of servicing?"

She wrapped her arms around his neck and let him feel the length of her body against his. "Desperately."

Walking backward, he began leading her toward the door. "We must take care of that, then.

Come along. I've been eager to see you in my bed for weeks."

Grinning, she trailed him to his chambers, already compiling a list in her head of all the ways they would service each other today . . . and every day thereafter.

Chapter Twenty-Seven

✦

Epilogue

Brooklyn, 1898

The crowd was twice what they'd expected.

Katherine stared out at the faces, the hundreds of people who were here for the opening of the Brooklyn Modern Art Museum. Nerves bubbled in her stomach. Would they love the art she'd carefully chosen? Enough to travel across the river regularly?

The idea was risky. But, as her husband liked to say, the most successful projects all started off as someone's wild idea.

Speaking of Preston, her eyes drifted toward where he stood, tall and commanding near the side of the dais. Kit and Alice were there, as well, along with Maddie and Harrison. Her friends were smiling proudly at Katherine, while Preston cuddled the newest arrival to their little group against his broad chest. Though she wasn't yet six months old, Elizabeth Victoria Clarke went everywhere with her father. Even Brooklyn.

The borough president gestured to where

Katherine stood with her father. "Next, we'll hear from the Delafield family, whose name presides over the museum atrium."

They agreed that Katherine would speak, so she stepped up and told the crowd of her mother's passion for modern art and the intention to keep the museum free to visitors. She thanked Eva Mansfield, the architect who'd shared her vision for the massive Beaux Arts structure. Then the ribbon was cut, the museum officially opened and throngs of New Yorkers streamed up the steps and through the front doors.

"She would have loved this, Kitty Kat," her father said as he watched the crowd. "You've done a marvelous thing."

"Thank you, Daddy. I couldn't have done this without you and Preston, though."

"Nonsense. You had the vision from the beginning. And this ended up a much better location for what you were trying to accomplish."

"It is, isn't it?"

Rebecca, her father's second wife, approached, a big genuine smile on her face. "Congratulations, Katherine."

Katherine hugged her stepmother, kissing the other woman's cheek. They'd grown close over the last three years, and Katherine now considered Rebecca a friend. "Thank you."

The crowd obscured Katherine's view of her daughter and husband, so she merely waited, chatting with her father about the projects he and Preston were currently taking on. Joining the businesses had benefited both men, both financially and personally. Her father traveled more with Rebecca, while Preston was . . . relaxed. Practically easygoing these days. He loved nothing more than being home with her and little Lizzy.

When the number of people dwindled, she looked for the tall dark head belonging to her husband. She breathed a sigh when she found him—but noticed another very tall man standing with the group, a red-haired woman at his side. The woman turned slightly, and Katherine's stomach leapt into her throat. "Nellie!"

Nellie spun at the sound and her face broke into a huge grin as she rushed forward. The two women collapsed into each other, arms holding tight, as they both talked over the other. Katherine laughed as they parted, her eyes wet with tears of happiness. "I didn't think you were coming."

"And miss this?" Nellie swept her hand toward the huge marble structure. "Not on your life. Also, I brought you a surprise. Come, I want you to meet someone."

They walked toward Preston and the others. Her husband's mouth was curved into a knowing smile, but Katherine hadn't the faintest idea what was going on. Nellie took Katherine's hand and gestured to the very tall man with a perfectly styled beard and mustache. "Katie, allow me to present Mr. John Sargent."

Katherine's mouth fell open. "No . . . Is it? Oh, my goodness." It was all she could think to say in front of such artistic royalty. John Singer Sargent was one of the world's most famous painters, his portraits a status symbol among the wealthy and powerful.

His lips twitched as he bowed over her hand. "A pleasure, Mrs. Clarke. Eleanor has told me so much about you and I'm honored to meet such an important patron of the arts."

"The honor is all mine," Katherine gushed. "I cannot believe you're here."

"Eleanor insisted, and she can be rather hard to refuse."

Nellie merely batted her lashes at the famous man. "Charmer." She turned to Katherine. "I think you should give John a tour of your new museum."

"Oh, I'd be delighted. That is, if you are interested," she said to Mr. Sargent. Then she winced, remembering. "We had a difficult time getting one of your works to display in the museum. No one was willing to part with a portrait, so there are just a few landscape sketches from your early days before Paris."

"Indeed?" He swept his arm toward the entrance. "Then we must see about rectifying that. Shall we?"

"Yes, of course. Nellie, you'll come with us?"

"Wouldn't miss it," her friend said.

"Give me a moment, if you please," she said. "I need to speak to my husband."

Preston was standing nearby, bouncing Lizzy in his strong arms, his voice soft as he spoke to their daughter. Katherine slid a hand over his shoulder to get his attention. "Can you believe it?" she whispered.

Her husband bent to kiss her cheek. "Well done, sweetheart. I'm so proud of you."

"No, I meant Mr. Sargent. Can you believe he's here?"

"Yes, of course. You're now one of the most important figures in the art world."

That seemed unreal. She pressed her lips to Lizzy's forehead. "Are you coming with us?" He'd already toured the museum many times, but not with Mr. Sargent in tow.

Preston shook his head. "No, I want to get Lizzy home. We'll wait for you there. Then we'll celebrate alone, just you and me."

She knew exactly what type of celebrating he meant. "That sounds perfect."

"By the way, I've already commissioned Mr. Sargent to paint your portrait while he's in New York."

Her skin heated. "Oh, no. I couldn't possibly. It feels too self-indulgent."

"Darling," Preston said, "consider it a gift for me. Perhaps we'll put you in something akin to Madame X's revealing black dress with plunging neckline. Then I could hang the portrait in our bedroom and look at it when—"

"Stop. You're supposed to be a respectable family man now."

He leaned down and put his lips closer to her ear. "Reinette, I'll never be respectable when it comes to you."

"And thank God for that," she murmured, leaning against him for the briefest of moments. "I should go. They're waiting."

"I love you. Go, bask in your deserved glory.

Lizzy and I will rest up and await your return home."

He kissed her forehead, right there in public, then strode toward their carriage. She sighed as she watched his broad shoulders shift as he descended the steps. Would she ever tire of looking at him?

Perhaps Mr. Sargent should paint Preston, as well.

"Katie, stop mooning after the man and come on," Nellie called. "There's an entire museum to tour."

Katherine smothered a smile and tried to appear professional as she turned around. "If you'll both follow me, I'll show you around the collections inside . . ."

Acknowledgments

❧

Okay, let's get the historical facts out of the way first because, let's face it, that's probably why you're reading the acknowledgements. I'll keep them brief.

The French Ball was a real Gilded Age event that took place each year in New York City, exactly as I've described here. Thousands of people, drunken revelry, indecency every which way one turned. (Sounds like fun!) It was first held at the Academy of Music, then moved to Madison Square Garden. I had to work this event into a book eventually, right?

The Twenty-Third Street location Preston knew would become so important? That is now the home of the iconic Flatiron Building (originally named the Fuller Building). Erected in 1902, the Flatiron was the first skyscraper north of 14th Street. It was never one of the world's tallest buildings, just the coolest.

The Meliora Club is based on a real NYC private social club for women, the Cosmopolitan Club, which is still open to this day. (I'm ready to be an honorary member!) Abby Aldrich did in fact marry John Rockefeller Jr. and went on to found both the Cosmopolitan Club and the Museum of Modern Art in NYC.

The Adirondacks, especially Lake George, was the place where the Gilded Age upper class went "rustic." Many of the families had big lodges or camps up there, and a lot of them can still be visited today.

Now for the writer stuff. This story really was a beast. It took me a long time to figure out who these two crazy kids were going to be, and I couldn't have done it without the help of Tessa Woodward, editor extraordinaire. We spent a lot of time brainstorming on the characters and the plot. I'm always grateful for her guidance and support.

Diana Quincy read this book three or four times and never complained. I'm so thankful for her friendship and assistance in general, but she really put in overtime on this one! I owe her big time.

Thank you to the romance reviewers, bloggers and Instagrammers who make this crazy effort worthwhile. If my books have offered even one person an escape for a minute or two, then I've done my job.

Much love to the other authors in my life that keep me sane. There are too many to name here, but they know who they are, and I'm incredibly grateful for their friendship, support and crazy text-threads.

Thank you to the entire team at HarperCollins/ Avon who works on my books: Julie Paulauski,

Sam Glatt, Alivia Lopez, DJ DeSmyter, Erika Tsang, and everyone else behind the scenes. But I have to give a special shout-out to the cover team, Guido Caroti and Anna Kmet, who have gifted me with such breathtaking covers for this series.

And lastly, I'm so lucky to have such a supportive family behind me. Thanks to my husband (who also helped with this book when I desperately needed it!) and my daughters for putting up with me. Sorry about my perpetual disappearing act.

(And, if you've read this far, dear reader . . . know that I have a wild ride in store for your girl Nellie coming up very soon. Read on!)

Keep reading for a sneak peek at the fourth
book in the Fifth Avenue Rebels series

❦

The Duke Gets Even

Coming soon from Avon Books!

"The sea, once it casts its spell, holds one in its net of wonder forever."

—*Jacques-Yves Cousteau*

Off the coast of Newport, Rhode Island
June, 1895

𝔐ermaids existed.

At least Andrew Talbot, the eighth Duke of Lockwood, was fairly certain of it. At the moment, a creature with long limbs and red hair was most definitely splashing in the frothy waves near the beach. If not a mermaid, then a naiad, perhaps.

Though he hated the ocean, he'd come out here after dark to swim in the chilly, murky water of the Atlantic, his body requiring the bloody exercise. He hadn't expected to see anyone else. Who was out frolicking at this time of night, if not a mythical creature?

Bare legs flashed in the surf. A shapely arm followed. He continued to tread water, unable to look away. Then a form rose up in the foam, and long red hair flipped backward. A woman. A *naked* woman. He was entranced.

As if the moon pulled him toward her, he soon found himself in the surf, too. The water reached his waist, and he watched her tumble and roll in the waves, like a small child who'd been cooped up all day and finally had a taste of freedom.

What did it feel like, such freedom?

Lockwood had never experienced it, not truly. His life had been shaped and molded since birth, a line drawn on a family tree to future generations of the same. The weight of it all fell on his shoulders—the crumbling estates, the empty bank accounts, the judgment of long-dead ancestors—and there were days when he feared for his sanity. Not a soul would remember him, unless he was the one who failed.

A terrible legacy, that.

A splash snapped him out of his dark thoughts. Saint's teeth, she was beautiful. In truth he'd never seen a more captivating woman. The sight of her slim limbs, high breasts, and incredible hair wound through him like vines, expanding and twisting, strangling him until he had no choice but to dive under the cool water.

When he resurfaced, she was directly behind him.

Long arms twined around his neck and she wrapped her legs around his hips. Bare flesh pressed soft and warm against his back. "About time you arrived," her husky voice said in his ear, like a whisper of silk over his soul.

He shivered. The right thing to do would be to let her go. To put his hands up and acknowledge the mistake. His title as a gentleman demanded it.

But he was tired of always doing the right thing.

For once, couldn't he act instead of think? Feel instead of strategize?

Heavy breasts rubbed on his shoulder blades,

and despite the cold water his cock responded, thickening and rising against her calf. His problematic heart thumped behind his ribs, the beat echoing between his legs. He couldn't seem to move or speak. Frozen by sensation.

Perhaps a shark would swim by and eat him. All his problems would be solved, then.

Sadly, his third cousin would inherit the title. Tooter, as he preferred to be called, was a complete nincompoop. Lockwood would wrestle the damn shark with his bare hands to prevent that travesty from coming to pass.

"I thought you'd forgotten about me," she said, nibbling his ear lobe.

Say something. Tell her she's mistaken you for someone else.

Christ, she felt good.

When her bare quim met his lower back, his mouth went dry, and he began contemplating the practicalities of naked depravity on a beach. Better if she remained on her hands and knees, then no one would acquire sand in unfortunate places . . .

Now is the time to speak, before this goes too far.

Keeping his hands at his sides, he cleared his throat. "Madam, I believe you have mistaken me for someone else." He winced. Even to his own ears, he sounded stuffy and ridiculous.

Her hold loosened. "Turn to your right. I cannot see your face."

He moved as instructed—and she gasped, releasing him as if he was engulfed in flames. "Damn and hell! Why did you not say something?"

He could see her then, but he almost wished he hadn't. No matter what else happened in the coming years, he would never forget this face.

She was simply stunning. Flawless skin and delicate features, with green eyes that glittered nearly gold in the moonlight. Her lips were full and plush, with a small bow in the center of the top one, and the lines surrounding her mouth meant she smiled a lot. "I couldn't be certain you were real."

"What?" She bent her knees to hide her nakedness in the dark water. "Are you some sort of masher?"

"I beg your pardon, but you accosted me. I was swimming and minding my own business when you wrapped around me like a limpet."

She splashed him with her hand. "I thought you were someone else."

"Obviously."

Her gaze traveled over his chest and shoulders encased in the thin bathing costume. He resisted the urge to flex his muscles. For some inane reason he wanted her to like what she saw. "You must swim a lot," she finally said.

"I do." He hated every second of it, but he hadn't a choice. Like so many things in his life.

"Why this late at night, though? What if you drowned?"

That would be Tooter's good fortune, then. "I don't sleep well. I also prefer the quiet."

"Yes, I can understand that. It's peaceful out here at this time, before high tide rushes in."

"The perfect hour for midnight trysts," he teased.

"Stop. I feel ridiculous enough as it is. Incidentally, I'm sorry for throwing myself at you."

"I didn't mind."

"I suppose most men don't mind when a naked woman swims up and clings to his very fit body."

Very fit? "I cannot speak for most men, only me, and I liked it. A lot."

"I noticed." She smirked. "The water must not be all that cold."

He choked on a laugh. "My apologies. I wish I could control it, but alas."

"I'm quite fond of the organ myself. It's temperamental but has a mind of its own. Sort of like a woman."

"I like that comparison."

"Well, fair warning, I am able to say it because I am a woman. You cannot."

He moved to his knees, so their faces were on a more even level. "Is that how it works?"

"Yes. I love women and we have to band together as much as we can. Men are good for only one thing."

"Midnight trysts?"

She smiled broadly, showing him even, white teeth. "Precisely." Then her smile fell as her gaze darted to the cliffs. "Though I suppose I've been stood up tonight."

"My good fortune, then."

"Don't get ahead of yourself, Poseidon. I don't even know your name, only that you're English."

Poseidon? He felt his lips twitch. In any other circumstance, he would introduce himself. Yet he hesitated. The urge to remain anonymous with her, to forgo any and all reminders of his life on dry land, won out. Which meant he could not ask her name, either.

He hooked a thumb in the direction of the open water. "Perhaps I fell over from one of Her Majesty's ships out there and swam to shore."

"With that upper-crust accent?"

"I might be an officer."

"That would explain the lack of scurvy."

He chuckled. Normally he did not banter with women, but this was proving enjoyable. Indeed, when in recent memory had he felt this light, this happy? She was quick witted and clearly no innocent, so a servant from one of the houses? Or perhaps the daughter of a local shopkeeper. "Would you believe I've been months at sea with other men, no contact from a woman in all that time?" It was partially true, anyway. He'd given up his mistress a year ago, unable to afford anything for himself beyond a basic necessity.

"I might believe it, based on—oh, shit!" She threw herself at him, but not in lust. Her eyes were wide with terror.

He caught her and stood up, cradling her close. "What is it? What is wrong?"

"Something bumped against my leg. Something big. And do not tell me it was a plant because this was no plant." She tried to climb up his body, doing all she could to lift her legs out of the water.

"There's nothing here but harmless fish and turtles," he said, rubbing his hand down her back soothingly. "Furthermore, I'm a much bigger target. If something decided to take a bite out of one of us, it would definitely be me."

"You don't know that." She stared down at the water as if expecting a giant fish to jump up and attack her.

"I am absolutely confident you will not die out here. How about that?"

"You're laughing at me, but I don't care. I might look foolish, but I'll still be alive."

"You don't look foolish," he said with all seriousness. "In fact, you are the most beautiful thing I've ever seen."

She leaned back to see his face. It occurred then that he had an armful of naked, wet and lush woman, one who wasn't mistaking him for anyone else. One who didn't know he was a duke, but simply a man. When was the last time that had happened?

He tightened his hold slightly, wanting to protect her. Wanting to keep her close and warm, and drive away anything that dared to scare her. He didn't want to let her go.

When she trembled, he eased her under the water but stayed close. They floated together, bobbing up and down in the gentle waves. Was it his imagination or had her breathing picked up? "Have we met before?" she asked. "I feel as though I know you."

"We have not been introduced. I definitely would have remembered a woman like you."

"A woman like me?" She stiffened and floated away, and he had to hurry to keep up. "Loud and brazen, I suppose. Scandalous." She drew out the word, as if she heard it quite a bit.

"Absolutely not. I was thinking clever and unafraid."

"Hmm. That was a very good answer, but I cannot tell if you're genuine or not."

He slowly moved in closer, back to where they'd been a moment ago. "Why would I lie? We don't know each other. There are no repercussions if I insult you."

She bobbed on the surface, letting him hold her hand, maintaining their connection. "You, sir, are very good for my confidence. Pray, continue."

"More compliments, then. Let's see. You are gorgeous, but you likely know that. You curse like a sailor, which I find endearing. You have excellent taste in organs, and possess the most remarkable laugh."

The moonlight sparkled across the surface of the water, illuminating her shocked expression. Then she smiled and dragged her fingertips along his collarbone. "Beauty, charm *and* brains. The female population must absolutely adore you."

"I could say the same about you and the male population."

"I do my best. I plan on sampling as many of them as possible before I'm done, after all."

"Before you marry, you mean."

"No, before I die. I will never marry."

She said this so casually, but with a note of finality in her voice, and he couldn't help but say, "That's a bloody shame. You should belong to someone. A lucky man who worships the ground beneath your feet." Not him, unfortunately. The plans for his future had already been set. The ring was in his luggage, in fact.

"I'd rather not belong to anyone, if it's all the

same. Novel idea, I know, but I'd like to retain my name, my worldly possessions, and control over my body."

"When you put it that way, I suppose the only appeal is children and regular bedsport."

"Both of which do not require marriage."

"What of disease?"

"Shields."

He glanced around dramatically. "Have I traveled to the future, to a place where women have progressive ideas and independence?"

"Perhaps you are stuck in the past." She pulled her hand out of his and pushed off his stomach to swim away. Legs kicking, she dove beneath the water, then resurfaced and shook water off her face.

"I thought you were afraid of the water."

"Not with you here to protect me. Though I suppose you'll have to catch me first." She angled away from him and began swimming, water churning as she performed a very competent breaststroke.

She was no match for him, however.

Lockwood dove in, kept his face in the water, and started a hand-over-hand stroke. It required a flutter kick as his arms rolled up and through the water, like a windmill. Every few strokes, he rolled to the side and took a breath.

In seconds, he caught her.

She laughed and fell into his arms like she belonged there. "That is hardly fair. You swim like a god."

"I am a god, remember?"

"How could I forget?" She pressed close and

wrapped her arms around his neck. He could feel her warm breath on his cheek. There was no one else around for miles, as far as he was concerned. The water was their safe haven, the moon their only witness.

It was magical, a world away from responsibilities and marriages.

"Are you married?" she asked, as if reading his mind. "I sincerely hope the answer is no, that your wife isn't staying at one of the cottages."

"No wife. Tonight I'm at the inn near the train station." Real life began tomorrow. This was fantasy, a few stolen moments in the water with a beautiful stranger. So he made the offer without stopping to think of all the ways it could complicate his plans. "Would you like to come back to my room?"

She sighed near his ear. "I can't. My absence would be noticed."

Disappointment burned in his throat, but at least she hadn't refused on the basis of being uninterested. If she was employed at one of these cottages, she couldn't risk her position by disappearing with a stranger. "I see."

"It probably sounds silly but I've made a promise and must abide by it, even if it does ruin all my fun."

"And mine." He cupped her face and dragged his thumb over her jaw. They were drifting away from the beach, into deeper water, but he didn't care. He felt untethered by this woman, cast free from his moorings. Fitting they should make it literal, then. "This is likely wildly inappropriate," he whispered, "especially as you have already turned me down, but I would very much like to kiss you right now."

"And here I was waiting for you to ask," she murmured and moved to gently place her mouth on his.

Oh, thank Christ. Relieved, he let her control the kiss, her lips soft and curious as they brushed over his. Anticipation built between them, a slow slide into the depths rather than tumbling in. He followed, content to let their breath mingle as the water rocked them into the deep. After a minute or two, she shifted to wrap her arms and legs around him, and he held them above the surface, his body straining to tread water as they continued to explore one another.

Suddenly, she broke off and swam toward the shore. When she crooked a finger at him, he was lost. Diving, he grabbed her and towed her closer to dry land, just until he could stand on the sandy bottom. This time, he captured her mouth in a brutal kiss. He held nothing back, letting her feel how much he wanted her, and she returned the kiss with abandon. When he flicked at her lips with his tongue, she opened and he thrust inside that warm haven. Their mouths and tongues worked in tandem, like the lapping of water against their sides, and she held on, lightly digging her nails into his scalp.

"Harder," he said into her mouth, and her nails found purchase in his skin. The rush of pain made him feel alive, like he was sparkling inside, tiny crackles of energy and light in every vein.

His balls were heavy, his cock throbbing. He bit her lip, sharing a bit of that dark energy, hoping she liked it even a fraction as much as he did.

She gasped and clutched him tighter.

Suddenly, he was ravenous, his mouth slanting over hers at a frenetic pace. She kept up, her hands pulling at him while little whimpers escaped her throat. He let his lips wander over her cheek, along her jaw. Down her neck and across her collarbone.

He wanted to eat her alive.

"Are you certain you won't come back to my room?" He should not be asking, considering his pending commitments, but the words tumbled out before he could hold them back. One night, that was all he needed. One night with this woman before he settled into responsibility.

"I can't. I could meet you there tomorrow afternoon."

"I won't be there. What about here on the beach?"

"What time?"

"Midnight. Will you meet me?" His stomach clenched. He wasn't certain what he would do if she said no.

Looking up at him through her lashes, she whispered, "Another midnight tryst. I can hardly wait."

Then his mysterious red-headed siren hurried toward the rocks, where she stopped to collect her things before blending into the darkness. It had only been seconds, but he already craved her again.

How was he going to survive the next twenty-four hours until he could have her?

JULIA QUINN SELECTS

Looking for your next favorite romance? The #1 *New York Times* bestselling author of *Bridgerton* recommends these new books coming from Joanna Shupe, Julie Anne Long, Charis Michaels, and Beverly Jenkins.

THE BRIDE GOES ROGUE

"Joanna Shupe is the queen of historical bad boys!"
— Julia Quinn

MAY 2022

In Joanna Shupe's latest Gilded Age romance, find out what happens when the wrong bride turns out to be the right woman for a hard-hearted tycoon.

YOU WERE MADE TO BE MINE

"I am in awe of her talent."
— Julia Quinn

JUNE 2022

A rakish spy finds more than he bargained for in his pursuit of an earl's enchanting runaway fiancée in this charming romance by Julie Anne Long.

A DUCHESS BY MIDNIGHT

"Charis Michaels will make you believe in fairy tales."
— Julia Quinn

JULY 2022

Charis Michaels enchants us with a romance between Cinderella's stepsister and the man who can't help falling in love with her.

TO CATCH A RAVEN

"A living legend."
— Julia Quinn

AUGUST 2022

A fearless grifter goes undercover to reclaim the stolen Declaration of Independence in this compelling new romance by Beverly Jenkins.

Discover great authors, exclusive offers, and more at hc.com

The Chase by Lynsay Sands

For Scotswoman Seonaid Dunbar, running away to an abbey was preferable to marrying Blake Sherwell. No, she'd not dutifully pledge troth to anyone the English court called "Angel." There was no such thing as an English angel; only English devils. And there were many ways to elude a devilish suitor. This battle would require all weapons, and so the chase was about to begin.

You Were Made to Be Mine by Julie Anne Long

The mission: Find Lady Aurelie Capet, the Earl of Brundage's runaway fiancée, in exchange for a fortune. Child's play for legendary British former spymaster, Christian Hawkes. The catch? Hawkes knows in his bones that Brundage is the traitor to England who landed him in a brutal French prison. Hawkes is destitute, the earl is desperate, and a bargain is struck.

Four Weeks of Scandal by Megan Frampton

Octavia Holton is determined to claim the home she grew up in with her late father. But she discovers the house is also claimed by one Gabriel Fallon, who says his father won the house in a bet. They make a four-week bargain: Pretend to be engaged, all the while seeking out any will, letter, or document that proves who gets ownership. But soon they realize their rivalry might lead to something much more intimate . . .

REL 0522

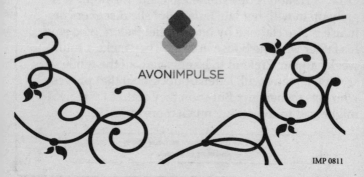